find you AGAIN

NASHVILLE STAR
SERIES

AVA HUNTER

Find You Again
Nashville Star Series, #2
Copyright © 2022 Ava Hunter

ISBN: 978-1-7374743-1-9

Find You Again is a work of fiction. Characters, names, places, angst and incidents are a work of the author's imagination and are fictitious. Any resemblance to real life events or persons, living or dead, is entirely co-incidental and not intended by the author.

Cover Design: Sarah Hansen/Okay Creations
Cover Image: © Regina Wamba
Editing: Eliza Dee of Clio Editing Services
Paperback formatting: Champagne Book Design

To women who stand tall and kick ass.

chapter
ONE

"**O**RDER UP!"

Alabama Forester winces at the shrill screech coming out of the kitchen. Mindlessly, she fills large tumblers full of ice and Coca-Cola, the sticky liquid splattering the front of her apron. Her gaze swivels across the room. A group of truck drivers crammed into a booth. Two young mothers bouncing babies at a small table. Hot pink graffiti scrawled across the front window: *To mess with Texas or not to mess with Texas, that is the question.*

She sighs. Great. Now her shift just got longer, thanks to some dickweed who thinks he's Shakespeare.

If anyone from Nashville could see her now, they wouldn't believe it. Smelling like fried grease, sloshing beer, schlepping food for the locals. It would mortify her teenage self beyond belief that she was back here. Hell, *she* can't believe she's back here. Back in her hometown of Clover, Texas, population 3,500, working at the local dive, Mill's Tavern, wearing a scratchy apron that could double as kindling.

Alabama's five hundred miles from Nashville, lying low like the trifling coward she is. Hoping, wishing, and praying that the last four months blow over.

Though she ain't too happy about the reasons that brought her home, she loves Clover. It's the town that raised her, Mill's Tavern the spot that kicked off her musical path. If only she knew how steep that path descended, right down into a fiery pit of what-the-fuck-did-I-do?, she might have rethought her next steps.

She might have rethought her life.

"We got burgers so rare the cow's still mooin' in the field."

The bubbly voice jars Alabama from her thoughts, and she glances up at the kitchen window. Her best friend, Holly—the fry cook, the manager, the emcee, and everything else under the sun—sets a plate stacked with a greasy hamburger in the window.

Alabama makes a face at the blood pooling on the plate. "Remind me to never let you write the menu."

"That's an insult to the chef," Holly replies, adjusting the red bandanna around her brow.

Alabama, suddenly feeling eyes on her, glances over her shoulder at the table of Carhartt-wearing truckers. One man's staring at her with wary concentration.

"They know me," Alabama says as she balances another Coke on the tray.

Holly sticks her head out of the kitchen window for a better look, her neon pink lipstick making Alabama wish she had on a pair of shades. "Of course they know you. You're Clover's claim to fame."

"Thanks a lot."

"That's not what I meant."

"Look at them."

"They just want an autograph from our pop-country princess."

"Bullshit. They're leerin', Holly." Alabama sighs, adding the last plate of food to her already-full tray.

Holly grins. "Speaking of leerin' . . ." Her curly blond head disappears. Then she's back, her phone in her hands, the *Nashville Star* website called up on the screen. "Did you see Broody McBroodster made the *Star* today?"

Alabama scoffs at the headline. *Country Music Star Griff Greyson Arrested on Disorderly Conduct Charge in Nashville.*

In the picture, Griff, being escorted out of Robert's Western

World, looks worse for wear. Like something rough and bitter scraped off the grill for the first time in two years.

Holly swipes to the next photo. "I think he's punchin' somethin' here. Or maybe he's holdin' a beer."

Alabama forces a half-hearted shrug. Griff doesn't deserve an ounce of her sympathy. "And everyone'll still love him," she says in a dry drawl. "It's the name of the boy's game."

With a groan, she hefts the tray. While she can tool around with her old six-string any day of the week, a tray of food and Cokes is nearly besting her. "Remind me why I'm doin' this again?"

"Money. Cold hard cash, Al."

Money. She needs it. All because of one terrible mistake. Is this what she's going to be for the rest of her life? A waitress in her dusty hometown? She should be steaming her face in a sauna, not steaming her face on the grill.

"Yeah. Don't I know it," Alabama mutters.

"I know you hate it. But you gotta go out there. Fluff your hair. Put a smile on your face."

She evaluates the men in the booth. "It ain't the stage, Hol."

Holly wiggles her eyebrows. "It used to be."

The sizzle of the grill has her looking up.

Alabama lifts a finger at the black smoke that's churning out of the window. "Your buns are burnin', baby."

"Shit." Holly disappears, a storm of curse words and expletives filling the kitchen.

Drawing her shoulders back, Alabama starts toward the table with the tray. These beer-bellied clowns ain't scaring her. As she crosses the restaurant, she bangs her heel against the jukebox, de-sticking the Waylon Jennings song that's been playing on repeat for the last ten minutes.

She stops next to the booth, dropping first the Cokes, then the food with surly attitude. This is Mill's Tavern; they didn't come here for the service. "We got a buffalo chicken sandwich with extra sauce and three burgers with everything."

Ignoring his food, a trucker with a Bettie Page bicep tattoo says, "You're that girl."

Her heart's a ticking bomb in her chest. She can't escape it. The past. It's coming in hot.

Alabama forces a smile, wanting the floor to open and swallow her down. "You're gonna have to be a little more specific than that, buddy." She swivels her eyes around the table. "Can I get y'all anything else? Fry sauce? Ranch?" *A cyanide tablet?*

The trucker waves a meaty paw. "No, no, no. I *know* you. You're the singer from the papers." A wicked grin spreads across his face. "The singer who likes to suck—"

She snatches up a dinner fork. Fast.

Then, Alabama's jabbing it under his chin, the tines lightly piercing his fat jowls. "You finish that sentence, there's no tellin' what I'll do with this little ol' fork here."

The trucker gulps, nods.

She lowers the fork, swings it at the rest of the table. "Y'all hear me?"

Nods all around. Eyes on their food, the truckers quietly dig in, only glancing up at the chime of the door. The men straighten up, tipping hats. "Sheriff," one of them murmurs, giving a dirty side-eye to the fork Alabama now holds at her side.

The town sheriff stands there, hands on his straining belt buckle. His red, weathered face creases as he scans the table. "Howdy, folks. How's life treatin' y'all?"

Alabama flashes a bright smile. "Goin' fine, sir. These kind gentlemen were just sayin' how great the food is." She sets the fork back down on the wood table with a clatter. "Your usual?"

He tips his hat. "Yes, ma'am."

They head to the counter, Alabama stepping behind it to pull a tray of donuts from the glass case.

The sheriff, resting his forearms on the countertop, says, "You givin' those men hell, Bama?"

She grins at her father. "Learned from the best."

A grunt.

As the town sheriff for the last thirty years, Newton Forester always has been a stickler for the rules, not to mention a man of few words.

Alabama pauses as she sticks a French cruller into the bag. "Lord, Daddy, is this good for your diet? What would Doc Harper say about this?"

"You just worry about yourself, Alabama." The soft admonishment has her smile dying a slow death. The few seconds of thin camaraderie they shared already down the drain. "Which reminds me . . ." Her father pats his back pockets with gusto. "You got some mail today."

She blanches. Her stomach takes a nosedive. "What kind of mail?"

Her father slides an envelope across the counter and Alabama's heart drops when she sees who it's from. She doesn't have to open it to know what it contains. Threats. Humiliation. Reminders of every single one of her mistakes.

"Thanks." Shame burns her cheeks as she trades him the sack of donuts for the letter.

Her father nods. Cordial.

He can barely meet her eyes as he turns to leave.

Hell, she can barely meet his.

She'll never shake the look on her father's face when she showed up on his porch after the scandal hit the papers. He knew what she had done—tried to do—to get ahead. He heard the names the paper was calling her. But he wasn't angry. He was ashamed, embarrassed. To Alabama, that was worse than anger any day.

Still, he let her stay with him, and after a few months they settled into an uneasy routine. Fractured, but Alabama hoped they'd make it back to each other. They had to. He was her father, the one who put the guitar in her hands, who had raised her up after her mother had run off to California when she was a baby, who always did the right thing by her. He learned her honest and true, and though she had her share of screw-ups in her teenage years, they never reached this status of epic failure. They never ended up breaking his heart like this.

She guesses it's about time her father realized she's not his perfect little girl. That she ruins everything she touches.

At the thought, tears fill her eyes.

She needs a breather. Quick. Before she turns into a weeping puddle.

"Cover my table, will ya, Holly?"

Holly waves a spatula to show she understands, and Alabama escapes out the back door to the alley.

She glances down at the letter held in her shaky hands. She exhales a long breath, trying to work up the nerve to open it.

Four months.

Four months since her life blew up. Four months and she's still living with the fallout of that damn photo.

It was her fault. Her fault for trusting Mort, her ex-manager, who came to her like some shady savior when she was hustling nights at the Bluebird Café.

After years of waitressing days, of singing nights to get her music out there, Mort was a light at the end of a dead-end tunnel. She saw what he had done for the Brothers Kincaid and other artists. She had been in Nashville for nearly ten years and all she had to show for her sweat was an album of her own songs, put out years ago by some two-bit label. *Wild Wonder* barely made a dent, never got airplay. Mort promised to reinvent her, promised her a new album, promised she'd finally have a number one song.

And he did. He did it all—all for a price.

Alabama was with Mort for three years. Three years of swinging her hips and her hair and then being billed as Nashville's pop-country princess before he cashed in on his favor.

What Mort wanted was for her to frame Luke Kincaid after their recording session. It killed two birds with one stone— Alabama got her hit song and Mort kept the Brothers Kincaid on as a client.

So she did. She kissed Luke. A reporter Mort hired from

the *Nashville Star* snapped a photograph of the kiss. The plan was to send it to Luke's wife—Mort would squash the brewing scandal, and the Brothers Kincaid would stay on as a client. But the plan went to hell when Luke's wife crashed her car after receiving the photo. Her car accident spun Mort's entire plan in an entirely different direction.

Four months ago, the truth finally came out. The Brothers Kincaid fired Mort's scheming ass, and in retaliation, Mort released the photo to the world.

The photo billed Luke and Alabama as cheaters. Luke, wanting to protect his wife and preserve his marriage, released the incriminating texts that outed Mort and his scheme. Which meant they outed Alabama.

She never blamed Luke for that. He did what he had to do. And Alabama came out and admitted to the world that she was Mort Stein's lackey. Luke stuck up for her at a press conference; even his wife, Sal, came to her defense. But even that wasn't enough to get her back in the good graces of Nashville.

Harlot. Whore. Homewrecker. Those were just some of the names she was branded with after the scandal. As always, the tabloids twisted the truth. The things they said about what she did to get ahead with Mort churned her stomach and tore out her heart. None of it was true, but in Nashville, it didn't matter. She's taken full responsibility, owned her mistakes, but she's still getting billed as the bad girl of country music, still getting called trash in the papers, especially by the *Nashville Star*.

It's bullshit is what it is. She's had her entire career and reputation derailed, while Mort quietly fucked off and is working as an agent in New York City.

She was a fool for trusting someone as much as she did. People let you down. People lie. And you get fucked over.

Case in point: Exhibit A.

Huffing a lock of red hair out of her face, Alabama steels her courage. She slides a finger under the envelope flap and tears it open. Dread curdles her stomach as she unfurls the letter. She reads fast, skimming the legal bullshit, the lawsuit.

As if the disastrous press wasn't bad enough, Six String Records dropped her from their label and then promptly sued her for damages for participating in what they called a series of "unethical decisions."

And of course, the judge ruled in their favor.

Alabama's eyes blur as she reads, dizzy from the debt. It's more than she expected. More than she has. Christ, she'll have to wait a thousand tables to recoup beaucoup bucks.

She sticks one hand in the pocket of her apron, running a thumb over the old copper penny that lives there. It's supposed to bring her good luck. Fat chance of that.

Once again, Alabama's eyes focus on the letter's parting words: *Failure to pay the enclosed bill within thirty days will result in us filing an attorney's lien on your properties and wages . . .*

Lord, what else could go wrong?

chapter
TWO

"**G**RIFF GREYSON."

The sharp words have him peeling his eyes open. A red-faced cop stands outside the bars of the jail cell.

Griff stretches and yawns, the cold cement bench beneath him better than any bed he's slept in over the last two months. "Damn, man, can't a guy get a little extra shut-eye? You're interruptin' my beauty sleep." He keeps his drawl long and languid, wanting to piss off the cop, wanting to stay here a little longer. He already knows he's in for a world-class ass chewing from his manager. Every single person who's ever invested time, money, and energy into him is probably waiting outside the station with pitchforks.

Hell, if he knew he was gonna end up in a jail cell anyway, he would have stayed in Clover.

The cop bangs his baton against the bars. Griff grimaces. The clanging sound rattles his teeth, his hangover.

"Your bail's been paid."

Griff frowns. By who? He didn't think he had that many friends left. With a groan, he sits up, swings his legs off the bench and stands. He tenses his hand, makes a fist. Hopes the guy he took a swing at is feeling worse than him.

There's the heavy slide of the cell door, and then he's out. Silently, he follows the cop down the hall to Booking to collect his belongings.

He peers into the box, taking back what's his. Aviator shades.

A flask. Two condoms. The rings he wears on every single one of his fingers. He slides a signet ring on his middle digit, his chest tightening as he gives the box a quick once-over. He doesn't see it. "Where's the penny?"

The officer narrows his eyes. "The what?"

"The penny." Griff rips a hand through his lank blond hair. He slaps at his pockets, making sure he didn't miss it. "I had a goddamn penny—" He breaks off, spying the rusted coin at the bottom of the box. He snatches it up, tucks it safely in his palm and tosses the officer a wild grin as he slips on his sunglasses. "Lucky, you know."

Then he's outside, wincing at the harsh early morning sunlight. He takes the steps two at a time, ready to get the hell away from the Nashville Police Department. He's nearly to the parking lot when he freezes in his boots and groans.

Fuck.

Nikki. She's leaning against a trash can, blond hair teased to high hell, looking like she wants to eat him alive.

Nikki's a mistake. A bad mistake that won't leave him alone. He slept with her last year after a show in Petaluma. He'd had a few and she looked just right. He'd regretted it in the morning when she wouldn't leave his side, but after that, Nikki was like a dog with a bone. She had a taste and she wasn't letting go. She's still hanging around, ever the loyal, doe-eyed groupie. Ever the constant pain in his ass.

Griff almost walks himself back into the jail cell. But she's on him like honey. She reaches out and grabs his hand, her thin face rabid with excitement. "Oh my God, Griff! I can't believe they kept you in there all night!"

"Whoa. Easy, darlin.'" He winces at the shrillness of her voice. "You think you can crank it down a few decibels?"

She snaps a bubble in his face, the sound like a gunshot. "Whatever you need me to do, Griff, baby. You know that."

He slings an arm around her shoulders as they trudge across the parking lot. Maybe Nikki can get him a hot meal, some coffee, a stiff drink. Give him a ride home. Hell, he's betting even her bed could rival that cold bench back in the jail cell.

"Shit." He stops in his tracks when he sees the car.

The black Mercedes-Benz circles the lot like a shark. Griff drops his arm from Nikki, who makes a little mewling noise of protest. "*Griffy.*"

"I gotta deal with this."

Leaving Nikki to pout, he approaches the car and leans into the rolled-down window. "Bailing me out, Freddie? I didn't think you had an ounce of humanity left in that soulless skeleton of yours."

Freddie Gladstone, his ruthless bulldog of a business manager, shoots him a dagger of a death glare. "Griff," she says, her British accent chillier than the November morning. "Get in the bloody car."

"You toss in an ice-cold beer and you got a deal."

Freddie revs the engine. Her knuckles, white on the wheel, tell Griff she's one second away from running him down. "Now."

He slips into the car, glancing over his shoulder for a brief second to see Brian, his cousin and tour manager, sitting in the back seat, reading a magazine. No doubt he and Freddie are in cahoots for Griff's come-to-Jesus moment.

Griff reclines the seat as far as it can go. "Breakfast first. Then we talk."

Without words, Freddie punches the gas, burning rubber as she peels out of the lot. Ten minutes later, she's squealing through the McDonald's drive-through to park at the outskirts of the parking lot in the shade of a sycamore tree.

Freddie drops the sack in Griff's lap, her angular face contorted in disgust at the greasy deliciousness about to fill his stomach.

Adjusting the cuffs of her powder-blue silk suit, she says, "Now, about last night."

"What about it?" Griff mumbles, his mouth full.

A low sigh comes from the back seat. Brian, his hands on each of the headrests, pulls himself forward. "We need to talk, Griff."

"So talk."

An under-her-breath mutter comes from Freddie as Griff tears into a second Egg McMuffin, littering her pristine floor with oily wrappers. "Ugh. The smell will haunt me until the end of my days." Then she clears her throat and locks eyes with Griff. "I hope you can hear me over the sounds of you chewing your food like a pig at a trough." Freddie's wry tone switches over to one that's all business. "The man you hit last night won't press charges."

Griff shrugs. "What can I say? He got in the way. Of my fist."

"Griff, the guy's a bartender," Brian says. "He was doing his job, man."

Griff scowls at the memory of last night. As far as he remembers, he met some fans who bought him a shot, and when he finished it, he slammed it on the bar. Glass broke. People were pissed. The bartender wouldn't serve him another one, and that's when he hit him.

Freddie's stiff shoulders sag. "Aren't you tired? I'm tired, Griff. I'm tired of always sweeping your shenanigans under the rug."

He lifts his flask and takes a long pull, trying to drown out her words.

Freddie's right. He is tired. Tired of always sleeping alone, tired of the drinking and the women, tired of singing shit songs someone else writes for him. Hell, how many more nights can he sing about beer and trucks? He hasn't sung an honest song since he left Clover. But it's all he knows. It's what made him a star.

Rule breaker. Rebel. Rowdy like Hank. That's what he was when he first started out. He made his music, his money, his reputation by playing fast and loose. Shooting off at the mouth, shooting guns onstage. It was a damn fine act, and it worked.

Twelve years ago.

And now, now he's sunk. He's so stuck in his image he can't even remember who the fuck he is anymore.

If he tells anyone he's bored with it all, he loses face. If he sings what he wants, he's a sellout.

"Now that I have your attention," Freddie says, her clipped voice breaking through his thoughts. "Let me tell you about the damage your fist did." She pauses for effect. Then, "Curt and Sooz have walked."

The news has him blinking. He lowers his sunglasses. "What? I got no band?"

This is the third band he's lost in two years. The only one still stuck with him is Brian, and that's because they're family. His cousin is loyal as a dog, stupid as one too. But he trusts him. Brian got him off a bender in the unruly days of his early music career, and since then, Griff's made him tour manager, put him in charge of writing some songs, cleaning up his messes.

"That is correct. You 'got' no band, Griff. You also have a ho-hum reputation in the press." Flashing her phone, Freddie shows him the home page of the *Nashville Star* website. *Aging Country Rock Crooner Griff Greyson: From Bad to Boring?*

Griff stares, that old familiar anger bubbling in his veins. "What the fuck kind of bullshit headline is this? *Aging*?" he snaps. "I'm thirty goddamn years old."

Freddie smirks. "I'll be blunt. Your music is boring, Griff. It needs work. *You* need work."

He slumps in his seat, wishing the car were currently going eighty right now so he could toss his ass into oncoming traffic. Freddie continues. "Did you notice there was not one photographer out there this morning?"

"There was Nikki," Griff grunts.

"Yes. Thank God the walking chlamydia machine came to the rescue." Freddie purses her lips. "You're stale, Griff. Your last album was all covers. You play mechanically, like you hate it. No one cares about you anymore. If they did, your little antics would sell records. *You* would sell records. Which brings us to my next point."

Griff shifts in his seat and takes another long swig of his flask, Freddie's harsh words hitting below the belt.

"The label is threatening to cut you loose. That means no fall tour. No new album."

This time, Griff sits up straight, his fingers curling against the thighs of his blue jeans. His body rocked by a kind of tense terror he hasn't felt in a long while.

Fuck. He can't lose everything he lost everything for. Especially not the music. The music's all he's got. All he cares about in his scummy shit-ass of a life, even if he hasn't shown it the last three years.

"They can't do that," he grits out.

"They can and they will. If your fast fists sold records it would be a different story. But instead you're busting jaws and sliding down in the charts faster than the *Hindenburg* crashed and burned."

Griff runs a hand down his scruffy jaw. He's thinking. Quick. He side-eyes Freddie for answers. She's always been sharp, willing to shake out solutions by the throat if necessary. "Well, what do we do?" he demands. "Tell me you got somethin' for me."

Smugness radiates from her like a beacon. "I believe I may have found what the label would deem a suitable resolution." She runs a finger down the line of her short black bob.

He waves a hand, impatient. "You're killin' me, Freddie." Then he glances in the back seat. "Why's he here anyway?" he asks, hooking a thumb at Brian, who's been mute and useless the entire time.

"My next point is why Brian is here," Freddie begins.

"The label will give you one last chance," Brian says, holding his eyes, telling him to shut up and listen. "They're willing to keep your fall tour on the schedule, with the sole change of demoting it from an arena tour to intimate music venues—"

"That's a goddamn insult and you know it," Griff snaps. *Intimate music venues* is code for dive bars. It means he goes back to playing on peanut-covered floors behind chicken wire.

"—providing you do one thing."

"Well? What the fuck is it?"

Brian clears his throat. "They want you to add someone new to the roster. A new opening act." His eyes fall to the floor. "Alabama Forester."

Griff's jaw drops, his mind automatically sizzling at the thought of her.

Then—

"No fuckin' way," he growls, drilling a finger on the dash. He ain't having her here on this tour. He can't.

"You have little choice in the matter," Freddie says, cutting off Brian, who's opened his mouth to speak again. "It's the deal. If you want to keep the label, the tour, we add her."

"Not her. Anyone but her." He searches his hangover-fogged head. "What about Bella Hope? Or, you know . . . that Kelly girl." He snaps his fingers, lost on her last name. "The one with the weird warble. Kelly Karr."

"Carrington." Freddie eyes Griff. "They want Alabama. Despite her troubles in the press, the single she has out is still at number one, which is more than we can say for you."

"It's that song she cut with Luke Kincaid. 'All Night Long.'" Brian adds, as if Griff needs a reminder about the guy Alabama locked lips with. "It's still gettin' airplay."

Griff makes a sound of disgust. That song makes him want to step on Luke Kincaid's fucking neck.

Freddie continues. "In this social media world we're in, negative publicity is gold. People hate her. But they also like her music. CMI wants to capitalize on her . . . let's say bad girl image." Freddie smirks. "Sex sells. You used to know all about that."

Griff bristles. What he knows about is Alabama's highly publicized troubles with the media, the scandal with the Brothers Kincaid, the way Six String sued the shit out of her. He's also heard the gossip whispered around Nashville. What they're calling Alabama in the press, at parties.

Using her misfortune to sell his records leaves a bad taste in his mouth.

"Our styles ain't even the same," he grumbles.

"Does it matter?" Freddie asks. "No one is buying your records, Griff. They'll come to see her. Besides, we need someone with more bad press than you. She'll soften you up some.

In return, you keep your tour, stay relevant, and if merch sells, if album sales pick up, we'll do a winter tour. Maybe then they'll bump you back to arenas. Dive bars aren't fun." Freddie examines her long, manicured nails. "For any of us."

Her words, her plan make sense. Still, he tries again. "Not Alabama. We have a past."

The words are like poison in his mouth, shutting down his body, making him choke.

"Yes," Freddie says. "Brian already informed me. Which is why I'm sure it won't be hard for you to . . . do that thing you do so well."

Freddie makes a hand gesture that looks suspiciously like rubbing a button. A very female button.

"You want me to sleep with her?" He's gawking. Freddie's always been unscrupulous, but this . . .

"Why not?" Freddie palms invisible words across the air like she's writing her own tabloid headline. "'Ex-Sweethearts Reunite Onstage.'" She looks at Griff. "People love a romance. Good, bad, dysfunctional. It all sells."

He lets out a snarl of revulsion. "I'd rather go back to jail."

Freddie's laugh is clipped. "Don't be so dramatic. You've slept with half of Nashville. Why would this be any different?"

Because.

Because Alabama's different.

She'd never be just another girl to Griff. A long time ago, she was his girl. One he loved and then left in Clover.

"Right." Griff sits back in the seat, a harsh ache settling in his chest. "Fifty bucks says I'll have her in bed in a week. By the time we hit the Carolinas," he says dryly.

"A bet?" Freddie smiles in delight. "Why, you're absolutely savage, Griff. I love it."

"Only for you, Freddie," Griff says with a swagger he doesn't feel. How can he feel like anything else other than a gigantic asshole?

Freddie's phone clicks as she swipes over to an email, her

eyes metronoming as she reads. "Now, she's holed up in some two-bit town in Texas. I'll be reaching out to her tomorrow via phone to inform her she *will* join the tour—"

"I'll go."

"Pardon?"

"I'll go to Clover," Griff bites out. "I'll talk to her in person."

Freddie calling Alabama would be a fucking disaster. His manager has all the subtlety of a chainsaw. The last thing he wants is for Alabama to learn the truth about why they're bringing her on board. She's already taking a beating in the press. He can't imagine her finding out they want her because her tarnished reputation will make their tour gold.

Plus, he knows Alabama. She's stubborn as hell. She needs someone who can match her word for word, which makes that someone Griff.

Freddie waves a manicured hand. "Fine. Be my guest."

Brian's gaping at Griff. Staring at him like he's off his goddamn rocker. Which he is.

He knows what he's done. Volunteered to go back to his hometown, to finally face the place he fled twelve years ago without an explanation.

Freddie puts the car in gear and backs out of the parking spot. She sets her gaze on the windshield, her profile sharp and pensive as she says, "I hope you learned something today, Griff. You do things when you drink. Things I hope you regret. Things that could cost you everything."

His jaw, his fist clenches, and he turns to stare out the window. Story of his goddamn life. Starting with Alabama.

chapter THREE

I T'S SATURDAY NIGHT AND THE SOUND OF BELLOWING laughter rumbling out of Mill's Tavern makes Alabama's head pound with the force of a thousand hammers. It's not her shift, but she's picked one up for another waitress, a good deed she instantly regrets. She should be at her glossy apartment in Nashville, soaking in a bubble bath, a glass of wine in her hand. But she's not. Instead, she's dealing with aching feet from wearing heels today during the lunch rush. She stifles a groan and shifts her purse from one shoulder to another. Her hip's aching in that old familiar spot. Even after all these years, it still gives her trouble. Still has her remembering that night on the Ridge. The night that sent her life in another direction she never saw coming.

She's hidden her limp well. Even while parading around on-stage, no one would ever guess she had fractured her pelvis in three places. She gave the stage her everything and ignored the pain. *Stiff hips*, she told people if they asked. If they noticed any-thing at all.

She pushes open the double doors to the tavern. As usual, it's bustling. By night, the tavern transforms into a wild honky-tonk that could rival Nashville any day of the week. The jukebox cranks out Hank Williams at deafening levels. Waitresses bark orders as they tap the drafts. On the small peanut-littered stage, a microphone glitters in the neon light. Alabama can't help but smile whenever she sees it, knowing that she cut her teeth on that same stage.

After dropping her purse in the storage room, Alabama's

tying on her apron when Holly finds her. "Al," she says, her brown eyes buzzy and bright. "You got a customer askin' for you."

She arches a brow. "Who is it?"

Holly's mouth twitches at the corners. "Corner booth. You'll see."

Following her best friend into the bar, Alabama grabs a menu and scans the room. Sitting in the booth is a man with his head down, scribbling on a napkin. She frowns. If it's another look-ie-loo come to gawk, he's got another thing coming.

When she reaches the table, she props a hand on her hip. "You need a menu or do you know what you want?"

"Wow," the man says in a voice gravel-rough and whis-key-aged. "You must be rakin' in the tips with an attitude like that."

Her temper flares and her eyes narrow. "Buddy, I don't know who the hell you think you—"

The words strangle in her throat as the man raises his face. When his eyes snap to hers, recognition hits her like a lightning bolt and Alabama finds herself staring at the roguish smile of Griff Greyson.

Her heart picks up its pump as memories, as feelings of the past slowly curl like smoke inside of her. Except for a mere passing at events or catching him on TV, she hasn't seen Griff up close and personal for the last twelve years. Hasn't wanted to. Not since he left her in Clover, taking her heart and her dreams with him.

Still, she can't help her eyes tracing over his face, his body. Life on the road has aged him, but not in a bad way. In a rugged and weathered hot-as-hell way. Blond and tall, the stocky boy she knew has hardened into a wall of chiseled muscle. His face is covered in a scruffy beard. Only faintly can she make out the long scar from the left corner of his eye to the corner of his jaw. His eyes are still the same strange tawny gold color she remembers. Eyes like a lion, she used to say. A myriad of colorful tattoos wind their way around Griff's tan forearms, his shredded biceps. Alabama takes in all the rings on his fingers—skull, fleur-de-lis, horseshoe, a bright band of turquoise. Her heart hitches in her chest as her eyes travel to his hands. Those big broad hands that used to hold her tight beneath the bleachers, in the back seat of his old Chevy, in the swing on his mama's front porch, right before they moved in for the kill.

His grin is wicked. "Hey, Al."

She feels a small flutter of tenderness at the resurfacing of her old nickname. Right before she stomps on those old feelings and channels them into anger.

Yeah, she's fucking angry.

"What the hell do you want?"

His gaze lingers on her. As if he's clocking every difference between teen Alabama and adult Alabama. "How 'bout a beer?"

"Get your own damn beer." She flings the menu at him. The hard slap of plastic against his face has his expression darkening. "Read it. If you're sober enough to."

He gives his jaw a massage. "Guess I deserve that." Crossing his arms, he sits back and appraises her. "Alabama Forester. Workin' the night shift at Mill's Tavern." A suck of his lip. "Never thought I'd see the day."

Annoyance flares through her. Griff giving her shit about her life choices when most days she reads about him waking up in a gutter in Nashville is rich.

She tosses her hair. "And I never thought I'd see Griff-fuckin'-Greyson comin' to grace Clover with his pain-in-the-ass presence." She props a hand on her hip, smirking when he scowls. "What are you doin' here, Griff?"

"I want to talk to you." But the look on his face says he'd rather be doing anything but that.

"Well, I don't want to talk to you."

What she wants to do is scream at him. Demand an answer for why he left Clover, why he left her before they could leave for Nashville together. People always said you don't marry your high school sweetheart, but Alabama knew she and Griff had been different.

Or so she had thought.

"Shame." He runs a hand through his chin-length muddy-gold hair. "And I came all this way. At least the scenery is good."

Alabama resists following his eyes to the stage. She knows what he's trying to do. Bait her. And though she tells herself it won't work, tells herself she's over it, she can't fight the past.

She remembers it all. How Griff's mama bought him a guitar and they taught themselves how to play. How they sang every Saturday at Griff's place and begged the owner of the tavern to take pity on them and let them sing on Sundays after church. How the first tip they ever made was two cents tossed in a cheap guitar case by a wasted patron. And when Alabama cried out back behind the dumpsters that they'd never amount to anything, Griff took her face in his hand and kissed her like she was a melody. He told her the pennies were lucky. They each took one, and then and there, they made a vow. He'd stick around in Clover an extra year until she graduated and they'd go to Nashville. Together. They even had a name for their band: the Copper Hounds.

But all those dreams went up in dust after the accident on the Ridge. When she looks at him, the only thing she sees is all the love she had for him, and that last goodbye she didn't get.

Griff stretches in the booth. "You should hear me out. I got good stuff to say."

She shakes her head, turning on her heel to walk away. "You got nothin' I wanna hear. I'm leavin', Griff."

"Won't talk, huh?" She's horrified when he slips out of the booth and starts walking backwards to the stage, his arms held out. "Maybe we should let the audience decide, huh? See what they say?"

He hops on the stage to wild hoots and hollers, the tavern patrons recognizing that their golden boy is back in town. Even Holly's dimming the house lights.

Alabama rolls her eyes. Damn showboater. His antics, his

cavalier attitude, irk her. Peacocking around onstage when his focus should be the music. Although she doesn't know what she's griping about. She did the same thing.

"What do you think, folks?" he drawls into the microphone. Feedback reverberates, clears. "Can y'all clap if you think I deserve a second of this pretty lady's time? I think we might get along, but she's a little shy."

Alabama snorts.

Scattered applause. Alabama glances over her shoulder to see Holly clapping along with rabid enthusiasm. "Really?" she asks her friend.

At least Holly has the grace to look shamefaced.

"Sing a song!" someone shouts.

"A song?" A sly grin curls Griff's lips. He pins his gaze to Alabama's. Her stomach flips, recognizing the look. Shit. Nothing good's coming from this.

Griff pretends to think on it. "Suppose I could." He wraps a hand around the mic, the devil in him ready to cause trouble. "How about one from Alabama Forester's repertoire?"

Her cheeks burn hot with embarrassment. She knows what he's about to do. Trot her horrid pop-country songs out onstage for a crowd that's loyal as hell to Willie, Waylon and Hank.

"Maybe 'Little Black Dress' or 'Leather and Lace' or even—"

Griff's voice dies a slow death as Alabama steps forward and rips the plug from the microphone. "Outside," she hisses, resisting the impossible urge to drag Griff offstage by his throat. "Now."

"Now was that really so damn hard?" Griff asks when they're outside.

His stomach clenches from nerves, and he almost tells Alabama to walk back in the bar and get him a drink, but he knows she'd knock him flat on his ass.

Alabama, her arms crossed, stalks across the alley, ensuring at least five feet kept between her and Griff. "You're an asshole," she snaps, shooting him a vicious glare.

He knows he is. He wasn't trying to embarrass her in there, just get her pissed off enough to talk, but he knows he did just that. He saw her face. Cringing at those shitty pop-country songs. He saw it in her eyes whenever CMT interviewed her. She hated those songs. A bet he'd place good money on.

Pushing was always one tactic Griff used to get Al to talk. She was a live wire snapping. You had to push her until you saw flames.

Griff rubs the back of his head. "It worked, didn't it? We're out here. Talkin.'"

"Then talk." She lifts her chin, her face pale and unreadable in the soft glow of the back door light.

Griff's heart flips in his chest. He tried not to stare back in the tavern, tried to focus instead on busting her balls, but now— now it's all he can do. Nothing could have prepared him for the up-close vision that is Alabama Forester.

The tall, lanky girl from years ago has given way to a woman with a body that has curves in all the right places. Her simple white T-shirt and blue jeans practically look hand-painted on. Her long red hair is an even deeper copper color than he remembered. He can't help but lose himself in Alabama's face. In her long dark lashes, her eyes the color of bare stone, the slight gap between her two front teeth that still gives her that adorable earnestness he's always loved. It's the girl he remembers. The woman he's never seen onstage. Down home. Drop-dead gorgeous. Even if the look she's currently giving him means to incinerate him.

"Griff?" Her soft drawl calls him back. She lifts her arms slightly, lets them fall back to her side. "What do you want?"

Her voice, tired, cautious, hangs in the space between them.

Keeping his face calm, his emotions in check, he says, "I want you to come on tour with me."

Her eyes narrow. "What?"

"I'm supposed to go on tour next week. The label wants you to open for me."

She scoffs. "You're unbelievable. Take your offer and shove it, Greyson."

Griff clenches his jaw, any effort to restrain himself gone. "Goddamn it, you're still so fuckin' infuriating, aren't you?"

"I'm infuriatin'?" Her eyes flash. "You come strollin' in here twelve years later. Everyone loves you because Griff Greyson can do no wrong, when you ain't never even been back home, not even when—"

She snaps her mouth shut, refusing to finish the sentence. But it doesn't matter. Griff knows what she was going to stay. He missed his own mother's funeral. Like the asshole he is, he didn't even try to make it back from his overseas tour. It's not that he hates Clover—he hates what he left. What he lost.

Alabama's guilty gaze is on the ground.

Griff tries to ignore the growing pit in his stomach.

"It's nothin' fancy," he says, picking up the conversation. Her gray eyes slide toward him. "Dive bars. Twenty cities. Six weeks on the road."

A long silence. At first, he thinks she'll walk, shut him down again, and then she says, "Gee. You're really sellin' it."

Griff shrugs. "No skin off my back if you come or not. I don't want you," he says, more harshly than he intended, causing Alabama to flinch. "CMI does."

Alabama considers the offer. Then her face turns sour. "Why would a label want me?" Her words, doubtful and lost, have his stomach flipping. "I'm a train wreck."

A wave of guilt crashes over him. Freddie's words in his head, the real reason for bringing her on board. He takes a rallying breath, trying to remind himself why he's here. That this is about saving his label, his tour. It's not about Alabama. Not one damn bit.

"Because you're a good singer," he grunts. "And I told 'em that."

Her mouth forms a tight line at the words. "Spare me your favors, Griff."

He sighs. He gets what he gets. And it's a wall. A big brick wall with barbwire wrapped around it. That woman's on fire. Angry. Haunted, too. He sees it in her eyes. She never let go of the past. She's never forgiven him. Hell, he's never forgiven himself. He knows he left her without an explanation. Without an apology. He deserves every single ounce of her wrath because she deserves the truth.

But what would he tell her? That the accident was his fault? That he has nightmares every night of rolling that Jeep? That the memory of Alabama saying in that soft serious drawl of hers, "Griff, I think we're idiots. I think we're hurt," still has him wanting to break down bawl like a baby?

He did that to her.

Maybe if she knew the truth about why he left, maybe it would—

No.

It's too late now. He can't get close to her. Not again. All he's good for is hurting her. And he won't do it. If he has to cut his hands off to keep his distance, so be it.

"While you're here . . ." He watches as Alabama digs around in the pockets of her apron. She unveils the copper penny they earned so long ago. "You should take this."

His breath stalls in his chest as she finally, fucking finally, closes the distance between them. She presses the small disc into his palm.

Griff clutches the penny in his sweaty hand and stares down at it, trying desperately to ignore the sting of pain she's just flattened him with by this one simple act. He knows what she's doing. Knows she's getting rid of the last piece of connection between them. But it doesn't stop him from saying, from choking out the painful words, "That's yours."

"I'm not lucky, Griff," Alabama says, her eyes downcast. "Not anymore."

He opens his mouth to respond, but before he can, a bright light flashes, blinding them both. Alabama utters a stunned exclamation, her cry like a starter pistol.

Griff, gripped by some primal instinct to protect her, revs into action. His heartbeat pounding in his ears, he grabs her arm and pulls her behind him. Quick, he snatches up an empty beer bottle from the ground. Blinking away bright sunbursts, he scours the darkness. "What the fuck?"

Alabama's hand drifts to Griff's shoulder, and at her touch, he freezes. Her lilting drawl floats soft in the night. "It's the *Nashville Star*. They got all their damn reporters out here houndin' me for a story."

"Well, they got it now," Griff grumbles, thinking about the photo that'll be in tomorrow's *Nashville Star*. Apparently, Alabama is too, her brow creased by a bothered frown.

"That's the last thing I need," she says, dropping the hand from his shoulder and moving dazedly away from him. "A picture of you and me . . ." She trails off, no doubt thinking of Luke Kincaid and that entire mess. Griff clenches a fist. He could kill that guy for hanging Al out to dry. For throwing her to the wolves.

"So go on tour with me." He floats her a crooked grin. "Let's give 'em somethin' to talk about."

Her eyes drift to his hands, his fist wrapped tight around the neck of the beer bottle. "It's gonna be like that? The whole tour?"

He flinches at the cool tone in her voice. That's precisely the reason he's dreading her presence on this tour. She comes along, he's a changed man. He already knows it. He can't have that. He'll cross lines, boundaries he's sworn off forever.

She flaps a dismissive hand. "Go on, Griff. Get outta here. You got better things to do than slum it in Clover."

"Think about it," he says gruffly. "I won't be here in the morning."

Then he's moving fast for the door.

He's already praying for sunrise. First chance tomorrow, he's getting the hell away from Clover. And Alabama Forester.

chapter
FOUR

THE BAR'S SILENT EXCEPT FOR THE SOUND OF HOLLY'S broom sweeping the peanut-strewn floor. As soon as the last patron stumbles out of the bar, Holly drops the broom, scattering peanut shells, and latches onto Alabama's elbow. "What happened out there?"

Alabama teeters, holding tight to the sticky beer glasses she's cleared from a table. "With what?"

"With what? Don't you mean with *who*? No way," Holly says when she sees Alabama clamming up. She plucks the glasses from Alabama's grasp, sets them on the bar, and sits Alabama on a stool. "You are not hangin' me out to dry. Dish. Now."

Alabama groan-laughs. "Okay, okay."

"So? What happened between you two?"

Alabama's smile fades. "There is no *us two*. Not anymore."

She glances at the door where Griff had stormed out hours earlier. His hands in his pockets, his cowboy boots burning rubber across the hardwood floor. Ready, willing and happy to get the hell away from Alabama.

Then, because Holly's waiting, she says, "He wants me to go on tour with him."

Holly's jaw unhinges. "And?"

"And I said no." Alabama shakes her head at the frown lines appearing in Holly's brow. "He can get someone else. Lord knows he probably has a harem waitin' in the wings." She stands and moves behind the bar, where she starts violently stacking bottles of whiskey.

Holly's staring at her like she's had a lobotomy. Maybe she has. "Are you crazy?"

"I'm not, but I'm sure you're fixin' to tell me why."

Though Holly's a cry-on-her-shoulder type of friend, she's also a call-you-on-your-shit, put-you-in-your-place soul sister.

"Al, you need the money." Holly's voice is a reproving hush. "This is a one-way ticket to payin' off all your legal bills. Not to mention Six String."

Alabama flinches. Holly's right. The minute Griff showed up with his offer, she knew the tour would be her straight shot out of debt. But Griff being the source of that money, the one serving the offer to her on a silver platter, has her digging her stubborn heels in. It's bad enough he showed up looking damn good in those blue jeans. Now he's gotta be the one to save her. No thanks. Hard pass.

"I can't work with him. Whenever I think about him, I want to kill him." Alabama puts away a bottle of Bulleit. "We just don't work anymore."

"You're thinkin' about this all wrong." Holly tosses a rag over her shoulder and sashays across the bar. Alabama cocks a brow. Holly continues. "This ain't about that sleazy womanizer who broke your heart back in high school. This ain't about the fact that Griff Greyson looks like one fine, juicy slice of outlaw. This is about you, honey. This is your chance."

"My chance to what?"

"To prove everyone wrong. To take the stage again and show them the real Alabama Forester. You don't need Griff." Holly takes her by the shoulders and gives her a good shake. "You're a pro in this business, Al. You've had some great songs. Sometimes I think you forget that."

Alabama smiles, loving her friend's fierce cheer-up sesh. "Sometimes I think you oughta be the voice inside my head instead of me." She dips to lift a box of limes ready for the fridge. As she stands, a sharp pain shoots through her hip and she sucks in a pained breath.

Holly winces in sympathy. "Your hip?"

Alabama nods, grinding her teeth against the endless throbbing pain.

"I'm telling you, Al, you gotta stop wearin' heels. They're killin' you."

"Oh, so you're a doctor now?"

"No. I just pay attention to when my best friend is in pain." Holly takes the box from Alabama, balancing it on her hip. "Go change your shoes. I'll finish up tomorrow's prep."

She floats Holly a thankful smile and hobbles to the storage room. She flicks on the fluorescent light and is immediately greeted by a hissing noise. A small sigh of relief escapes her as she seats herself on a wooden crate. Dipping forward, she slips off her heels, slides on the comfortable slippers she's stashed behind the bread boxes.

Taking a moment, Alabama exhales and kneads her right hip. She closes her eyes, a mistake, because suddenly, the memories take over and she's back on the Ridge.

She took her daddy's Jeep without asking. One of the first big fat mistakes of her life. She let Griff drive them up that dark dirt road to the Ridge, a sandstone cliff overlooking Lake Lynn. But the accident wasn't his fault. Alabama had been egging him on, telling him to gun it, and he did. They were young. Teenagers. Reckless, wild and in love. She thought they were invincible, and then Griff hit a soft shoulder and rolled the Jeep like it was a wagon wheel. They fell ten feet down the cliff but, luckily, landed on a rocky ledge before they hit the bottom. She remembers waking up upside down, her seat belt the only thing holding her in until help arrived. They took both her and Griff to a hospital in Austin. While Griff had a gash on his face, they released him the next day. Alabama fractured her pelvis in three places but was up and back to normal by the time the summer was over.

Griff stuck around until she healed, then he left.

But did she really heal? She thought so until she saw Griff tonight.

Anger curls her fist. Griff's got some nerve showing up like this. Like he didn't wreck everything in their past. Just another man, another person promising sweet nothings. How long until it blew up in her face? Until they lied, schemed, screwed her over. It was all the same. With Griff. Mort. Landry.

Landry Jones was the first man she had loved since Griff, only to have him take the one song they wrote together and suddenly leave her for a record deal and an agent.

But she never let that get her down. She said fuck him and moved on. It was an attitude well practiced after Griff disappeared. She didn't have time to nurse a broken heart. After she graduated high school, she packed up her guitar and left for Nashville. She was determined to make it without Griff, determined to outshine the person who had left her behind in Clover.

Only she didn't.

For Griff, his rise to fame happened fast. For her, it took five years of waitressing in Nashville before she scraped together an album and an agent. And even then, she couldn't even touch Griff Greyson's star status. Which was what made it easy, so damn easy, to partner with Mort. She was so desperate, so hungry to make it, she nodded yes to auto-tune, embraced the pop-country princess label, let everyone else write her songs.

Mistake after mistake after fucking mistake.

Alabama hunches forward and cradles her face in her hands. Everything's a mess. She's broke as hell. Her father's lost any pride he ever had for her. Her reputation's in shambles.

This is her life now, and she was content to leave it like that until Griff showed up. Though his offer has her seeing red, it also has her seeing something she's been missing.

The music. The real Alabama.

She doesn't know who she is anymore. For years, she's been painted up, primped out, jumping through hoops to get scraps meant for the boys. Shit, she didn't have a number one song until she recorded with Luke.

This could be her chance to change all that. To prove to the world that she can sing. That she can write her own songs and damn good ones at that.

She always told herself she fulfilled her dreams. But were they the right dreams? Were they really hers? Or were they someone else's?

She doesn't know. But she could find out.

Straightening up, Alabama digs around in her apron for her car keys. She glances at the clock on the wall and grins. Two a.m.

Perfect.

With a sigh, Griff crosses the creaky floor of his mama's bedroom. The old stone house feels about as run-down as he does because working up the nerve to call Freddie and tell her Alabama flat out declined ain't easy. Hell, he'll just wait until tomorrow. Go back and throw himself on her ice-cold mercy. Shit, commit to rehab or sleep with whoever they fucking want just to keep his label happy.

He flips the penny high into the air and catches it in his palm. He places it on top of the dresser, next to his own. His eyes snag on the color—copper—and a flash of Alabama's hair, her face, sideswipes his mind.

A frustrated growl escapes Griff at the unwelcome image. Thinking about how goddamn gorgeous she turned out to be is already reinforcing his need to leave Clover and everything associated with Alabama behind. Like this damn penny.

He scowls and rips open his dresser drawer.

Griff puts both pennies in the drawer, burying them among socks and various odds and ends. When his hand bumps against something square and hard, he frowns and pulls it out.

His jaw flexes as he stares at the small box. He doesn't need to open it to know it's Alabama's ring. He had worked two jobs that entire summer just so he could save enough money to propose by the end of it. They were young, and he knew they were in for a hell of a talking-to, but he didn't give a damn. He knew what he wanted, and that was Alabama.

Only the accident on the Ridge had changed everything. Just like the Jeep he had flipped, that night tossed all their hopes and dreams ass over teakettle.

Still, he forces himself to look at what he lost. Everything he gave up because he was a fucking idiot. He opens the box. The sparkle of the diamond seems to mock him, and Griff chokes down a deep well of bitterness.

He closes his eyes, not even bothering to try and stop the memory from coming. It's stuck so deep in his mind it'd take a winch to get it out.

He had been drinking that night when Al pulled up to the kegger, at the helm of her daddy's Jeep, asking him to drive. He should have said no, should have told her he had a few beers, but he didn't, and he got behind the wheel.

And then he was in the hospital, the side of his face stitched back together, frantically waiting for word on Al, when her father, Newton, took him aside. Her father had never liked him, but he had always held his peace. But that night he finally unleashed. That night in the hospital he told Griff he knew he had been drinking. Had threatened to charge him with drunk driving and toss his ass in jail. "Is this what you're gonna do?" Newton had said in that intimidating baritone of his. "Drink yourself stupid on the road with my daughter? Drag her down with you? Kill her?" He crossed his meaty arms. "Don't think, boy. Leave. Or go to jail."

Though a teenage Griff had outwardly scoffed at Newton's threats, deep down, he was scared shitless. The thought of his mama, of Alabama, hearing about what he had done . . .

He couldn't hurt them like that. So he ran. Ran from Alabama all the way to Nashville because her daddy told him to.

Griff stares at the ring, his heart pounding hard at the pain of the past.

What kind of fucking man was he?

It was the biggest regret of his life—leaving Alabama. He swore when he made it big he'd go back and get her. Only he never did. The guilt of hurting her was too strong. Her father was right. He'd just get her hurt again, drag her down with him.

He'll never love anyone like he loved Alabama. All the women, they don't mean a goddamn thing. Love 'em and leave 'em, and no one gets hurt. It's the Griff Greyson way of life.

It's how he survived day after day in Nashville. Missing Alabama didn't feel so bad, not when he loved the wrong women, stumbled out of bars, swung a fist at anyone who pissed him off.

Still, he still can't help but wonder what would have happened if he stayed and they went to Nashville together. Would they have made it? Would they still be together?

Griff lets out a long breath and snaps shut the box. He buries the ring beneath a rolled sock and slams the dresser drawer closed, earning the toppling of a few picture frames. Then he stalks to the bed. Zipping open his duffel bag, he snatches up a shirt and crams it in. He meant what he said. He's leaving before sunrise. Sticking around in Clover is bad for his health, and what his health needs is a drink.

He searches the room for the bottle of whiskey he stashed. He's pouring out a fistful into an old tumbler when the glint of headlights through the window catches his attention. A truck's coming down the old dirt drive to his mama's house. Griff checks the bedside clock. Late or early depending how you look at it. Either way, company shouldn't be calling at this hour.

He shoots back the shot.

Storming to the closet, he snatches up the shotgun and heads to the front door, ready to light the late-night caller up with a warning shot.

He flings the front door open and pounds down the porch steps. Then he frowns. Alabama's hopping out of the rusty truck, barefoot, her hair a trail of fire behind her, lit up in the headlights.

"Shirtless and holdin' a shotgun. How'd a girl get so lucky?" Her soft drawl's a lilt in the dark.

Griff lowers the shotgun, his heart pumping fast. "It's two thirty in the mornin', Alabama. What the hell are you doin' here?" he snaps, unhappy about her driving around on unlit back roads in the dead of night.

She merely arches a brow. "You don't gotta growl at me like some ol' ex-con. I hear you." She juts her chin. "You can put that gun away too."

He leans the shotgun against the porch railing. As he watches her long legs walk across the grass, his eyes narrow. Is she limping? Yeah. Definitely a limp. His stomach fills with lead as he realizes it's a carryover from the accident.

Alabama takes in the run-down farm. Empty stables, rusted wind chimes, cracked and crooked shutters. Her lips purse. "This place has seen better days."

"Been on the market five years," Griff says, crossing his arms.

"Poor thing," Alabama murmurs. "I always loved this house."

Griff knew she did. His mama's house was like a second home to Al. She was always over, helping his mama with dinner, talking about music. His mama, Della, was the best type of woman. She was always there for Alabama—and Griff. His father left and his mother worked her ass off in her small salon to give him a good life. And she did. She gave him a guitar, and her last name, and the tools to be a good man.

Too bad he never used 'em.

He grunts. "Ain't never gonna sell."

"That's because it's run-down." Alabama moves closer to the front porch. She runs a finger over the chipped paint on the railing. Griff's eyes hold on her face, swirling up images of her and him singing all night long on the front porch as his mama sang right along with them. "A fresh coat of paint will do wonders."

"You came over to tell me that?"

Her eyes flick to his. "Oh, yeah. I moonlight as a home renovator. Didn't you know?"

Griff shuts his eyes and rubs his temple. Alabama's giving him a headache like no other woman ever could.

"Al," he presses. The whiskey's burning a hole in his stomach. "Why're you here?"

"It's tomorrow." She points at the starry horizon. "You won't be here, remember?" Her smile's resigned. "I'll do it. I'll do the tour."

Griff sniffs. "You said no. What makes you think I want you now?" He keeps his voice cool, tough, even though his heart's just skipped all kinds of beats.

Her expression flattens. "You want me, Griff."

The blunt statement has the front of his pants stiffening. He can't deny it. He wants her. On tour. In his bed. But it'd be wrong; it'd be a risk he can't take. He won't do that to her, not again.

"What changed your mind?"

She gives a little shrug. "I figure I can do somethin' I'm good at or sweat my ass off at the tavern for the rest of my life. So, I choose door number one."

The dry grass crunches as she sidles closer to him. The closest she's been all night. So close Griff can smell her perfume—coconut and vanilla. Her scent makes him heady. She braces her back against the railing so they're side by side, staring out into the illuminated dark. "Plus, I want this too," she says, her drawl soft and serious. "I need it. Bad."

He frowns, unsettled by the tone in her voice. "What's goin' on, Al?" He turns toward her, leaning against the porch column.

"It ain't been so easy lately." Before he can ask, she sighs. "I'm broke, Griff. I got a mountain of legal fees from tryin' to break from Six String. If I don't pay 'em in thirty days, they're gonna turn me over to collections."

The admission hits him like a stack of bricks. His stomach twists. He was right—she wasn't working at the tavern for shits and giggles. Al's in trouble. He sees it in her face, in those sad lines of stress around her mouth that she shouldn't have yet.

His jaw flexes. "You should have called me."

She laughs. "Please. We ain't seen each other in twelve years."

That's not entirely true, although he'd never tell her that. He always kept tabs on Alabama. He knew when she first arrived in Nashville that she was busting her ass waitressing at the Hungry Cow. He'd show up when she was on break, slip some extra cash into her tip jar. At parties, when he knew she'd be there, he'd leave first so she didn't have to worry about running into him.

He wanted to make it easy on her, but he knew what he was really doing—trying to make it easy on him, his guilt.

She looks at him. "So what do you say? We gonna do this or what?"

"We're on," he says. "We'll get you a contract tomorrow."

A little grin lights up her face, the change in her expression so startling it has Griff seeing the lanky, goofy girl from years ago. "So you're making contract negotiations now?"

His mouth kicks up at the corners. "Might as well."

"Well, in that case, I have some demands . . ."

"Oh, I'm all about the demands."

Alabama's lower lip pushes out as she thinks on it. Then, she says, "I get to sing my own songs." She juts her chin like he'll say no. "Three every show."

He blinks. "That was an option?"

Her face loses its lovely smile. "Everything was an option with Six String."

"You'll get that," he promises. His chest swells; he wants to give her everything she asks for and then some. Wants to beat the absolute shit out of everyone who took away that fiery spark in her eye. "And that's a promise."

She makes a little noise of disbelief and steps away from him. "If it's a Griff Greyson promise, I won't hold my breath."

The coldhearted jab punches him in the stomach. Because she's right. It's what he does: push everything and everyone away. Love the wrong way because the right way costs too much.

But he keeps his face stoic, his only dead giveaway the muscle clenching tight in his jaw.

The moonlight illuminates her hourglass figure as she walks away from him, and Griff twists the horseshoe ring around and around on his finger.

He did his dirty deed for Freddie, and that's it. They'll do the tour. Alabama will get her money and he'll keep his label.

All he's gotta do is stay away from her. Stay drunk. Chase her away like he did before. That's all he's good at.

chapter
FIVE

A WEEK LATER, ALABAMA BOARDS THE BUS FOR THE Straight to Hell Tour, feeling like she's already halfway there. She's the first to arrive. Griff's late, per usual, leaving her with a parking lot full of nosy news media to avoid. The schedule has them in Louisville tonight, performing at Graham's Grotto, a dinky dive bar with a rep as bad as Alabama's.

She finds her bedroom at the end of the hall, next to Griff's. As she unpacks her things into the marble-top dresser, she has to keep reminding herself that this isn't new to her. She's been here before. Only six months ago, in fact.

When she told her father she was joining Griff's tour, he had responded with a grunt of disapproval. "I don't know, Alabama. I just don't know."

Alabama doesn't know what she's doing either, but Holly was right. Sure, her career's seen better days, but it's not over. No way in hell. If Mort fucking Stein can still land clients, then she sure as hell can have a comeback. All Griff has done is pave the way. Her mind flashes back to last week. Griff bare-chested, his jeans slung low on his waist. He looked damn good, but he also looked wary as hell when she agreed to go along.

He doesn't want her here any more than she wants him around.

Distance, Alabama thinks, setting a photo of her and her father on the dresser. Keep a Grand Canyon of distance between the two of them and everything will turn out just fine.

It isn't lost on her that—except for Holly—Griff's the only one who's kept faith in her. She's here because she can sing. Even

Freddie, Griff's bulldog of a manager, had looked her over doubtfully. But she didn't let any of that bother her. Because for once, Alabama has a kick-ass contract, and that contract gives her the freedom to sing her own songs. She has boatloads of 'em. Songs Mort made her shelve. Songs he said weren't good enough. He had her singing like some country Britney Spears when she wanted to be Dolly.

Her eyes land on her guitar. Truth be told, she's giddy with excitement for this opportunity. For once, she'll do the right thing: take control of her life and let her love of music—not fame—drive her. If she can survive six weeks on the road with Griff, she'll have enough money to pay off her legal fees and, by the time it's over, get the hell away from Griff Greyson and start fresh. Easy.

Real easy.

A commotion outside has her attention drifting. Peering through the window, she sees Griff sauntering through the parking lot full of news media. He's got a bottled blonde tucked under his arm, and Alabama rolls her eyes at his token entourage. She knows about his reputation as a womanizer. He went through 'em like Tic Tacs. Griff's no different from any man she's ever known. Everyone loves, everyone lies, and everyone leaves. Especially in the music business.

Alabama meets him at the front of the bus as he's disentangling from the blonde. Before he can escape, she grips his hand and pulls him back for a sloppy kiss.

A pang of jealousy rolls through Alabama, and instantly she's angry with herself. She's not looking to rekindle the past. Just her career.

This is what got her in trouble in the first place. Cozying up to Griff is *not* an option. Hell, he's the one who dumped *her* way back when. The only thing she's on this bus to do is shake her bad image, to do things her own way, to keep it platonic no matter how good a tattooed Griff Greyson looks.

Alabama angles her gaze down at Griff where he stands at the foot of the stairs. "Bad night?"

He grips the bar and pulls himself up so they're standing on the same stair. Inches apart. Alabama bristles as his chest brushes against hers. His musky scent's tainted by floral perfume. On his breath—booze and spearmint. He lifts his sunglasses to look at her, those yellow eyes of his pinning her down. "I'll tell you right now, sweetheart, bad life."

There's the flash of a camera.

Griff braces a hand on the wall beside her.

Alabama's heart beats unsteady in her chest; she's unable to tear her gaze from his. He's got her shivering in her skin like she's seventeen all over again.

Damn Griff Greyson.

"Griffy," whines the rail-thin blue-eyed blonde below.

"Your puppy dog's cute," Alabama tells Griff. "What's her name?"

"Nikki," he grunts, instantly looking uncomfortable at the conversation.

Alabama gives the girl a bright smile, only to be greeted by a middle finger.

Griff groans.

"Mmm." Alabama lifts a brow. "Seems like she has real good manners. You must be proud."

His lips lift at the corner, but he doesn't look happy. "Look, you gonna bust my balls or are we gonna get the hell on the bus?"

Alabama wets her lips. Extends an arm. "After you."

He stares at her for an extra-long beat, then brushes past her, his scarred face twisted up into a scowl.

Alabama follows, heading into the lounge at the front of the bus. She bypasses Griff, who sits on a couch, to settle into the small dinette near the kitchen. She wraps her arms around herself and forces her eyes away from Griff, unwilling to let the girl or Griff get to her.

She's not here to make nice. She's here to sing.

The door blows open again and Alabama glances up in time to see Brian Rodgers, Griff's cousin and tour manager, barging onto the bus. In his hands, he carries Griff's duffel bag and guitar case.

At the sight of Brian, Alabama inhales a steeling breath. Brian's always been a slimy little weasel. Even in high school, he was always a hanger-on, jealous of Griff, trying to lurk in his shadow. It was never Griff's fault; Brian just never had the drive. All he was was a hall monitor with a hard-on for power.

And a hard-on for Alabama too, apparently. Junior year, homecoming, he cornered her after the dance. Alabama promptly kneed him in the balls when he went in for a kiss. She never told Griff, not wanting to hurt their relationship, which supposedly has stood the test of time. She's heard Brian's the only one who hasn't quit on Griff, or faced his drunken wrath.

Brian nods solemnly at Alabama. He wears a Griff Greyson T-shirt two sizes too small, the thin fabric stretched tight around his paunchy stomach. "Alabama. Good to see you."

Alabama flashes a tight smile, tucking away the childhood memories. Clean slate, right? Although, it does give her a smug sense of satisfaction to see him doing Griff's grunt work. "Hey, Bri. Long time."

Brian's face breaks into a broad grin. "No doubt. Hey, look it, we got the Clover gang back together."

Griff smears a hand over his face, his expression pained. "Christ, Bri."

Brian looks at Griff. "Nikki followin' us on the road?"

Alabama's body goes rigid.

"Guess so," Griff says with a two-shoulder shrug. "She's got a car, she's comin'. Not like I can stop her."

Brian chuckles. "Man, that's a woman approachin' stalker status if I've ever seen one."

"I'm afraid stalker status is my job, Brian."

The feminine British voice sneaks up on them and Alabama glances toward the doorway.

Freddie, the manager she had met earlier this morning, stands as starched as a shirt in the doorway, looking like she's ready to deliver last rites.

Griff stretches his arms out across the top of the couch, his hands opening up in greeting. "Hell, Freddie, you hitchin' a ride?"

She laughs, but there's no humor in it. "No. I am here to give a few house rules before I go. It's in your contract, but since no one ever reads the bloody things, I am here to reiterate. And Brian is here to keep you two in check."

Freddie's eyes scan the room. "Now . . ." She smooths an invisible wrinkle on the front of her silk skirt. "While you are allowed a commotion or two, Griff, it is of the utmost importance that you stay out of trouble. You stay out of jail. You work on that temper of yours."

Griff lifts his hands in mock offense. "Why am I gettin' all the flack?"

"Maybe it's because you do all the flack?" Alabama quips, not even bothering to play nice.

Griff rolls his eyes, his tattooed biceps flexing as he crosses his arms and kicks a boot up on his knee, apparently deciding to settle in for Freddie's lecture.

Freddie's laugh is a delicate burst. "Oh, you're delightful," she says, her brown eyes swerving to Alabama, sinking into her like fangs. "And you . . . you sing. You just do what you've always done."

Griff listens from his perch on the couch. He smirks, bored, all bad boy machismo, but the grin doesn't reach his eyes. In fact, his spine's gone stiff from Freddie's words, as if another feeling's overtaken him entirely.

Alabama's eyes narrow. What is it? Guilt, anger, annoyance?

And then she's hit by another thought. Is it all an act? The outlaw cowboy image? Firing guns onstage? Burning guitars? She can't tell anymore. Couldn't pick the real Griff Greyson out of a line-up if she tried.

Griff's eyes lift to hers. "What?"

His voice sharp, cool.

She clears her throat and looks away, embarrassed at being caught staring. "Nothin'."

"And remember . . ." Freddie's crisp voice cuts through the tension. "You throw a fist or you miss a show, you're done. That goes for both of you. Is that clear?"

Griff smirks, tucking his lank blond hair behind his ears. "Crystal."

Brian, taking that as his cue, launches into an endlessly long description of the tour and what they'll be doing and where they'll be singing and who they'll be meeting on every stop.

Alabama forces herself to listen even as Griff's eyes glaze over from boredom.

But there's only one fact that matters.

She and Griff—they're on the bus. They can't get away from each other now.

After arriving in Louisville, Alabama disappears to get ready for the show, while Griff stretches lazily on the couch. All he wants to do is take a nap, sleep off his beer buzz, cleanse his system of Nikki. She's like a tick. Always hanging on, following him to the next town. He saw the way Alabama was looking at her today. Though it gives him a slight thrill to think he's pissed her off, he also hates her thinking Nikki's his.

She's not.

None of the girls are. Years of having a different girl every night just don't cut it no more. He's been on a sex freeze for a while now. Longer than he wants to admit. Besides, all the girls, they're all the same. Cheap thrills. Nothing serious. Nothing like Alabama. No woman could compete with her.

Griff feels the couch lurch as Brian sits beside him, jarring him from his thoughts.

He lowers his sunglasses, glares at his cousin as he leans up on his elbows. "I'm tryin' to sleep, man."

Ignoring him, Brian taps the top of Griff's boot with a pen. "You got anyone I should add to the list tonight? Griff?"

But Griff doesn't answer him.

He can't.

He's too busy staring at Alabama, who's just come down the hall. His eyes narrow at her outfit, no doubt picked perfectly to mess with his head. Every curve of hers—breasts, waist, hips— is hugged by a metallic miniskirt, a rhinestone belt, and a tight black top. Her sky-high heels are the cherry on top.

Fuck.

His dick, his heart clenches. She looks so damn good it hurts.

Brian's eyes metronome between Griff and Alabama. "Let's see your set list," he says, snapping his fingers at Alabama.

With a sigh, Alabama hands it over. Griff gets her frustration. She's a pro; being micromanaged by a childhood-friend-turned- tour-manager is no doubt a pain in her ass.

Brian's lips quirk in amusement as he scans the songs. "'Butterfly Anthem'?"

The frown on Alabama's face deepens. It's a shit song, but someone making fun of it is off limits.

"Lay off," Griff says. "We all got songs we don't like."

"We do," she says. "I especially hate 'Tailgate King.'"

Griff busts out with a belly-deep laugh, too impressed to be insulted. The song, it's one of his own. One toward which he feels an especially fierce loathing. "Brian wrote that."

Alabama flashes a shit-eating grin. Pins her gaze to Brian, who's turned beet red. "I know it." The proud jut of her chin tells Griff she can hold her own, tells him she doesn't need him to come to her defense.

"Mikey's got your guitar onstage," Brian grumbles, handing her back the set list. "It's ready when you are."

Alabama pauses at the door. A wince crosses her face as she

presses a hand into her side, near her back. There's the barely in-audible inhale of air.

Griff sits up and leans forward. "Hey. You okay?" He sur-veys her quick, careful.

"Fine." She flashes a faint smile. "Just stiff. It's not a big deal. I'm used to it."

Guilt sweeps over him like a dry breeze. Knowing that her hip is still hurting her all this time later has him feeling like a gi-gantic asshole. Christ, he didn't even know. But it's his own damn fault because he didn't stick around long enough to find out.

Alabama's expression resets itself to a cool, calm facade. No telltale signs of pain, no nothing. She gives Griff a little wave with her fingertips. "I'll try to rock-and-roll it up for you."

Griff settles back into the couch, anchoring his boots to the floor, because all he wants to do is get up and go to her and make sure she isn't hurting anymore. "You do that."

The minute the door shuts, Brian laughs. "Man, they're gonna eat her alive."

Griff shrugs, trying to shake the worry nagging at him. "Freddie's got a reason, so she's here. I just sing."

"I still think it's a bad idea."

"You think what's a bad idea?"

Brian snorts. "The way you're looking at her. You got that ol' cartoon wolf tongue thing goin' on."

"Just another girl," Griff says mildly.

"Bullshit. You're still hung up on her."

Annoyance fills him. Griff leans back on the couch, adjust-ing his aviators. "I'm tryin' to sleep, Brian. Tryin' to get some goddamn peace and quiet, so shut the fuck up."

But Brian continues chattering like he hasn't heard him. "Hey, I don't blame you. We're gonna get rich with that thing on board."

"I'm gonna fire your ass you keep talkin' like that." He keeps his voice light, easygoing, even though his fists curl at the way Brian's talking about Alabama. She ain't just another girl and she sure as hell ain't some *thing*.

"Yeah, well. I know you and Freddie made a bet, but my advice—steer clear of her. She's bad news. After what she did to Luke Kincaid, she might work on hangin' you out to dry next."

A hot hit of anger rushes through him.

The last thing he wants to do is talk about the Brothers Kincaid. Two of them ditched Griff on his last tour, leaving him without a bass and a fiddle player. Then they came back from nearly a year-long hiatus to bust his ass in the charts. Everyone thinks Luke's a saint when it's Alabama taking the beating in the press. Besides, thinking of Alabama locking lips with Luke Kincaid doesn't exactly endear the guy to him.

It makes him livid.

"You believe that shit?" Griff asks.

"You don't?" Brian shakes his head sagely. "She ain't the girl you remember, Griff. Get that through your skull before she gets under your skin."

Doubt wraps itself around his mind, Brian's words like a soundtrack on repeat. Sure, Griff's known her forever, but does he know who she is now? Maybe he's been in the wrong defending her. Maybe she did do all those things they said she did. But he can't believe that—he didn't the first time he heard it, and he won't now. The thing to do is get answers from Alabama.

Brian's smug voice cuts in. "Although the way it's lookin' now," he says, "I'd say you're in good shape. It's pretty clear she can't stand you."

Griff growls and snaps his eyes shut. He knows what Brian means; he saw it on Alabama's face the second he set foot on the bus. She's gonna be treating him like a grimy gym sock this entire tour. Which is just fucking perfect. The farther apart they can stay, the better.

There's a hard knock on the door, and then it's swinging open to reveal Mikey, their stage manager. His face is calm, yet tinged with panic.

"We got trouble, Griff."

chapter
SIX

THE CHANTS OF "WE WANT GRIFF, WE WANT GRIFF" hit Alabama's eardrums like small pebbles of doom. The ragtag audience at Graham's Grotto telling her time's up as boos and half-empty water bottles land onstage.

She can't sing. Not a lick. Her throat refuses to work. She had been so confident earlier on the bus, ready to take the stage like a boss. And she did. She belted out the first five songs like clockwork and the audience loved it. Mostly her fans, but she had even seen some of Griff's tapping a toe. But when it came time to sing her own song, one she knew better than her own skin, she froze. Like a deer in the headlights, wondering what she was getting herself into, right before the big Mack truck of reality slammed into her.

Jesus. She'll be in the press again. She can already see the headline coming down the AP wire: *Alabama Forester Looks Dumb as Shit.*

Her heart in her ears, the hot stage lights burning a hole through her, Alabama closes her eyes, bracing for them to laugh her right offstage when there's a hand on her shoulder, a gritty drawl in her ear.

"I don't think she likes y'all." Cheers and hoots erupt all around her as she opens her eyes to see Griff Greyson leaning into the mic.

A broad grin fills his face. He turns his gaze toward her, his eyes searching out hers for a melody they don't yet know but will, and it's like she's back in the past, back on his front porch with their guitars and sweet tea and pens and notebooks.

"What do you think, Alabama? Maybe we oughta shake things up with a little Willie Nelson number." He glances down at her set list and makes a face of repulsion. "Because let's be honest, no one wants to hear 'American Doll.'"

Anger flares in her at the laughter rippling through the audience. But it's enough to get her shaking off her stupor. She flashes a syrupy sweet smile. In her best southern belle voice, she says, "That's mighty kind of you, but I got this, Greyson."

She goes in to grab the mic, but he wraps a hand around it first.

He flashes another cocky grin. "Oh, I don't think you do, sweetheart." There's another chorus of applause in the crowded room, louder than it had been for Alabama.

Alabama can only watch in disbelief as Griff signals to his band and they strike up the first few chords of 'Highwayman.' Regretfully, because it's suck it up or get fucked, Alabama follows his lead.

The audience raises cell phones high.

They sing in unison. Their voices twin, Griff's sound like a buzz saw to Alabama's earthy drawl. It's the first time they've ever sung together as adults, and Alabama can't even appreciate that. Because all she can do is burn.

The second the song is over, Alabama throws the guitar pick at Griff.

An "Oooo" rises in the crowd.

"Asshole," she hisses and storms off the stage.

She's pissed. Pissed at herself for screwing up her first show of the tour, pissed that she's going to be in the papers *again* tomorrow, pissed that she got roped into sharing a song, a stage with Griff, and even worse, pissed at Griff for saving her pathetic ass.

Minutes later, he comes strolling through the curtain, a lazy swagger in his step. "You're welcome, by the way."

Alabama stops at the top of the stairs that lead down to the exit and whirls on him. "I didn't thank you."

"Well, you should. You were like a wet mop up there." A smug smirk crosses his face and Alabama wants to wipe it away with her fist. The last thing she needs is some muscle-bound cowboy with a chip on his shoulder telling her how to sing.

"No one wants to hear 'American Doll,'" she snaps, mimicking Griff's dismissive tone onstage. She narrows her gaze. "What gives you the right?"

"What gives me the right?" Griff clenches his jaw. "How about my openin' act's singin' some shit song that'd barely get anyone else past the front door at Tootsie's?"

She scoffs. "Oh, now you care about your tour? From what I hear, you're too busy actin' like an asshole up onstage to give a damn about the music."

His expression darkens. "Good. Get it all out." He lifts his hand, beckoning her closer with his fingers.

She takes a step toward him, as if accepting his challenge. Griff remains silent as she approaches, his only tell the vein straining in his temple. "I can handle this myself," she says, in a tone of lethal quiet. She doesn't want a bailout. Not by anyone, and especially not by Griff. "I don't want your help, Griff. I don't *need* your help."

"Sure seems like it."

Her fists clench, and she stares him down. "You left. You don't get to suddenly pretend like you care about me twelve years later. *So just stop it.* And walk away. Like you always do."

Something like pain flashes in his eyes, infinite pain, but it's gone before Alabama can make heads or tails of it.

Griff, stone-faced, snaps his fingers at someone in the shadows. "Mikey, take her back to the bus."

"I can get back myself, thanks."

She rips her arm away from Mikey and then spins around on her heel.

She needs to get away from Griff. Fast.

Two in the morning and the sound of laughter shakes the entire bus. Alabama exits her room to see the front of the lounge packed with people. She wades through the haze of smoke and conversation to see Griff sitting on the black leather couch, a beer in his hand. There's a brunette with thigh-high boots tucked into his side.

When Alabama hovers in the corridor, Brian gives her a nod. "We wake you up?" he asks in a tone that says he doesn't care. He's in the dinette, counting money from the merchandise sales. Alabama can't help compare his expression to the same one Mort would wear. Greedy as hell. He doesn't care about the music or Griff. All he cares about is getting rich.

"You did," she says coolly.

Before she can silently escape, Griff glances up, his tawny-colored eyes sliding to hers. The girl he's with looks Alabama over from head to toe—scanning her bare legs, her long T-shirt and ratty hair—and softly snorts. "Who's that?"

"No one," Griff drawls, his voice husky and bored.

The girl giggles and marks her territory by scooting herself up onto Griff's lap.

Resentment curls Alabama's stomach. She can't deny it anymore. She's jealous, like some damn teenage girl. In fact, teen Alabama would haul this girl off Griff's lap by her hair and toss her out on her ass.

But she ain't that girl anymore, and Griff ain't hers.

The truest two facts she knows.

Alabama watches as Brian pushes another beer on Griff, watches as Griff fumbles with the lighter to light a cigarette. Her gaze narrowing, she takes in the cemetery of beer cans, the empty whiskey bottles. Griff, his face drawn, looks worse than she's ever seen him.

As if he's read her mind, Mikey steps close to her from

where he'd been refilling the small fridge with beers. "He started drinkin' the minute you left the stage."

Her stomach drops. "Shit."

"He could barely finish his set." Mikey's hushed voice betrays worry. "It wasn't a missed show, but . . . it was close."

That seals it. She pins her gaze to Griff. "We got a six o'clock show tomorrow."

His brows lift, but his voice remains deadened. "So?"

"So. That's early. You gonna be able to take the stage feelin' like shit?"

He sneers. "I'll do better than you did tonight."

The girl giggles and the scornful sound slices through Alabama like a knife. A reminder of what she lost. A reminder of what she can still lose.

Freddie's threat ringing in her head—they miss a show, they end the tour—Alabama tries again. "You keep drinkin' yourself silly, you won't be able to play."

Griff knocks back the entire beer in three deep gulps. He wipes his mouth on his arm. "Guess you'll see tomorrow."

"No, *you'll* see tomorrow," she warns. "Crack of dawn I'm gonna be in your room wakin' your ass up."

Keeping his eyes on her, a smirk on his face, Griff calmly cracks open another beer.

Mikey swears under his breath, and Brian snickers.

That's it.

Not missing a beat, Alabama strides forward.

She rips the beer from Griff's hands and tosses it in the trash.

"Hey!" he snaps.

He stumble-staggers to standing, tossing the brunette off his lap.

The room goes still as death.

Griff gets close to her, his eyes blazing with fury. "What the fuck do you think you're doin'?"

Her heart thundering, Alabama crosses her arms and squares

up. "Givin' a damn about you, Griff, because it's clear no one else out here does."

He laughs, a bitter, broken sound. "The only reason you give a damn about me is because you need me." His upper lip curls in contempt. "Without me, all you'd be good for is playin' your shit songs at shit-ass Mill's Tavern in that shit mess of yours you call a life."

She jerks back like he's slapped her. The blow of his words, their stinging truth, has her turning on her heel and striding fast for her bedroom. Stupid man. She ain't putting up with this shit. Doesn't know why she cares, why she tried. It's clear Griff's only looking out for himself, just like he did in Clover.

"Alabama . . ." Griff's voice follows her down the hall. The shuffle of his footsteps as he stumbles after her.

She doesn't stop. She can't stop. She stops, she'll break, and she'll never give Griff Greyson the satisfaction of seeing her fall.

She throws her bedroom door open. She whips around to slam it shut, but Griff wedges his boot in, propping it wide open.

Her gut twists as their gazes collide. She doesn't know what she expected—that same ire and fire he directed at her in the lounge—but not regret and remorse. She's so stunned her hand tightens around the doorknob to hold herself up. Griff's face is raw, frayed down to its absolute edges, like he's trying to hold it together and barely succeeding.

"Al," he says, broken-voiced. Tentatively, he reaches out to fiddle with a long lock of her red hair. The strand disappears in his palm as he cups the side of her face. A lick of heat sweeps down her spine as he grazes a calloused thumb across the curve of her cheek. "I didn't mean it," he whispers. "I'm sorry. I'm so damn sorry."

She closes her eyes, her entire body a shudder. She wants to break in half at his touch. "Please. Let me have this, Griff." Her voice shakes. "Don't ruin this for me."

"I won't. I swear it, Al. I won't."

His softly uttered words, a promise she doesn't know if she can believe, have her opening her eyes.

Griff's moved closer. His big, broad hands clutch her around the waist, and then they drift down to grip the hem of her T-shirt. Slowly, so slowly, he pulls her into him.

Alabama's cheeks warm. Her heartbeat surges through her, a pulse in her chest, a pulse down below. It's a reminder of how they used to be. How they'd bicker until steam started pouring out of their ears and they started tearing each other's clothes off. How sparks always flew between them, but they made up like none of it mattered. Like nothing would ever stand in their way.

Apparently, Griff feels it too because his eyes haven't left her face. Not once.

Desire curls in the pit of her stomach. The urge to grip Griff by his dirty T-shirt and pull him into her bedroom has real teeth.

A shrill giggle in the hallway sets the alarm siren off in her brain.

What the hell is she doing? Griff's drunk.

Griff's drunk and she's just another girl to him.

This—whatever *this* is—is not an option. All Alabama's doing is falling back into her old ways. Falling into *his* ways.

The thought's acid.

She jerks away from him.

"Al," he says, reaching for her.

"Go to bed, Greyson," she says, lightly pushing him out of her doorway. He staggers drunkenly and looks at her shame-faced. "Go to bed and sleep it off."

She shuts the door. Her breath, her heart, held still in her chest until she hears his soft pad of footsteps heading down the hall.

chapter
SEVEN

THE SOFT RUMBLE OF THE BUS SHAKES GRIFF AWAKE. Rolling over in bed, he gives a kill-me-now groan at the harsh sunlight assaulting his retinas. Blindly, he reaches over onto his nightstand for his sunglasses. He slips them on. For a long minute, he lies there taking inventory of his condition. His mouth's ashtray-dry; his body feels as if he drank the entire state of Tennessee.

And his head . . .

He searches his mind for memories of last night. All he gets are foggy images—cigarettes, seven and seven, bottles of Bud Light, some brunette whose name he's already forgotten, and Alabama—

"*Fuuuuuuck.*"

Griff closes his eyes, his slow swear like his last dying gasp. And it should be.

He insulted her last night. Worse, he insulted her and then put the moves on her. Griff squeezes his eyes shut tighter, trying to block out the image of her face. Hurt. Walking away from him. Closing the door in his face.

He can't deny the entire blow-up was his fault. He got blitzed last night after she called him on his bullshit backstage. Brought that girl back to the bus to fuck with her. He doesn't know why in the hell he cared about what she said. Why her words affected him so fucking bad.

If she wasn't so damn stubborn, she could have just let him help her without blowing everything up. Fucking woman. All she's doing is stirring up old memories of Clover, of the way they used to be together, of the old Griff Greyson.

The one who actually gave a damn.

He doesn't want that. It's too hard and people get hurt.

All he wants to do is get through this tour with his head on straight and his dick in his pants. But last night . . . tempers were high. He can't deny he was horny as hell—and he didn't want that brunette on the couch. He wanted Alabama. And she fucking knew it.

At the bright chirp of his cell phone, Griff buries his face in his hands. It's like a knife tearing into his temple.

Not even bothering to answer, he stumbles out of bed. In the bathroom, he fumbles with the bottle of aspirin and dry-swallows three pills. He's crawling back into bed, considering getting some more shut-eye, when the phone sounds again, its bleating chirp muffled. He glances at the clock. It's only ten.

"Goddamn," he groans, flipping the covers off the bed to find his phone sandwiched beneath a pillow.

He snatches it up without bothering to look at the caller ID. "What?" he growls.

"Your greeting needs work, Griff." Freddie's clipped voice lashes his eardrum.

A long pause, then, "What?" he says, a bit softer but no less gruff.

"Have you seen the papers?"

He flops back on the bed. He doesn't need more bad news, more shitty press. "No, I haven't. What'd I do now?"

"A good thing. And for once, it doesn't involve fistfights or fornication." The sound of a keyboard clacking fills the line. "I'm sending you the link. It's you and Alabama onstage. You helped her out last night. Apparently, people like your music, your sound."

Griff sighs. Their sound.

Christ, they hadn't had a song together since Clover.

"Your set was a bit shorter than I would have liked, but barring any further setbacks, I'm willing to overlook that."

Griff chuckles. He's not sure how Freddie does it. She's gotta have eyes in the back of her head or spies on the inside or some shit like that to constantly be aware of Griff's mistake-making ass.

"These are good headlines," Freddie goes on. "Even if fans are skeptical, the press is still reporting positively. Or in terms you'll understand, they're eating this shit up. I want more of that. More of the two of you together onstage. More of you playing the rugged, yet dashing, gentleman."

Griff clenches a fist at Freddie's insinuation that he was just using Alabama, that he's playing a part. He wants to tell her it wasn't planned, it just happened, that Alabama needed help and whatever she needs he'd give her without a second thought.

"Fred—"

"Do not disappoint me, Griff. This tour is off to a smashing start."

"Is that it?"

"Yes." He hears the smile in her voice. "You may go back to your hangover."

The call ends with a click. Griff pinches his temples and lets out a frustrated growl. His head hurts like hell, and all he wants to do is go back to bed, but he can't stop thinking about Alabama. His brain is unsettled by all the shady shit Freddie keeps asking him to do. To slap a label on Alabama. To just use her like everyone else. When all he wants to do is . . .

Christ. He doesn't know anymore.

Once again, Griff's mind drifts.

Last night. He doesn't know what came over him. He had sworn up and down he would stay away from her, but the sight of Alabama looking too goddamn gorgeous nearly undid him. Her long, bare legs, her shock of red hair, her deep Texas drawl that intrudes when she's hot and bothered. That fiery girl he had loved came back to him. Calling him on his bullshit, going toe to toe, pouring out his beer—Alabama was the only woman who could ever put him in his place.

He smears his face in his hands, knocking his sunglasses cockeyed. Fuck. What's happening to him? She's making him soft. Making him the man he was when he was with Alabama.

A sharp knock on the door has him wincing. No doubt Brian coming to lay down some life lessons. "Go away," he snaps, leveling his voice with the threat of death.

The door swings open to reveal Alabama. Griff's stomach tenses at the sight of her. She stands in the doorway, wearing a white sweater dress, her face stony, a bottle of water in her hands. "Get up."

"Go away."

Griff lets out an *oof* as the bottle of water slams him in the stomach.

"Damnit, woman," he snarls, ripping off his sunglasses to glare at her.

She frowns down at him. "We got a show in Lexington tonight. And I warned you, Griff. Tomorrow's today." Griff feels himself hardening beneath the sheets. The bossy tone of her voice turns him on like nothing else. She bares her teeth. "Get. Up. Now."

He does. He drags himself out of bed to stand in front of her, lifting his arms in a *what-now* gesture, and then drops them at his side.

"You tell me what we're doin' at least?"

"There's a weight room at the hotel." She tosses her glossy red hair. "I called ahead. We'll be there in ten. You're gonna get dressed and get your ass in there, and get it together. Go sweat it out."

He nods, as if he has a choice in the matter.

"Listen." Griff slicks a hand through his hair. "About last night, what I said—"

She lifts a palm. "We all do dumb things when we

drink," she says, and the knot in his throat tightens. "Already forgotten."

"Still," he says, holding her eyes. He needs to get this right, to make sure she knows he means it. "I never should have said it. I acted like an asshole to you and I'm sorry."

Alabama pulls herself up straight, her thin shoulders stiff. She studies his face, her gray eyes reading him like no one else can. "This is the last time I do this," she warns. "I ain't babysittin' you. That ain't what I signed on to do. I signed on to sing and I hope you'll let me do that."

"I got it. And I will. I won't wreck this for you." He stares at her and then nods. "I promise. No fights. No boozin.'"

Griff's heart soars at the hope that brightens her face. And then and there he knows he can't let her down. Not again. She deserves this tour. More than he does.

"Thank you." Though she gives a curt nod, a familiar softness flickers in her eyes.

Then, she points a lean arm toward a pile of clothes stacked on a corner chair. "Now march."

Griff grunts. "Yeah, yeah." He tosses her a look as he sniffs a T-shirt, checking its clean factor. "You enjoyin' this, ain't you, sweetheart?"

Her gorgeous face breaks out into a sly smile. "Enjoyin' watchin' you sweat it all out, no doubt."

Griff steps into the bathroom, not even bothering to hide a groan at every ache and pain that runs through his body. "I hate you for this," he tells Alabama as he dips his head to chug the trickle of water from the faucet.

He hears her smile through the door. "You better sing your ass off tonight, Griff Greyson, because if you don't I'm gonna kick it. To high heaven."

After her set, Alabama takes a spot backstage, watching Griff as he performs "Get While the Getting's Good," a rollicking number from one of his very first albums.

> Are you gonna get while the getting's good?
> Are you gonna be that girl who says she could?
> Change my mind, move my whole damn world
> And then you take what you get and give the blame
> Because you know there ain't no shame
> In gettin' while the getting's good,
> Girl, get while the getting's good . . .

Griff's moving slow, but he's clear and focused, singing with his typical cocky confidence. His voice sounds better than ever, rough and ragged. Goddamn gorgeous, if she really wants to admit it. Sure, he's hungover and hurting, but he's hiding it well and that's all that matters to Alabama.

She needs this. She needs this tour and she and Griff have to pull together to make it a success.

> Don't need to stick around to understand
> Don't need to see him to know I ain't your man
> So pack your bags, you done what you could
> And get while the damn getting's good . . .

Despite her crossed arms, her emotionless face, Alabama can't help but tap a toe at the charming sound. It's a terrific song. Griff's entire first album was a knockout, had won him Male Artist of the Year at the ACMs. She remembers angry-eating ice cream as she watched it on TV with Holly. He had thanked his mama, thanked Jim Beam, and then promptly booked it offstage. He was high as a kite, and she—and the world—knew it.

There's a soft rustle in the dark and then Brian's standing beside her. His arms crossed against his two-small shirt, he wears a headset attached to his mouth, a somber expression. He watches Griff for a long second and then says, "You two sounded good tonight."

She nods. "Yeah. I thought so too."

The admission has her gritting her teeth.

They sang together again onstage. After her first few songs, Griff had graced the audience with his presence. She still doesn't like it, him stepping in to smooth things over with his fans, but she didn't fight it. They sang a cover of "Pancho and Lefty," and then Griff left her to finish out her set.

Brian's headset erupts with the sound of buzzing voices. His brows lift and then he sighs. "I gotta go help Mikey out of a jam." A small smile overtakes his face. "You got this, Al."

"Thanks," she says softening, surprised by Brian's bolstering words.

She watches him retreat to the shadows and returns her gaze to the stage.

For a split second, Griff glances over, his gaze sweeping over her. She stiffens, her heart ricocheting in her chest as if it wants to leap onstage with him. Then she scowls at herself, at her traitorous internal organs. Griff's eyes are already forward, focused back on the audience.

Why is she even bothering with Griff? Why doesn't she just let him sink, blow his own boat up? Well, she's on that boat. And Alabama's done sinking.

Still, she can't help but watch him, can't help but wonder if that boy, that sweet boy from Clover, is still in there. Somewhere. She saw a glimpse of him this morning in Griff's apology. It was sincere. Honest. Shame in his eyes. He meant it, and that meant a lot to her. There was no trace of the edgy bullshitter who put up a tough-talking front last night. No trace of the man who had taken her in his arms and tried to—

Alabama's thoughts are blasted out of her brain at the sound of an electric guitar sizzling onstage.

She presses fingers to her lips, smothering a laugh.

Their sounds are so damn different. Sounds she never would have pegged them for. While Griff is all countrified rock and roll, Alabama's pop-country. When they played together back in Clover, at Mill's Tavern, they somehow bridged that gap. Their sound walked the line between old school country and rock and roll.

And no matter what, their songs always had heart.

Alabama's phone vibrates. She pulls it out from the waist-band of her skirt and checks it. A text from Freddie. *Keep up the smashing work!*

Below it—an attached screenshot of a headline from the *Nashville Star*.

Despite Rocky Start to Tour, Alabama Forester's Voice Finally Takes Center Stage

She smiles softly, trying to ignore the thrill of excitement, of happiness, she feels at one measly—albeit positive—headline.

Once again, Alabama's eyes settle on Griff.

She doesn't know if she trusts his word, the promise he made this morning to toe the line, but it's all she's got, so she has to hang on to that.

Because she can do this.

She and Griff—they can do this.

They have to.

chapter
EIGHT

THE DEVIL DOG LOUNGE IN MYRTLE BEACH IS A grungy bar out on some country dirt back road. It's late, after midnight, after a show that killed it. Griff, the band, and Alabama are in one of the best moods they've been in, and ready to celebrate. Tomorrow's their first day off in a week. And so far, Griff's been a poster child for good behavior. There's no drinking to excess, no missing shows. He's kept it professional, and she's kept her distance. Talk when you need to; shut the hell up when you don't. The way it should be. The way it's gonna be.

The tour's also getting good press. For once, the *Nashville Star* isn't so focused on her sex and instead is focusing on her songs.

Which puts Alabama in a very celebratory mood.

She glances down the bar where Griff and his band—the Gunslingers—have bellied up. Scotty, their drummer, orders shots of tequila. As he passes them down the line, he catches her eye. "You doin' this, Red?"

Accepting the shot, Alabama raises it in a toast. "Anything worth doin' is worth doin' right." She shoots back the tequila, swallowing through the burn as Scotty cracks out a gunshot of a laugh.

She smiles, finally feeling as if she's found her groove with the band. Sure, the communal bathroom sucks and the closet space is lacking, but she doesn't mind sharing a bus with the boys. They treat her like one of their own. Anything to be back onstage again, to be singing her songs. Although, so far, her songs have been met with a lukewarm reception. She knows it's because they're older; she needs to write new material, but she can't work up the nerve. She's worried about clamming up again. She didn't like the way it made her feel. Vulnerable and anxious. It opened up a whole new world that was scary and strange and foreign. What if she can't do it anymore?

"Another?" Scotty asks.

She nods, glancing down the bar at Griff, who's got Nikki pressed up against his side. Singing with Griff—it's not something she bargained for. It gets her hot and bothered more times than she wants to admit. Sharing a mic with him, his low voice unfurling like a spool of velvet so close to her ear she shivers. So far all they've done are covers, but it's made her think of the past and the songwriting sessions they used to hunker down for. It was like sex. Writing their songs. The closest, the most passionate they had ever been.

"Man, y'all sure made the whole stage rattle tonight," says Coop, the big, burly bass player. He ashes his cigar on the bar, much to the chagrin of the scowling waitress.

"You should've heard 'em back in the day," Brian supplies and Alabama fights to hold back an eye roll. His smile's proud, like he personally introduced the two of them.

"No way." Scotty gapes at Griff. "Really?"

Griff, not looking happy with his cousin volunteering the information, turns his empty shot glass between his scarred knuckles. The glass clinks against the metal of his rings. "Really."

"Man, how did I not know this?" Scotty drums his hands across the bar top and whistles. "Now that's a story I'm gonna need."

Alabama leans back from the bar, voice neutral. "Ain't no story. We knew each other in the past. We sang together once upon a time. The end."

Griff lifts a brow but doesn't say a word.

"I knew there was somethin'," Scotty muses. "The way the two of you sing . . . like fire and gasoline."

"Combustible," Alabama mutters under her breath.

"You wanna sniff something out," Griff says easily, slapping Scotty on the back like he can kick him into a different gear, "sniff me out a goddamn drink."

At that, Scotty rattles off an order for a whiskey neat.

Alabama quickly surveys Griff. A decision she immediately regrets. Because when Nikki leans in to nuzzle Griff's neck, Alabama has to fight the urge to scrape out her eyeballs.

The tips of her ears burn, and she looks away.

Good Lord, what's wrong with her? Getting back in the saddle with Griff ain't even a thing. It ain't even an option. It's a mistake is what it would be. And yet, she can feel it. Every time she gets close to him, onstage, on the bus, she can't help but go back there. To Clover. To the way she used to feel. Damn near close to spontaneously combusting from lust.

Lust she can work with.

She turns to Coop. "Another."

Coop looks impressed. "Man, girl, you keep continuin' to impress." He looks past Scotty and Brian to Griff. "Greyson, you think she can outdrink you?"

Scotty passes down a shot. "Now that's a bet I'd put good money on."

"How much?" Alabama asks, wiggling her brows before shooting the white-gold liquid back down without so much as a second thought.

Tonight, it's her turn to have fun. To make mistakes, to drink herself silly. She hasn't had a good time in so long. Besides, they're off tomorrow. Griff can get as drunk as a skunk because that's what she plans to do.

Two more shots are set in front of her. Scotty whips out a wad of dollar bills.

Griff stares slack-jawed as Alabama downs the shots in quick succession.

"Hey, take it easy," he says, his face hardening.

The tequila's settled her nerves, loosened her tongue. She

smiles sweetly and gives a one-shoulder shrug. "Didn't you hear, Griff? I'm just as bad as you."

Brian snorts.

Griff does his best to scowl but ends up busting up into a laugh instead. "You could never back down from a challenge."

"I seem to remember you pokin' a bear a few too many times," Alabama banters. She nudges Coop with her elbow. "You should see the scar he's got from tryin' to race a bull in a go-kart."

"No shit." Coop laughs. "Who won?"

"Don't answer that," Griff says to Alabama, his lips twitching.

"Griffy," Nikki whines. "This is boring."

Alabama has to bite back a grin at the annoyed look that crosses Griff's face.

But when Griff stops his conversation to check in on Nikki, Nikki shoots Alabama a smug smirk.

Alabama feels her temper flare, her fists curl against the hem of her dress.

Just then she's saved by a good-looking cowboy in a bolo tie. "You wanna dance, darlin'?" he asks, a playful gleam in his big blue eyes.

She leans back and grins. "You know what, I would love that."

"Great." He puts out a hand to help her off the barstool.

She lets out a sharp gasp as she slides off the stool. The cowboy grabs her hand, steadying her. "You okay?"

She plasters a smile on her face. "Right as rain."

Damn heels. Her hip might as well be made of steel.

As the cowboy spins her out onto the dance floor, she catches Griff's profile. A thundercloud's rolling across his face, dark, silent and dangerous.

She shakes it off. Whatever's got a burr in his saddle, she ain't gonna sit there and be jealous. He's the one who broke her heart. Not like he cares. He's barely made eye contact the entire night. No. The only thing she is to Griff is a bad memory.

Soon, the world, and the dance floor, is spinning. Alabama feels lightheaded, her cheeks flushed from alcohol, from the body heat of the crowded bar. When the cowboy pulls her into a quick two-step, she has to shout above the din to make her voice heard. "You're a good dancer."

He grins at her. "You wanna go somewhere a little more private?"

"What do you have in mind?" she asks, her entire body vibrating.

"C'mon." The cowboy takes Alabama by the elbow and leads her out the back door into the chilly autumn night.

Outside, his beefy arm pulls her close, and Alabama lets his mouth devour hers.

"Mhhh," she whimpers, her body instinctively pulsing with pleasure. God, how long has it been since she's had sex? Too long. Too goddamn long.

The cowboy lifts her up to set her on the deep jut of a windowsill. At that, a little giggle bubbles out of her. So this is her life now. Kissing some random cowboy she picked up at a cheap dive bar. Oh yeah, she's hit the big time. She's also drunk, feeling good and fine, and most important, horny as hell.

Alabama's eyes blur as she tries to focus on the stars above. Her whole body feels heavy, weighed down by her limbs, by the tequila she's imbibed. But this is fine. She tells herself she doesn't care what she does tonight. They're just two strangers who want to feel a good thing. This ain't nothin' professional she can fuck up. It's not a love she can lose. It's lust. It's just a guy in a back alley with his hands running rough over her body.

"It's not the same," she murmurs.

The man slips the strap of her dress down. "What isn't the same, baby?"

"You." Her head tilts back against the brick wall. She closes her eyes in pleasure. Letting the cowboy's kiss chase away any and every thought of Griff Greyson. "You're not the same at all."

There are three things Griff's good at: fighting, singing, and kissing pretty women.

Add a fourth to that. Pissing off Alabama Forester.

He saw her hasty exit minutes earlier with that busted-ass bolo-tie-wearing cowboy, moving fast like she couldn't wait to get away from him. He keeps his face forward, scowling at the rows of alcohol behind the bar. Watching that cowboy spin Alabama all over the dance floor ain't his idea of a good time.

At least she stopped drinking those damn shots. He already ripped Scotty a new one for pushing alcohol on her. Goading Alabama into doin' something is like waving a red flag at a bull. You just don't do it. Or you do it, and then you run.

Griff leans his elbows on the bar and rolls out his tense shoulders. He finally told Nikki to get lost. But that's not why he's bothered. He's bothered because he cares. Goddamn, does he care about Alabama. Always has. He can't fucking deny it anymore. Singing onstage with her night after night—it's a feeling more intense than lust. A tenderness, that same gotta know her, gotta have her feeling he had when he first saw her walking down that dusty dirt road with a cherry pie to welcome him and his mama to town.

And tonight, reminiscing about good times in Clover, just cranked on all those buried-deep feelings. Not to mention a rogue wave of guilt twenty foot tall. He's wanted to tell her so long why he left, but it wouldn't matter. He sees what she thinks of him.

He's a fuckup with a quick temper. A loser who left her. And she'll never forgive him for breaking her heart.

Griff stares down at his drink, his fingers digging into the cheap glass. He knows she's hurting, too. Physically. Her injury from the rollover. He sees the pain in her face night after night after finishing a set; she practically limps back to the bus. He even ordered Brian to put a stool out onstage so she could sit and rest while she sings, but she ignores it. Damn mule-headed woman.

A groan rips out of Griff, and he swallows the rest of his

drink. Twisting on the barstool, he scans the bar for Alabama. For that flash of red hair that always told him she was near. Except she's not.

Griff's spine goes stiff. He snaps his fingers at Brian, who's skirting the bar with a pool cue in his hand.

"Where is she?"

Brian halts in his tracks. "Who? Nikki?"

"No. Alabama."

Brian shrugs. "She went out back with the guy she was dancing with."

Griff tenses. There's a roaring in his ears, a strange kind of panic and urgency tearing through him.

Brian sighs, his mouth flatlining. "Dude, you're gettin'—"

He's up and moving before Brian can finish his sentence.

No one's seeing Alabama naked tonight.

And sure as hell not when she's fucking drunk.

Though he's no saint himself, has had many one-night stands, he never took a woman to bed if she didn't have her wits about her. It wasn't fair. To her or to him. And tonight, Alabama definitely doesn't have her wits.

He stomps across the dance floor and slams open the door to the alleyway. Instantly, he's greeted by neon light, by the buzz of a fluorescent beer sign.

The next thing he sees has his insides turning to liquid. Has Griff thanking Christ he made it here when he did.

Alabama's sitting on the window ledge, pressed back against the wall, her gray eyes unfocused and swimming. The strap of her dress hangs loose, flashing a peek of lavender lace bra. The cowboy has one hand on her cheek, while his other hand grips Alabama's shapely thigh.

Bolo Tie dips his head for her lips.

Griff stops him with a growl. "Don't you goddamn move."

Alabama's eyes pop open. "Griff?" she calls, searching for him in the darkness.

He moves toward her. "I'm here, Al."

Bolo Tie glances over his shoulder. "Hey, man, we're busy."

Griff clenches his jaw, his fist. Some big-mouthed cowboy trying to give him static ain't happening.

"Move," he demands, baring his teeth in a dangerous canine snarl. "Now."

It's an effort to keep his cool, an effort not to grab the guy by the throat. But he's got to restrain himself. If he hits the guy, he's broken his no-fight promise to Alabama.

He don't got much to give her, but he's got his word.

As Bolo Tie reluctantly steps away from Alabama, she looks at Griff, heavy-lidded. Then she arches a speculative brow like she's hell-bent on giving him trouble. "I can do what I want, Greyson."

He nods, staring at her. "You can. But not when you're three sheets to the wind and can barely walk a straight line."

He holds out a hand to help her off the steep ledge, but she ignores it and slides off herself. Griff blows out a frustrated breath and tries to take her elbow. Those heels she's in are a death trap. The last thing he needs is her falling and knocking herself out.

"Go away, Griff." Alabama shoves him, but she misses and stumbles, nearly crumpling to the ground before he catches her up in his arms.

"Easy, sweetheart," Griff says as Alabama sags against his chest. He wraps an arm around her waist to keep her steady, to keep her close to him. "I got you."

Alabama, her eyes all hazy, stares up at him. The strap of her bra slips down even more, revealing a healthy amount of cleavage.

Bolo Tie gapes at her like he can't believe what he's missing out on. Well, he sticks around any longer, he sure as hell ain't gonna miss out on Griff's fist connecting with his jaw.

Anger surges in him, and Griff turns to Bolo Tie while keeping a tight hold of Alabama. "Get lost," he growls, and Bolo Tie finally beats it back inside.

That's when Alabama's long, tall body goes limp. Before she can protest, he sweeps her into his arms. Her face lolls drunkenly into his chest. Her eyes flutter and Griff waits for her to pass out, but she rallies and laughs at the stars. "Oooh. I feel dizzy."

He makes a noise of sympathy. "Yeah, I know you do, sweetheart. You gonna puke on me?"

She purses her lips. "If you're lucky."

The flirty tone in her voice has heat spreading through his chest, his lower regions, but he pushes through his own need. He wants Alabama on the bus. He wants her safe. If the press gets a hold of this . . .

Hell, that's the last thing she needs.

When Griff reaches the bus, he bangs three times on the side. Sam, the driver, heaves the door open, blinking at Griff in the darkness. Then his eyes widen at the sight of a half-conscious Alabama cradled tenderly in Griff's arms. "Go back in the bar and get Al's purse and her things," he orders Sam. "She's okay, she's just . . . not a word to anyone," he warns. "I mean it."

Sam gives him an impressed look, and Griff bites back the urge to snap at him. Yes, he knows. For once in his life, he's picking up someone else. Probably the only person in the world who could make him give a damn about anyone but himself.

Once on the bus, he carries Alabama down the hall to her room. She sways slightly but stays sitting up when he sets her on the edge of the bed. He kneels in front of her, so close he can smell the sharp sting of tequila on her breath.

Keeping his eyes on her face, he drags the small trash can closer to her. "In case you need it."

"No way." She hiccups. "I'm not drunk."

Griff laughs. "Yeah, you are. You are very, very drunk, sweetheart." Then, cupping her slender ankle in his palm, he uses his other hand to slip off her high heel. Alabama lets out a sweet sigh of relief and rests her bare foot on the thigh of his jeans. As he removes her other heel, his eyes can't help traveling from her pink-painted toes to her slim calves to her creamy taut thighs. Alabama always had the longest legs he'd ever seen. And now, all grown up, she's nearly as tall as he is. And he's gotta admit, it turns him on. Mightily.

"Wait." Alabama giggles and his heart flips. Her laughter—girlish, light. He hasn't heard that kind of sound from her since Clover. It's a glimpse of the girl he loved, and he finds himself wanting more. Needing more.

"I am drunk, ain't I?" Her eyes go wide and Griff can see the pinfire patterns of gray. Dark and light all blending into one singular color of misty silver.

"Yeah, but it's okay. You're allowed to have some fun." He grunts. "Just not with him."

"With who, then?" She wets her lips. Her eyes bore into him. She tilts her head, her long copper hair spilling over a shoulder. "With you?" She leans forward. Her low neckline exposes the voluptuous curve of her full breasts. "With you, Griff?"

Shit.

He recognizes the look on her face—it's one he's had many a time. Red-hot want. A yearning that can't be satiated. And he knows—he knows—it's the same way he's felt all goddamn night. He wants Alabama and she wants him. Which is an incredibly bad, incredibly tempting idea. Because she's drunk and his dick's jumping in his pants.

He needs to go, to get the hell outta here and beat it back to his room to beat it off.

He clears his throat, readying himself to go. "Al, I—"

Only before he can, she kisses him.

Her lips, sweet and wet, meet his. His entire body tenses at the contact and then as she melts into him, he hooks an arm around her waist, pinning her against him. Christ, she feels like everything a woman should. Soft, full of curves, feminine, yet strong. A hard shudder rockets through Griff. His body's damn near ready to overheat from her nearness. Every part of him needs her worse than he ever has, is crying out to taste every inch of her.

She rakes her fingers through his hair and moans into his mouth.

This kiss is all Alabama, and yet it's a far cry from the girl he knew. His girl is a woman and she's doing things to him that he never knew she could do.

Things like make really bad decisions.

Fuck.

That thought has Griff's growl of lust curdling in his throat. That thought forces Griff's brain to regroup, to man up and recognize just what the hell is happening. Alabama's goddamn gorgeous, and all over him, and drunk.

She's drunk as shit.

As much as it pains him, literally, he forces himself to tear his lips away from Alabama's. He does this, he's no better than Bolo Tie taking Alabama out back into the alley.

She sits there, panting, a stunned look on her face. Then she leans in, trying to kiss him again, to go back for round two, but Griff braces himself. He cups her bare shoulders. Holding her upright, he presses her gently away from him.

"No, Al. We can't."

"Griff . . ."

Alabama's pleading whisper nearly rips him in half.

"Oh, we're gonna do this," he tells her, brushing a finger across her cheekbone. His mind's already made up—he's having Alabama. "Just not now. Not tonight." He tucks a long lock of copper hair behind her ear. "You're drunk and I ain't that guy and you deserve better."

She nods, her eyes downcast, her expression disappointed.

"Let's get you some water, sweetheart, then get you into bed."

After a careful glance at Alabama, who sits with sagged shoulders, Griff exits the room to fill a glass of water in the small bathroom. He stares back at his harried reflection in the mirror, willing his cock to play dead, wondering how in the hell he got to be such a goddamn saint.

Alabama, he thinks. It's the closest to heaven he's gonna get, his lips on hers. That's not to say she ain't playing the devil with that hot-as-hell body of hers.

When he returns to the bedroom, he swears.

Alabama's passed out cold, lying on her side, one slender arm dangling off the bed, her fingers splayed.

Griff goes to her. Gently, he scoops her into his arms and then lowers her into the bed. Her head rolls off the pillow to her right shoulder, a thin veil of copper hair obscuring her pale face. He brushes a tender hand across her brow, his heart wrenching violently. She looks so fucking gorgeous, so vulnerable and strong at the same time.

Griff covers her with a blanket and then trudges over to a corner of the room, where he settles into a chair. He knows the proper thing to do is leave, but he ain't taking the chance on her waking up and getting sick with no one around to help her. He'll stay, wait a few hours to make sure she's okay, and then he'll go.

Griff gives Alabama one last long look, watching the slow rise and fall of her chest as she breathes. As he stares at her, he knows his mind's made up. He's told himself time and time again he wouldn't do this with her, he'd stay the fuck away, but he can't fight it any longer.

He wants her.

In every way he can possibly have her.

chapter
NINE

ALABAMA WAKES UP IN LAST NIGHT'S CLOTHES WITH a warm blanket wrapped around her. She lies there, in the cool, quiet darkness of her bedroom, blinking away an uneasy sleep. She can feel the memories of the evening swirling around her, and she mashes fingers against her brow like she can work out all the kinks. Kinks like too much tequila. Like a cowboy. Like—

Oh, good Lord. Oh, shit.

The memory hits her like a sledgehammer.

She sits up in bed with a strangled gasp.

Griff.

She kissed him.

A flush of hot shame washes through her. Alabama groans and buries her face in her hand like she can block the image of Griff's lips on hers. She had wanted him—so bad she could feel the ache in her bones. Wanted him to take her to bed and treat her like just another of his women. Wanted him to wrap his hands in her long red hair and pull.

But all he did was stop her. Stop her before she could go too far, before she could beg.

She groans again.

Thank God he turned her down. She can't get mixed up with another man she works with. The memory of kissing Luke Kincaid, the embarrassment she felt when it all came out . . . she has no choice but to keep it platonic.

Besides, there is no past; there is no Alabama and Griff.

There is just Alabama. Her tour, her money to make, her reputation to get back. No matter how much her body is screaming at her that she's a damn fool.

She bites her lip, wanting to tear into it and taste blood as images of last night flit through her memory. Griff coming to her rescue, giving the cowboy the boot, carrying her back to the bus, slipping off her shoes, tucking her into bed.

She groans. She *is* a damn fool. She never thought she'd be saying this, but thank God for Griff Greyson. While she didn't feel danger last night, she had put herself in a dangerous situation and she's grateful to Griff for watching out for her when no one else was. For taking care of her when she was at her worst.

She sits there in the dim light, her world spinning with awareness, until the crack of the door gets her attention.

Oh, God. Double shit.

It's Griff.

"Hey there," he says, sauntering in without bothering to ask permission. He looks put-together. Sober. Showered. Sexy as hell. His muscles strain against the fabric of his tight white T-shirt. She watches as he sets a cup of coffee on the nightstand beside an already-full glass of water, then cracks the blinds to let in a thin sliver of light.

She waits for it. A snide comeback, a rude remark, but there's nothing. Only his intent gaze on her. "How you feelin'?"

Alabama winces but manages a smile. "I'm okay. Embarrassed."

"Nah," he says quietly. "Don't be."

She draws the sheet up around herself and inhales a sharp breath. "About last night . . . you got me out of there before I made a fool of myself. It wasn't a dangerous situation"—here, Griff's face tightens—"but it could have been. I'm sorry."

He leans back against the wall. "You don't gotta be sorry about anything." His eyes hold hers. "I'm just glad you're okay."

"Me too. I'm glad you were there. Thank you," she says, meaning it.

"You're welcome, Al."

And it's like something passes between them. A truce of some kind. A surge of emotion, a gratefulness that their orbits are still orbiting.

Alabama takes another breath. Better to get it all out now. "Also, I'm sorry for sloppily kissin' you last night."

He grins. "I ain't so sure about that. Best sloppy kiss of my life."

The word *kiss* sets something off in her and Alabama glances down at the bed, trying to ignore the wistful rush of heat in her thighs, her belly dipping so far down she can feel it in her toes.

"Well, sloppy or not, it was inappropriate, and I didn't mean it," she says hastily, tugging the fallen strap of her dress up on her shoulder. "When I drink, I get . . . wild."

"Wild," he echoes. The arch of his brow tells her he's wondering what exactly constitutes a wild Alabama Forester. "I knew there was a name for the girl I saw last night."

She floats him a stern look and a humorless laugh. "Griff."

"C'mon," he says, suddenly all business, apparently deciding not to torture her any further. He pushes off the wall and crosses his arms against his chest. His tattooed biceps bulge. "Hydrate, drink your coffee, then get yourself cleaned up."

She gives him a half-smile. "What is this? Payback?"

"Payback? I'd be lyin' if I said it didn't cross my mind, but hell, I ain't that cruel." A slow grin spreads across his face. "We're goin' out."

"Where?" She takes a sip of her coffee. It's heavy with cream and sugar, and Alabama feels a flutter in her chest. Griff—all this time, he's remembered.

"We're gonna buy you some boots."

At her sigh, he gives her a hard, no-nonsense look. "You're hurtin', Alabama. Every night you're onstage, your hip's givin' you grief."

She stares down into her coffee. "That's not your problem, Griff."

"Bullshit."

She looks up, stunned.

There's anger in his voice, but it's not directed at her. The hard angle of his jaw tells her he's angry at himself. A pang of sorrow tears at her heart as she sees the years of guilt etched across his rugged face. Years of blame and shame that have stuck with him all this time.

Griff's harsh voice takes on a kind of vicious tenderness. "You're in pain, and I ain't havin' that."

Alabama, at last, admits, "It does hurt. The more I'm onstage, the less I sit, it locks up. It's gotten worse over the years."

He gives her a sharp look, and she wonders if he'll bring up Clover. But he doesn't. Instead, Griff swallows and moves closer to sit at the end of the bed.

"My scar hurts," he says, and her eyes leap to his face. "Every time it rains, it aches. And every time it aches, I remember that night and what I did to you."

Alabama looks at him, wanting to cup his scar beneath her palm and tell him that it's okay. That she never blamed him for the accident. That all she wants is an explanation for why he left.

She shakes her head. "It was my fault as much as yours. I'm the one who stole my daddy's Jeep—"

"And I was the one drivin'—"

"Because I asked you to. I'm the one who wanted to go joyridin' up on the Ridge. I told you to man up and speed up, remember?" He chuckles grimly, and she goes on. "We were both wild, Griff. That's why we worked. Back then."

She can't help the dig, but once she says it, there's a strange tightening in her chest, a rush of regret that what happened last night won't happen again.

"Right," he says, meeting her gaze head-on, and Alabama's breath hitches. The look in his eyes—brazen? Defiant? Hungry?—leaves her speechless. But before she can fully puzzle out Griff's piercing gaze, he says, "So how 'bout those boots?"

She smiles. "Okay. Boots."

Alabama sits on a bench in Tommy's Fine Boot Fitters, Johnny Cash on the speakers above, watching as Griff gives the frazzled clerk a list of boots a mile long. He's all confidence and action as he rattles off Alabama's shoe size and the brands they want and the ones they don't. The clerk, a skinny teen girl with braces, clearly nervous at being in the presence of Griff Greyson, is doing her best to follow his demands.

Alabama can't help but smile. It's their first day off in a week and Griff's spending it with her, doing the most mundane activity alive, shoe shopping. She steals a glance at his tall, broad-shouldered form. Griff's changed into jeans and a button-up with the cuffs rolled up to expose arms corded with muscle and tattoos. With his dusty boots and his aviators, he looks like just a guy. A guy she would have known in Clover.

A slice of regret hits her at the memory of the past. They used to be so good together. Hell, ever since this morning it feels as if they've arrived at something. What that is, she doesn't know. Only that their old conversation came back simple and effortless. The bond between them familiar, bordering on friendly. She hates that it was this easy, wishes their connection would have died the second Griff left town, but even twelve years later it's still kicking. She could always talk to Griff. Being with him, being part of his pair, always made her feel wild and strong. Together, with their tempers, the two of them were like gasoline on a flame. But it wasn't dangerous, and it wasn't mean. It was determined. They pushed the other, worked anything out with loud voices but kind mouths. They listened, but more importantly, they took care of each other. Which was exactly what Griff did last night.

She pulls her mind back to the present as Griff moseys over, fingers hooked in his belt loops. "That does it," he says. "Now we wait. Gonna take her an hour to find everything."

"Think you scared that poor girl to death," Alabama quips.

"You scare me to death." He sits next to her on the bench. He toes her heels, kicked off her feet, strewn on the ground. "Paradin' around in these around every damn night. Would wear me the hell out."

Though his voice is gruff, she hears the concern in it.

She smirks. "Tough cowboy, huh? Pair of little heels got you down?" She keeps her voice light, teasing. She's not in the mood to rehash this morning and talk about the accident. It gets them too close to the past, to where they used to be.

Unless Griff's going to tell her his reason for leaving Clover, she wants to leave the past behind them. And it's on the tip of her tongue to say just that when she suddenly busts out laughing.

The look on Griff's handsome face has suddenly morphed into an expression so disgusted it could curdle milk.

"What on earth's got your face so ugly?"

Without a word, he lifts a finger to point at the speakers above them.

Alabama listens. And hears it. The Brothers Kincaid's catchy new single "Second Chances." Luke's smooth voice rings out in a passionate southern drawl.

> I woke up early one mornin', answerin' the dawn of sun
> My wife was beside me sleepin', dreamin somethin' in her mind
> Lord, I lay in bed just starin', like a lovesick son of a gun
> Because second chances don't come easy and I'm grateful that she's mine.

Alabama frowns at Griff's surly scowl, realizing he's serious. "You really dislike the guy, don't you?"

She doesn't know whether to be amused or shocked by Griff's fury. By the tender look of protection blazing in his eyes.

"Dislike ain't strong enough a word." He turns to her. "If I ever see Luke Kincaid, the two of us, we're gonna have words."

"What'd he ever do to you?"

"You mean besides throw you under the bus?"

"Luke's not that bad."

His eyes practically pop out of his head. "Not that bad. Christ, Al, he sold you down the river."

"'Sold you down the river'? Really, Griff, who talks like that?" She shakes her head. "And he did not. Mort outed us both. All Luke did was protect his wife and his band. He's gotta be loyal to them. Not me." She bumps her shoulder to his. "Besides you're just jealous the Brothers Kincaid don't have to act like assholes to sell records."

"Yeah, well, I still think the guy's a prick," Griff grumbles, leaning forward to rest his elbows on the thighs of his jeans.

"It ain't the same for guys," she says softly. "Hell, Griff, you went to jail, you hate Clover, you weren't even born there, and you still got a statue in our hometown." Griff frowns as if he's just now realizing her truth and doesn't like it. Alabama continues. "You take any girl to bed and you're a saint. I make one bad decision and I'm branded a slut for life."

A contrite look crosses Griff's face. But Alabama's not done. Something's turned on inside of her. A hot flush of embarrassment, yes, but also a purging of the soul. It seems like everywhere she goes, she has to admit, to deny, to deflect. She's sick of it. Sick of running, sick of sticking her head in the sand, sick of saying sorry. Nashville's a big city, but it's got small-town fangs. It will never let her forget.

No one knows the real story but Alabama—why she did what she did with Mort.

"I hear what they're saying about me in the press. I know what you heard. That I'm a whore. That I slept with Mort. That I'll suck anyone's dick to get ahead." Griff winces. She plows forward, wanting to make sure he hears her and understands. Because even though they've been estranged for years, she realizes it still matters what he thinks of her. Even if the truth is an embarrassing hot mess of petty bullshit.

She peers at Griff. He's frowning her way, his tawny eyes clouded and wary. "I've made a lot of mistakes. Kissing Luke to set him up for Mort was a mistake, and I did do that, Griff. I own that. But all that other stuff . . . I'm not that girl. I would never—"

"I know that."

She blinks. "You do?"

"I do. You don't deserve any of that," Griff says fiercely. "Not you, Al. I know you."

"Used to."

He sighs. "Alabama . . ."

Tears spring to her eyes. Unbidden, but she can't stop them. Just the belief, the conviction in his voice . . .

He's been the first person to stand by her. To stand up for her. Even her own father hadn't backed her during the mess with Six String.

"You should've seen the way my daddy looked at me," she whispers, a tear slipping down her cheek. "I embarrassed him. He always taught me to do the right thing, and I didn't. He'll never look at me the same way again. He hates me."

Griff grabs her hand. "Don't do that to yourself," he says, turning his entire body toward her. "You're so damn strong, Al. Everything you've faced, you just keep comin' back. Sure, you made a mistake, we've all made mistakes. You can't go on blamin' yourself forever."

She raises her eyes. "You takin' your own advice?"

The look on his face, the conversation from this morning, says he won't.

He lets go of her hand. Instead of answering her question, he says, "I never for a goddamn second thought you did any of the shit they're sayin'. Never." He runs a hand through his hair. Hesitates. "But I gotta ask, Al—and feel free to kick my ass— but why? Why'd you do it? You didn't need any of it. Hell, with or without Mort Stein, you were on your way to a number one song. A platinum album. You would have made it. I know it."

She sees him trying to piece it together.

The girl he knows.

What she's told him.

What she did.

She gave him everything but the why.

She stares down at her hands. That's the part no one knows. Not even Holly. The part she kept out of the press conference.

Now, she owes him the truth. She owes herself finally saying the words aloud.

Her throat threatens to close up, but she braces her body, steadies her voice and says, "I wanted to beat you."

Griff blinks, surprise creasing his face. "What?"

"The only reason I ever came to Nashville after you left Clover was to beat you. If you could make it without me, I was gonna show you I could make it without you. And when I met Mort, I thought he was the fastest way to get ahead. The fastest way I could get me a number one song and prove to you I was as good as you were." She nods, staring at the ground, lost in the past. "I thought, all it was was one kiss. How much damage could it do?" She laughs grimly. "Turns out, a lot, in fact."

Alabama exhales a breath, the admission like a weight released. She wasn't expecting to bare all in a boot store today, but she did. Surprisingly, she feels better.

She lifts her head to stare at Griff.

His jaw is open and gaping. She can't tell what she sees in his eyes. Regret. Maybe guilt. She knows it was a hell of a story to lay on him here and now, but it was something she had to do. For herself and for him.

Griff smears a hand over the back of his head. "Damn. Al, I—"

But whatever he was about to say is cut off by the reappearance of the clerk. She stands in front of them, a tall stack of boot boxes swaying precariously in her arms. "Okay, we've got the classic calfskin cowboy boot here with a round toe and a one-and-three-quarter inch heel . . ."

Alabama gives him a quick side-eye. "We'll talk later."

"Oh, you better believe we'll talk later," Griff says, his face as dark as a storm cloud.

chapter
TEN

I T'S DUSK BY THE TIME THEY LEAVE THE BOOT SHOP. GRIFF
walks slow beside Alabama on the Oceanfront Boardwalk,
taking in her stance, her lightened limp. She's ditched the
heels and is wearing her new boots. A honey-colored pair of
Luccheses with elaborate stitching.

"How do they feel?" he asks.

Alabama stops in her tracks and does a little twirl. The hem
of her long-sleeved yellow maxi dress flares up, exposing her
long slender legs. Griff's stomach flips. "Fit like a glove," she
says. "They feel good too."

"Good." He nods. "Get those worn in and you'll be golden.
I want you wearin' those every damn night you're onstage, Al. I
don't want you hurtin' no more."

"So what? You're my big strong protector now?" Alabama
teases.

She's goddamn right he is.

Ever since they'd left the boot outfitters, Griff's been gripped
by a hollowness in his stomach. The admission that Alabama had
partnered with Mort Stein to stick it to him left him reeling, left
him chuckling, left him admiring her even more for fighting to
make her dreams happen without him.

But it also did something else to him. It pissed him off. He
saw the pain in her eyes. Saw how shitty she's been treated in
this industry, in the press, because of one stupid mistake. Lord
knows, Griff's had his share of fuckups and he's still been able

to sell records, to survive unscathed when Alabama's never been given an ounce of the respect she's owed.

It makes him sick to think that's exactly why she's here. To use her sex to sell his records. It makes him want to beat the shit out of himself. He can't imagine how she'd feel about him if she learned the truth.

What if he told her? Told her everything. About the ring. The real reason he left Clover. Why she's really on tour.

Griff's cyclone of thoughts stops swirling when he realizes Alabama's stopped. His gaze drifts to her. She's standing beside him, frozen, the only sound in the air the carnival-like cacophony of the Boardwalk.

"What's wrong?" he asks.

As if in answer, there's a soft rustle of footsteps behind them.

Alabama stiffens, listening. She glances back over her shoulder and then at Griff. "Paparazzi?"

Griff goes hot all over, a torrent of anger bubbling beneath the surface. His eyes narrow as he scans the shadows. "I don't know."

Instinctively, he moves closer to her, gripped by an urgent need to get her out of there before they can get another goddamned photo of her. "C'mon," he says, lightly pressing his palm against the small of her back.

As they continue down the brightly bustling boardwalk, Alabama keeps close to him, her hips brushing against his, their fingertips grazing each other's in their effort to match each other's stride.

A soft chuckle escapes Alabama's lips, as if she's been lost in thought this entire time.

He looks over at her. He can't help the catch of his breath at the way the moonlight ripples across her copper hair.

God, she's beautiful.

"You know I don't even like heels," Alabama says, breaking the silence. "Guess I've been wearin' 'em because I'm so used to 'em." Her red lips purse. "It's how Six String wanted me to look. High heels, short skirts. At first, I didn't give two hangs about it. I came to Nashville to be famous, and that's what I was gonna do. But it went on and on, and I couldn't even write my songs. I was stuck singing that syrupy shit that had you cringing." Alabama shakes her head. She breaks eye contact and looks away. "Those last few months with Six String . . . I barely even remembered who I was or why I loved the music or what my own voice sounded like."

Griff stays silent, listening, wanting to hear more about this Alabama Forester. A woman he's admiring more and more.

Her laugh rings out over the crash of the waves. "Now, all I've got is hundreds of haters and a number one song that doesn't even feel like mine."

Her brave words, her earnest honesty topple something in Griff. A similar feeling he's had all these long damn years. It's no one's fault but his, but still. He got hooked, and he got hooked good. By the time he realized what was happening, it was too late to get out. He liked the money, the fame, the high so much he was stuck.

"I'm fake," Alabama says in her soft lilt. "All thanks to me and Mort."

"If you're fake, I'm fake, Al," he says, and she turns surprised eyes his way. "Hell, I'm the fakest son of a bitch you'll ever meet."

They pause next to a railing, a secluded spot on the pier that overlooks the beach. Alabama sets her bags down and turns her entire body toward him. She doesn't ask him to go on, but he does. The look on her face tells him she's listening and to Griff, someone listening, truly listening, is worth all the whiskey in Tennessee.

"You and I—we took the same deal, I think." He slicks a hand through his dirty blond hair. "I ain't wrote a song since my first album. The first five years I can barely remember. I liked gettin' drunk, smokin' dope, startin' fights. I liked it and the label liked it and it sold records. But it got to where I couldn't figure out where the real Griff Greyson began or ended."

Her brows bunch in concern.

He goes on. "These last five years I've been drier than Oklahoma. What I'm doin' ain't sellin'. I'm tired of raisin' a ruckus, but I don't know how to do—to be—anything else."

"Me too." She's staring at him with sad, understanding eyes. "When you try to change, they won't let you."

"They got you so goddamn pigeonholed—"

"No one will take a risk on you doin' somethin' different."

"I sing songs someone else wrote. And I hate 'em, Al." He clenches a fist. "I fuckin' hate 'em."

She's nodding. "Same. I don't connect with any of mine. I mean, 'High Heels, Higher Expectations.' What the hell kind of song is that?"

They crack up.

When she sobers, Alabama says, "At least you *could* have written your songs."

Regret slams him in the gut. He squandered his opportunity when Alabama never even had it.

"Yeah, but they're a load of hokey bullshit. They don't mean anything. Not like the songs we sang."

The words land between them like unfinished lyrics.

Alabama averts her eyes, and he's hit with a hard realization. She doesn't want to talk about the past. When suddenly it's all Griff can think about. Being with Alabama has him remembering the guy he used to be, the songs he used to sing, the man he wanted to become.

"We wrote some damn good songs," Griff hedges. There's an ache inside of him. One that wants Alabama to pick up the trail, to tell him she remembers, that she still feels that way too.

A smile works its way across Alabama's lips. "We did. Our sound was so different," she muses, staring out at the water. "You always wanted to sound like Kristofferson, all badass and renegade."

"And you had that gut-busting voice like Loretta." He chuckles. "You were a wild card, even back then."

"Wild card, huh?"

"Hell, yes. You had this spirit. Guts like no one I ever seen." He cuts her a look. "You still do."

"Hmm. I like that." Her eyes brighten. "And I did. Somehow, someway, we met in the middle and it worked." She meets his gaze. "Our songs *were* good, Griff." She shakes her red head, exhales. "Man, I really loved those days."

Griff loved those days, too. Days where he and Alabama would spend all day penning a song. They'd work it over together, just right, and they'd bicker over everything. In the end, that's what made them better. That's what made them *them*.

Alabama's soft voice brings him back to the present. "No one would even recognize us now. Not even our past selves."

She's right. Past Griff knew what he wanted. Alabama. A music career. Only he gave up one for the other and he's regretted it ever since.

"Remember the name of our band?" Griff peeks over at Alabama, her pretty face pensive.

She lifts a challenging brow. "The question is, do you?"

"The Copper Hounds, and our first gig was gonna be at the Bluebird."

"You got it, Greyson." Alabama turns her face to listen to the faint strains of music from a nearby restaurant. A soft chuckle escapes her. "Wow. Guess we're really barin' all tonight, huh?" She leans against the railing, bracing her back against it to face Griff. A shiver runs through her body and she hugs herself.

"Speaking of barin' . . ." Griff steps close and runs a finger down her collarbone, watching as goose bumps break out over her porcelain skin. "You cold, Al?"

She keeps her body slightly rigid, like she's trying to refuse his touch, then she smiles. "I remember this move. The pretend-to-care, then cop-a-feel."

"That's harsh." Griff braces his arms on either side of her, his rings nicking the metal railing. "You know it wasn't like that. I always cared. But I was a red-blooded all-American boy. I had needs."

Alabama tilts her chin. There's a flirty glint in her eyes. "Clearly you still do," she says and, for emphasis, glances down at the ever-stiffening crotch of his pants.

Griff's brain is going places. Dirty places. He knows he needs to rein it in. He knows he left her. Knows he owes her an explanation, knows she needs it, but that explanation would shatter one truth for another.

But Griff sees the woman Alabama is—strong, stubborn, and hot as hell—and wants to bring the past to the present. If she'll let him.

Lowering his hand, Griff grazes fingertips across the curve of her breast. "We had some good times, didn't we, Al?"

"We did," she says, breathless. "But we can't do this, Griff."

"Why not?"

"Because. Because we've both had our drunken moments, and now . . . now we have to be adults about this and . . ." Her words trail off as Griff dips his head to brush his lips across her neck. "Oh," she says, her head lolling slightly, her long red hair cascading like a waterfall.

The arch of her body is insistent. She's feeling him. And goddamn if he doesn't want to feel her.

His hands curl around her shoulders, Alabama making a needy little noise at the contact.

And that's his pistol start. All he needs to make his next move.

Wordlessly, Griff hauls Alabama to his chest and kisses her. Hard. Like nothing else matters. Like she's his only one. Because she is. Griff knows it ain't lust he's fighting. It's something else. Something deeper. That feeling from the past never faded and tonight, he's goddamn owning it.

Alabama gasps as her lips meet his. For a second, she resists, and then she's moaning his name, pressing her body against

Griff's. Her arms wind around his neck, her touch hungry and claiming, and a canine growl escapes Griff.

It's then Griff knows he's sunk. The minute he tasted her lips, he knew. Knew everything he's been doing is over. Fucking up, screwing around, getting drunk.

It's Alabama. All he wants, all he needs.

He doesn't deserve her, but he's got to have her. He wants this second chance more than he wants air. He wants to show Alabama everything she's been missing. And most importantly, right now, tonight, he wants to take her back to the bus and—

"You son of a bitch."

Griff stiffens at the shrill voice, and Alabama goes statue-still in his arms. He closes his eyes, wishing, willing it to go away. Because he knows who it is. And it ain't no one good.

Grimacing, willing himself to look, Griff glances over his shoulder. Nikki stands on the entrance of the pier, hands propped on her hips, her eyes dagger-sharp and deadly.

It fucking figures. His one bad mistake from his past coming back to haunt him. Tonight of all goddamn nights.

Alabama's expression flattens. "That's why we can't do this," she hisses.

Ripping herself out of his arms, she backs up against the railing. The chill she's giving off colder than the Arctic.

"There ain't nothin' between us," he tells Alabama and it's the truth. "Hasn't been for years. She's been following me since my last tour and I can't get rid of her." He holds up a placating hand. "Stay here."

Her snort of doubt follows him as he turns on his heel. He hates leaving Alabama because she's two quick seconds from tearing out of there, but he's got to talk some sense into Nikki.

"You asshole," Nikki says viciously. Griff catches her elbow as she tries to hit him and marches her off to the side of the boardwalk.

"Have you lost your goddamned mind?" he demands. "You can't keep showing up like this. We're done. No more."

"You don't mean that." She goes in for a kiss, but Griff gently but firmly moves her away.

"I do."

He knows he's done Nikki dirty in the past. He regrets leading her on, treating her bad, using her only when it benefited him. He's a selfish asshole prick who should've changed years ago. It's all true, and he was the worst kind of man.

But now—that's all over for him, and all he can do is recognize that and apologize.

Nikki grips his bicep with fierce strength. "You and me— we're, we're together."

He shakes his head. "Now that's where you're wrong. I never meant to lead you on, Nikki, and I'm sorry I did."

She looks away from him, her eyes glazed and empty.

A curl of unease snakes down his spine when he sees she's staring at Alabama. Her expression angry, almost desperate. And then she smiles.

Unnerved, Griff gives her a shake, wanting her eyes off Alabama. "Hey, you hear me? Stay away. For good."

She whips her face toward him. Her smile twists up into a hideous grimace. "You'll never love anything."

Griff's stomach clenches. But before he can reply, Nikki slams a palm in his chest. "You deserve what you get, Griff Greyson."

There's a flash of yellow and red as Alabama strides past him, her long legs headed for the bus.

"Hey," he hollers, ripping a hand through his hair, frustrated as hell. Damn women are making him crazy. "Where you goin'?"

"Away from you," she tosses back.

"We're done, Nikki," he says, his eyes still on Alabama.

There's no one else for him.

Not anymore.

chapter ELEVEN

ALABAMA'S WALKING AWAY NOW. BEFORE SHE GOES down this road with Griff. Again. For years, she's kept her distance, preferring to compete instead of pine, wanting nothing from him. And now, after a week of being in his orbit, he's got her back in his clutches. The smooth talker that he is, he had her seeing the Griff from years ago, the what-could-be, the what-she-always-wanted. Hell, he had her kissing him. Her body feeling things it hadn't felt in years.

Well, she ain't doing that. No goddamn way.

She can't compete. She won't.

All she can do is get away from him. Fast.

Anger roars in Alabama's ears, louder than a freight train as she marches toward the bus. It's parked some feet away from where Griff had ordered Sam to wait for them.

She's nearly to the stairs when a hand grips her arm and whirls her around.

Griff stands there, shopping bags hanging off his arm, a crooked smile on his face. He's hustled to catch up with her; his breath comes in small pants. "Those boots make you fast, Al."

She yanks her arm from his grip. "Take my boots and shove 'em up your ass, Griff."

The roguish grin drops off his face. "Sweetheart . . ."

"Save your sweetheart for someone else, because that ain't me."

She bangs on the side of the bus. Instantly, the locks click and she grabs the handle. Somewhere in the distance, a bright boom of a light. Cursing the photographers, ignoring Griff, she opens the door, climbs the stairs.

Blessedly, the bus is empty.

"Goddamnit, Alabama, would you listen to me?" Griff's heated voice is at her back.

There in the darkened lounge, she spins around to face him, clenching her teeth. Griff stares at her, his forlorn eyes pleading with her for another chance.

Well, he doesn't get one. Not again.

"There's nothing to say," she says, digging her heels in. "I won't do it, Griff. I won't be another one of your girls."

His golden eyes widen, right before his face darkens. "Now wait a goddamn minute. You think you'd be just another girl to me?" Disbelief and anger stain his voice.

"I do." She closes her eyes, opens them. "I think I risk everything and you risk nothing, and at the end of the day, or night, or bed, or whatever, it'd be a mistake, *my* mistake and I—"

But whatever she planned to say next never makes it out because Griff's lips get in the way, crushing hers as his big hands grip her waist, pinning her against him. His lips are sweet and hot, muttering sharp reprimands—curses at himself, at her, for both being idiots—as they hover over hers, devouring her mouth.

She brings her arms up to shove him away, to hit him, but her body won't let her, and her arms drop helplessly to her side.

Everything falls away. Every ounce of protest, of anger, dies a slow death. It's just her and Griff. Big-time adults with big-time lust.

Alabama kisses him back, almost as roughly, as if to show him she can give as good as she gets. He rips away from her, his pupils big and blitzed. A desperate man, near over the edge, looking at her like she's his undoing.

His hands come up to grip her face, the coolness of his rings intermixed with the heat of his palms. "I want you, Alabama, and no one else."

Her breathing speeds up and her chest heaves.

Magic words? Maybe.

For now.

Their lips meet again and then Griff's walking her backwards, walking her down the hall, neither of them saying anything between kisses, between hungry gasps of air.

He picks her up when he gets to his room and carries her inside, lowering her onto the bed. Kneeling in front of her, he peels off her boots. Alabama tingles at Griff's touch, his hands running up and down her legs, creeping higher to caress her inner thighs. Her body's rocked by a trembling shudder. Just his touch, it's a spark—it's Griff. It's better than she remembers.

When he glances back up, his eyes pin hers.

"What about tomorrow?" Alabama breathes. Despite the heat building, she can't help worrying, wondering, playing it safe.

Griff flashes that savage grin again. But when he speaks, his voice is serious. "Tomorrow's ours."

Alabama shakes from the promise, from words she'd never thought she'd hear, from a man she never thought would say them. Her heart pounds in her chest. They're just words, but coming from Griff, they're more. They feel like a pledge, like a badge of honor he will wear and then some. And she realizes she trusts him—still, despite everything.

Griff slides a hand up her knee to part her thighs, then stills. "Tell me to stop. You'll kill me, but I will." His yellow eyes bore into her. "Tell me to stop."

He's waiting for her, to give her approval, for her body to respond to what he's offering, for her to take charge. Her brain tells her *stop*, but her body broadcasts a single screaming message: *let go*.

Pretending's a thing of the past. She wants Griff, wants this high to last all night. All her reasons why they can't do this, that she's falling back into bad habits, it all slips away. She just doesn't care. Her body can only hold out so long.

"No." Her hands grip his broad shoulders, her long pink nails digging in, making their mark. Claiming. "Go."

A sly, greedy smile spreads across his face. "Oh, I'm goin'. Slow," he says, leaning in close to brush the curve of her throat with his lips. "Believe me, I'm gonna take my damn time tonight."

With a kind of vicious reverence, he ravenously kisses her legs, moving up her shins to her thighs. He spreads her thighs, and she moans as he presses a kiss to her sex. He hisses his approval when he finds her already wet. Then Griff pulls back to stare, his eyes riveted on her, his grin slow, his breath a hot, predatory pant.

"I want to feel you, every part of you. Explore what I've been missin'. It might take all night, but I'm gonna do it."

Alabama shivers at the husky desire in his voice. Impatient, she tears at his shirt, dragging it away from his body with one slick hand. Grinning at her, Griff lifts her dress up and then it's off, leaving Alabama clad in only her bra and panties.

Griff's eyes widen as his gaze drifts up and down her body. His eyes soften, losing some of that feral hunger. "Jesus." His voice is hoarse. Appreciative. "You're goddamn beautiful, Alabama."

A hot blush creeps across her cheeks, but she basks in his compliment. Because Alabama knows what he means.

His body—Griff's all grown up. Alabama takes her time drinking him in. His broad shoulders, stocky V-shaped build, and beautifully muscled arms and chest. A thatch of golden hair leads a trail up his stomach.

Then, Alabama lets out a squeal as Griff's on his feet, scooping her up with one arm. His biceps, his tattoos rippling as he easily drags her backwards to the middle of the bed.

Alabama arches in his arms, her need too intense for words. A groan escapes Griff. She follows his eyes to see him staring. One of her breasts has come free of her bra, a taut rose-colored nipple standing at attention. Unable to help himself, Griff lunges, catching her breast in his mouth. His tongue licks and strokes concentric circles around her beaded nipple, slow swirls that have her going flat-out insane.

The sensation has Alabama crying out, her eyes rolling back in her skull. Griff keeps a tight grip as she goes limp in his arms.

His eyes, hooded and dark and dangerous, find her. "I'm not sure I can go slow." He lays her down on the pillow.

Alabama wets her lips. "I'm not sure I want you to."

One muscular arm props him up as he hovers over her, and then his other hand is drifting. Down, down, down it goes, his thumb hooking into the hem of her panties to slowly drag them off. His fingers dip inside of her with an expert gentleness. She sucks him in and she hears a sharp exhale of pleasure from Griff. Alabama writhes as her heat pulses around him. She's already wet, thrumming with need and sick of being teased mercilessly.

"Oh God . . ." Alabama arches helplessly. She thrashes her head. Her hips rise and fall. "More, more," she begs.

Griff slips two fingers inside her. Her abdomen quivers. Her head snaps up, and she flings an arm around Griff's neck, dragging him down to her. She moves greedily for his lips, needing more from him, needing release. As if in answer, he cuts off her gasp, sucking in her air. Her body responds, drinking in his hot breath. His tongue flicks against hers and Alabama lets out an agonized moan. She's over the edge and he knows it. He's got her surrendered.

"Griff . . . please . . ."

She whimpers when Griff breaks the kiss, his clever fingers slipping out of her to find her clit. His fingertips move expertly. No more teasing. He knows slow circles, smooth strokes do the trick, has always known. Alabama's brain overheats at his familiar touch and her body shakes. Her stomach feels as if it's being pulled up to the stars.

A golden yellow light fills her vision and then Alabama's trembling, shaking, pulsing as waves of pleasure crash over her. Crying out, Alabama bucks her hips up against Griff's abdomen, her pleasure pulsing against him, imprinting him with slick trails of her arousal.

Before she can collapse against the bed, he clutches her tight to him. Alabama, writhing in pleasure, lets loose one last violent tremble of her body before she sinks limply into his grip.

Griff's gaze meets hers. All seriousness. All business, all for her.

"What's next, Al?"

Sex. It's what she wants. It's what he wants. Fighting it is no longer an option.

Her stomach flip-flops from nerves, from exhilaration, from that age-old first-time feeling.

She and Griff, they were each other's first, and the sex back then was fumbling and awkward and illicit. Stealing moments whenever they could, but it had been true. It had been real. And now. Now Griff's all smooth moves and clever hands. And Alabama—she ain't too bad herself.

She smiles, blissed out beyond belief. "Right now," she says. "Right now is what's next."

He lifts a brow. "Yeah?"

"Yeah. Get a condom and we're golden."

He settles her gently back against the pillows, then reaches into his nightstand, digs down deep, and grabs a condom. His eyes, having never left her face, crinkle as he grins. "However you want it, sweetheart, you tell me."

Her stomach tightens. There's something in his eyes that tells her this is all for her, that his pleasure comes last and he won't enjoy himself if she isn't.

A slow smile spreads across her face. "Hmm," she says, sitting up on her elbows. "Well, I tend to like it like this . . ." She flips herself onto hands and knees. When she glances back over her shoulder, Griff's suddenly gone very still except for the flexing of his cock. "What do you say, Greyson?"

His lips curl in approval. "I'd say . . . what am I goddamn waitin' for?"

A rush of heat fills Alabama.

So much for staying away from Griff Greyson.

chapter TWELVE

G RIFF'S WHOLE WORLD, NOT TO MENTION HIS COCK and balls, are on fire. He's got Alabama all to himself. His entire body had been buzzing after their conversation, their kiss on the pier, and now it's damn near ready to combust. He's finally gotten through her barriers and is back to the girl he knows. Only the girl he knew is now a woman, and all he can do is stare.

He's unable to tear his gaze away from the gorgeous-as-hell sight that greets him. Alabama on her hands and knees, half-naked, waiting for him. Her hazy gray eyes bid him closer, her luscious ass high up in the air, her hair like flame, her skin like rich cream.

It's torture. Straight-up torture.

Slowly, he makes his way toward her. He wants to revel in every curve and contour of her flawless body. She shudders as he positions himself behind her. But he doesn't take her. Not yet. He runs his hands over her soft curves, her tight ass. Alabama trembles from his touch.

"Griff, please," she begs. "You got me goin' crazy . . ."

"Not yet." Griff drapes himself over her, his breath hot against her ear, and presses kisses to the side of her mouth, her neck, her jaw. Giving her a playful bite on her shoulder, he whispers, "Waitin' feels good, don't it?"

She groans. "You don't play fair."

"Who said I'm playin'?"

With an expert hand, he quickly removes her bra. Her plump

breasts spill out into his waiting palm. He runs a thumb over her soft nipple, stroking it to a hardened peak. Alabama lets out a throaty gasp and throws her head back, her eyes fluttering.

Grinning, he wraps a hand in her long red hair and tugs, firmly yet gently.

"Griff," she moans. "I can't . . . please . . . fuck me."

Her words snap him like a whip.

Quickly rolling on the condom, he backs up to take her in. A surge of pleasure washes through Griff at what he sees. Plump, she's plump everywhere. Lips, ass, clit.

With a ragged growl, he grips her around the stomach and slides into her. Alabama gasps, and every muscle in Griff's body tenses at the feel of her. The bellow of ecstasy he lets out shakes the room. Christ, she feels fucking good. Like heaven. Like his cock's been dipped in warm honey. With trembling hands, he grips her hips, his fingers making the sexiest dimples in the sides of her creamy thighs.

Alabama arches as he drives himself into her. Drives himself into her with a vicious hunger he's never had before. Insatiable. Ravenous.

Deep. He's so goddamn deep inside of Alabama.

Alabama cries out, but before he can stop, ask if he's hurt her, she murmurs her approval. "Faster, Griff . . . faster . . ."

She dips down lower, her bare breasts dragging against the bed, her long red hair falling like a veil across her face. And then she's rocking with him, swaying her hips in a figure-eight. Showing what she likes and taking what he gives. It's the sexiest thing he's ever felt—that combined with Alabama tightening around him. Viselike. His teeth grit as Griff's endurance is tested. His determination to last is swallowed up by the urge to let go.

He's gonna come. Fast.

"Oh, God," Alabama gasps, her fingers clenching sheet corner. Her body bucks against him. "Oh God . . . like this, Griff, yes, just like this . . ."

She pulses around him again, and he gasps at the sensation.

His cock's going to explode any damn second. He closes his eyes. "Alabama . . ."

"Griff, please . . ."

Her voice, breathy, begs him to let himself go.

With a savage cry, he hammers against her one last time. And then he's spilling into her, pain mixed with pleasure, savoring the feel of her body pressed against his. In response, Alabama's throaty cry mixes with his, all kinds of satisfied and serene.

For a long second, their ragged breathing is the only sound in the room. Then Alabama lets out a purr of pleasure and sags into the pillows as if she can't stay upright any longer.

Griff catches her around the stomach and drops beside her. He unrolls the condom, careful not to spill its contents, and leans over the edge of the bed to chuck it in the trash.

And then he's tucking Alabama tenderly against his side so they're facing each other. He brushes away her veil of hair, adjusting her in his arms so he can see her face. She's smiling. She lets out a laugh and covers her face with her hand. "I can't believe we just did that."

His lips graze her temple. "Better than high school."

She gives him a look. A warm blush creeps across her cheeks. "Griff."

"What?" He traces a finger down her cheek. "It was."

Alabama rolls her eyes. "Yes, thank God for both of us being well experienced in the sack," she says dryly.

"It was good back then. It was good now." He searches her eyes, searches out her face for any trace of regret.

Instead of responding, Alabama reaches out a finger to trace the ink on his bicep. "I remember this."

The copper penny. Griff remembers having the tattoo artist make it the same color as Alabama's hair. Then, her fingers fluttering with a delicate grace, she bypasses the penny and stops at a crudely drawn guitar with the word "Outlaw" on its fretboard. Griff's first tattoo in Nashville.

She lifts a brow. "For the love of the music, right?"

He chuckles. "Right."

She pauses on a strand of bright blue flowers. At the tilt of her head, Griff offers, "Texas."

"Ah, bluebonnets."

Then she's onto the Waylon Jennings–inspired tattoo: a large W inked along his forearm. His heart hitches when she stops on a delicate cursive script. His mama's name—Della Ray—scrawled on the inside of his elbow.

Alabama looks up at him with sad eyes. "We missed you at the funeral."

He stares at her, his chest expanding at her words. "You went?" It's news to him.

She frowns like she's insulted he never considered it before. "Of course I did, Griff. Your mama was an amazin' woman. I loved her—I wanted to be there."

"She loved you too, you know," Griff says hoarsely.

Alabama lies back in his arms. She looks up from under her lashes curiously. "Why ain't you been home, Griff? Everyone's wonderin'."

He tightens his grip around Alabama but stares at the ceiling. Guilt, reality hovers around him like a storm cloud. He's been avoiding going home because of the memories. Because of what he's become, his selfish, drunken life, and what he's lost along the way. The shame of Alabama's father threatening to arrest him. The shame of never coming home for his mama's funeral. The shame of putting Alabama in the hospital. The thought of facing her father has his anger at a simmering boil. He wants to put a fist in the old man's face for telling a stupid kid what to do.

Hell, put a fist through his own face for being a stupid kid who listened.

He takes a harsh inhale of breath. And because Alabama's waiting, he says, "Goin' back to Clover, it was never an option for me, Alabama."

"Why not?" When he doesn't answer her, she leans up on her elbows. Reaching out, she presses a palm against his left eye, against his faded scar. He shivers at her tender touch. "Is this why you left?"

He wants to tell her. So fucking bad. That he didn't sleep for weeks after he left her. That he's still got the ring he bought her. That he doesn't want to ruin the memory of the man she thinks her father is. She was hurt, she needed her father, and she didn't need that burden laid on her then.

Only what about now?

But he swallows, choking back the truth that threatens to bubble up, and just says, "Al, it is what it is."

A brief flash of anger appears in her eyes. She wants an answer, she's burning inside for one, but she won't beg for it.

"Look, sweetheart, I'm sorry," he says, wanting to defuse the situation. He just had the best fucking night of his life and doesn't want to chase her away or piss her off. He reaches out to pull her into his arms. "I know you want more, but the fact of it is that I'm an asshole, Alabama. And that's one thing you didn't know about me." He lets out a long breath, as close to the truth as he can get. "I left because I wasn't good for you."

Shrugging off his touch, she leans back to look at him. The confusion on her face is heartbreaking. "What're you talkin' about? You were the best one for me, Griff."

He grunts. "I was an asshole."

This time, she lets him draw her back into his arms, and even though she curls up against his chest, she doesn't relax. She's quiet for a long time. Whether she agrees with him or is silently gathering more ammo to argue with him, Griff can't tell.

They lie there in the quiet. The only sound the bus's low humming. He presses a kiss to her temple, breathing in her hair, the scent of her coconut shampoo, and he's back in Clover. Christ. Griff closes his eyes. How can someone smell the same after all these years? Smell so damn good it tears at his lungs like wildfire. She's here in his bed, a place he'd never thought he'd find her again. It's too damn dreamlike for words—lying next to Alabama.

He's about to doze off, Alabama in his arms, when he feels the bed shift.

Griff sits up, his eyes following her curves as she slips out of the covers, slips from his grasp. His chest tightening, he reaches out to snag her wrist. "Hey, where you goin'?"

She stares down at him, her expression unreadable. "Back to my room." She disentangles her wrist from his grasp.

He frowns, unused to this. Usually he's the one telling the girls to get out. But not Alabama. The thought of a night like this never happening again, of him missing Alabama in his bed— he ain't having that. He wants her here in his bed, in his arms. Where she belongs.

"The hell you are."

A little line appears between her brows. "I won't be that girl, Griff."

It's like a kick to the ribs.

"I told you, you ain't."

She gives him a look that says she doesn't believe him and dips to scoop up her clothes. He watches as she slips on her panties, then her dress.

Griff slides to the edge of the bed, his eyes on her. "Damn it, Al. This ain't a one-night thing for me." He's already decided he won't play games. He knows what he wants and he wants her. "We're doin' this. Doin' us. I found you again and I ain't lettin' go."

Her eyes widen at the boldness of his words.

"Think on it," he says before she can refuse him.

"I will." She meets his eyes. "Tomorrow."

He grabs her hand. "Now."

"Tomorrow, Griff." The soft smile she gives him calms him. Barely. She squeezes his hand. "It's late. And we gotta sing in Savannah tomorrow."

Griff lets out a breath. "Al . . ."

"Thanks for the boots." The flirty smile in her voice softens when she says, "Good night, Greyson."

The click of the door and then she's gone, leaving Griff sitting there in bed. A little voice inside of him screams at him to get up, to go get her back, but he lets her be. Roping Alabama ain't his choice. But he sure as hell knows this ain't no one-night stand.

Normally, he'd reach for a bottle, a stiff drink to soothe himself, to make him drift off into a dreamless sleep, but all he can do is think about Alabama. She's rocked his world—and not just in the sack. Everything he gave up is back, here if he wants it, and he knows what he has to do. He won't take his life or his time with Alabama for granted anymore.

And though Griff knows she doubts his womanizing ways, knows she's refusing to get involved with another man she works with, knows she's closing herself off because he left her first, he ain't giving up. He's gonna show her this is a second chance they can't pass up.

He doesn't deserve her, but he wants to deserve her.

Griff flops back in bed, allowing a rare smile to spread across his face. He gets to be the man who proves her wrong. A damn honor. A privilege.

And he's gonna enjoy every goddamn second.

chapter
THIRTEEN

FTER A RESTLESS SLEEP, ALABAMA WAKES EARLY. SHE exits her room, and after a quick glance at Griff's shut door, she pads down the hall to the writing room just off the main lounge. Hell, if she's gonna screw Griff Greyson, she's gonna make damn good music while doing it.

The writing room is a small six-by-six square with low couches and tables for penning new tunes. While she's surprised Griff's bus has something like this, she's thankful. It's a delightful little slice of quiet away from all the on-the-road chaos.

She sinks into a chair and opens her notebook. Blank pages. She hasn't written anything since Clover and figures a new notebook equals a new start.

Although judging how things went last night, she probably set herself back to the Stone Age.

Alabama grimaces and rubs her brow, a fresh headache on the horizon.

She's lost her damn mind doing what she did with Griff. She tried to keep it strictly professional, and she couldn't. It wasn't a mistake, but it can't happen again. She wants nothing from him.

Except his body. Those blue jeans. That cocky grin as his mouth sucked on her—

"Idiot," she mutters, a hot flush coating her cheeks, and scribbles that note in the margins.

She needs to stop this now. She knows she danced around a promise last night, a promise to keep this going, which isn't a good look for her. She's trying to drag her reputation out of the gutter, not kick it in any further. If this got out . . . she'd only be seen as the woman who puts the moves on every man she works with. Griff, he'd be fine, probably even score another record deal out of it. She'd lose any shot of having a serious career. The career she's always wanted. This is her chance, and she can't give that up for anyone. Especially Griff Greyson. Especially not when he left her first.

But last night, that doesn't track for the man she pegged him for. She saw what he was asking her, what he was telling her. He's in. Committed. The raw bluntness of his words had her fumbling for a response. She couldn't find one, couldn't decide on her answer, so she took her boots and she ran.

She slept on it.

And now . . . now the shitty thing is—she wants Griff.

Alabama doesn't know how she can deny it any longer. Her heart, the past tugs at her, leads her down a path she's walked before. She wants to keep this going, this whole what-if thing between them.

She wants to keep it casual. But still.

Still her and Griff.

Shaking off her foolish lust-filled thoughts, she turns her attention to her notebook, remembering a line Griff said last night. About the two of them.

I found you again and I ain't lettin' go.

So she puts pen to paper and scribbles "Find You Again." It's a damn good title. Could be a damn good song.

A small smile curls her lips. She should get Griff in here and really bust out this song. Like the old days. Like the good days. Why the hell not? As much as she hates giving the cocky son of a bitch credit, they were good together. They may as well make something together if they're going to do this *keep-it-casual-only* fling.

And that's all it is.

Casual.

A sharp rap sounds on the door.

Tucking her notebook under her arm, Alabama rises, ready to just do this thing. Ready to throw herself on the mercy of Griff Greyson and let her hair down and have some fun.

Only, when she swings the door open, the smile slips from her face. She blinks. "Brian."

"Good mornin'," he says. His big brass buckle glitters, his meaty fingers hooked through his belt loops. Alabama fights the urge to laugh. The pose is straight-up Griff's.

"Mornin'. You know, I was just on my way to get Griff." Her voice is overly loud in the small room.

Brian leans an arm in the doorway. "Do you need Griff?"

She stares at him. "What?"

"I thought you were trying to make a new start, Alabama," Brian says, stepping inside the room and shutting the door behind him. "You do the tour with us, you keep your hands off the merchandise, and maybe, just maybe, you'll get new rep again."

She clenches her jaw but keeps her voice light. "I don't know what's got you on a tear, Bri, but—"

"Cut the shit, Alabama." Brian's face is so twisted she doesn't even recognize him. "I know what you two are doin'." He shakes his head. "Griff's barely hangin' on as it is. He doesn't need someone like you messin' with his career."

"You mean *you* don't need someone like me around Griff," she shoots back, instantly knowing what's up Brian's ass. The fun, the games, the women, the easy cash cow are gone. "Helpin' him, showin' him that things don't have to be how they are."

"Think of yourself, then." Brian's gaze narrows. "You won't get far if you keep fuckin' Griff. The press is gonna find out. And won't that be a shame."

Alabama goes still. Her face burns at the threat, at the thought that Brian knows about her and Griff and is using her past to scare her away from him. Pompous little prick weasel. He's always been a sore loser, ever since she chose Griff over him.

She meets his stare dead-on. Draws herself up. "You don't know what the hell you're talkin' about."

"Don't I?" He takes a step forward. Into her space. "He wears you down, Al. *Lets* you down. But you know that better than I do, don't you? You know he'll never be satisfied with just you."

"Why're you telling me this?"

"Because it's an easy fix. All you gotta do is give me what you're givin' Griff. Should come as second nature to you."

Her eyes blur with hot tears. Unfairly pegged by Brian. By everyone, the world.

"Fuck off, Brian."

She moves to leave, but he lashes out and snatches her wrist.

"I am your boss," he hisses.

"Griff's my boss," she fires back. "And if he knew you were touchin' me he'd put your head through the damn wall."

"Leave Griff alone."

Though her heart's in her throat, she keeps her voice even, determined not to let this asshole get to her. "You're hurtin' me, Brian."

His grip loosens, but he doesn't let go.

The only sound is the rumbling engine of the bus as it tears down the freeway. Then Alabama wrenches her wrist from Brian's grasp. Rage floods her veins as she stares him down. "You touch me again and I'll skin you. My daddy's a cop. I know where to hide the bodies."

Before he can say anything, she rips open the door and slams it shut behind her.

Fucking creep.

She breathes heavily, feeling violated and rocked. Her heart pounds out a flatline in her chest. Her eyes sting, but she won't cry. Her daddy taught her better than that. Take no shit.

Only Brian's words have dragged her down, replanted her feet firmly in reality, rudely ripped away everything she was hoping for.

She'll never outrun Mort's Alabama. That girl making bad decisions. Foolish choices. Trusting everyone but herself.

No. She can't do this again. She can't mess up, and she can't have everything. She can't have Griff. She has to back off from the possibility of them.

Even though it's the last thing she wants.

"Where are you?"

"We're in bumfuck nowhere, Freddie," Griff says as he leans back against the kitchen sink to watch the scenery zip by. Cows, fields, churches. "Where on the goddamn green earth would you like us to be?"

"And tonight?"

"The Cowtail Saloon. Savannah."

"Very good." He hears her nod over the phone. "A test, Griff. To make sure you stay on the straight and narrow. Believe me, I don't like these weekly check-in sessions. They are a pain in my ass just as much as yours."

Automatically, he reaches for the flask he keeps in the breakfast nook but stops himself. Getting blitzed ain't on the agenda today.

"By the way, did you happen to see the photos?"

He grimaces. Oh yeah, he's seen the photos. Lugging Alabama's shopping bags around like he's her personal fucking shopper. Still, a smile crosses his face. Yesterday—talk about a goddamn great time.

He smears a hand down his face. "You want a new pair of shoes next, Freddie?"

She chuckles. "I like this photo of you, Griff, a shopping bag in your hand. It almost makes you look . . . domesticated."

Griff clenches a fist. Freddie can give him shit all she wants but he doesn't regret that photo for a second.

"You know who else likes you? The people. They're connecting with you. They like you and Alabama together."

Griff closes his eyes on her name.

Morning couldn't have come soon enough and now that it has, she's nowhere to be seen. He's acting like some teenage horndog, all sweaty palms and rock-hard erections, but that's what she's doing to him. Making him sweat. Making him think of every single dirty thing he wants to do to her.

And Alabama, either she regrets last night, or he scared her off. He fucked up and went too fast.

His ears snag on Freddie, reading captions and quotes aloud from social media sections.

"'Hottest country couple alive!!!'

'Hashtag relationship goals.'

'Love this, love their music! Here's hoping for a collaboration ASAP!'"

"I thought you weren't supposed to read the comments," he says dryly. He doesn't know the first thing about social media and couldn't give two shits, instead letting someone in marketing run his account. Anything that would have his idols rolling over in their graves, he ain't touching with a ten-foot pole.

"I read the comments, Griff. The label reads the comments. And they want more of this. More of you two together. Record sales of *Lonestar* are up, shows are selling out, which means big things."

"What kind of big things?"

"A winter tour. They're talking more cities, arenas, possibly even Europe."

A swell of pride crashes over him. The one person keeping the shitshow that is Griff Greyson together. "Yeah, well," he says, "It's all Alabama. She's been workin' like hell. Singin' her heart out every damn night."

"Not to mention the fact that she is an absolute ratings monster," Freddie trills. "Keep up the excellent work. It's a fabulous act you're pulling."

"It ain't no act," he growls in a voice full of venom.

Out of everything he's done, this is the real fucking deal.

Griff's heart lurches when he sees Alabama. She's exiting the writing room, eyes downcast, notebook in her hand.

"I gotta go, Fred," he says and ends the call.

He goes to Alabama, forcing himself not to seem too eager, to play it cool, when all he can think about is last night and what happens next.

"Good mornin', sweetheart." He reaches for her, but Alabama steps back. She leans against her bedroom door, her hand on the knob.

He lets his hands fall to his side. "Hey, what is it?"

She swallows. "Nothin'."

He juts his chin at the writing room. "You wanna get back in there, show me what you got?"

Suddenly, he's hit by inspiration, a determination to crank out a true Griff Greyson number. Not that shit he's been singing for so long. "We could work on a tune. Debut it at tonight's show." He grins. "Get back those two pennies we're owed."

"No, we can't," she says, her tone absentminded as she turns away from him.

He frowns. "Sweetheart, you okay?" He peers at her close. Her eye are red-rimmed, her shoulders stiff.

Alabama shakes her head. "I was wrong about last night. We can't do this."

"Do what?"

"Us."

He flashes a grin that's bound to get her temper fired up. "C'mon, Al. We'd be good together onstage."

"And in bed?" She crosses her arms tight against his chest as if she's trying to protect herself or freeze him out.

He groans, frustrated. "That ain't what this is about. You mean more to me than that. And you know it."

"It was just sex. One night. That's all it was."

Her words are a bucket of ice water.

Fuck.

His nostrils flare. Hell yes, he's angry. But instead of storming away in a huff, instead of clenching fists, he steps closer. He won't walk away from Alabama—never again. He wants to solve this quick, so he can make her feel better, so he can fix whatever's hurting her.

"It wasn't just one night, damn it. Talk to me."

He reaches out to take her in his arms, but she steps away.

She closes her eyes, inhaling a deep breath. Adamant. Angry. "No," she says. "We can't do this. Not anymore."

Before he can respond, she's turning on her heel, entering her room and closing the door behind her.

Griff blinks, staring at the shut door. He's never been so goddamn confused in his life.

"Fuck." He rests a palm against the door, his heart tearing a hole in his chest.

He doesn't know what's happened, but he knows he's got to fix it. He has to convince Alabama what she means to him. He can't let her walk out of his life. Not now.

Not again.

chapter
FOURTEEN

"I DON'T THINK I'VE EVER SEEN SKIRTS THIS SHORT," Alabama muses, one hand on her cocked hip as she stares at her closet.

"Pigeonholed again," Holly crows in her ear. "You gotta shake things up. You hate wearin' all of that, so why are you?"

With a frown, Alabama tucks the phone under her ear and stands. She rifles through her closet, the clothes the stylist picked out. Everything's short and low-cut, pink or some color that screams princess. Clothes meant for someone else. Someone other than Alabama.

"You know, you're right. I should just burn this whole bus down."

"Sounds rash. Maybe just wear something you like."

"No." She examines the gold metallic manicure she got in the last town over. Macon? Atlanta? She can't remember. "Fire's the answer. Flames and fury are the answer to everything."

Holly laughs. "And then how will you get to Birmingham? Maybe Griff Grumperson will fireman-carry you all the way to Marlow's Bar and Grill."

Alabama groans and glances at her door to make sure it's really closed. Closed tight. Against Griff. That's what she's been doing ever since they had sex. Shutting off. Powering down. Focusing on the music and not some man who keeps looking at her like she's his undoing.

It's been a week of keeping her distance from Griff, of leaving the room when he enters, of singing their one song and then exiting the stage straight after her set, of eating Thanksgiving dinner alone in her room, of watching to see if Griff brings a girl back to the bus. She's doing all she can to avoid him. She knows any close contact, cramped quarters, would be dangerous business. She doesn't have willpower around Griff.

It's how she got herself into this mess in the first place.

Alabama sighs. "That's the last thing I want, Holly."

"Really?"

"Really. It's called the ol' two-step avoidant shuffle."

"What?" Holly's hopeful voice deflates. "C'mon, y'all gotta make a comeback. I rescind what I said at the tavern. I'm secretly rooting for you two."

Alabama fingers a sequined jumpsuit and frowns at the scratchy material. "All I wanna do is buckle down. Just four more weeks and I get that big fat check on payday."

She's put off the lawyers until the end of the year, but she doesn't know how much longer she can stall until they come calling with collections. Or worse, another lawsuit.

"Sounds like Griff's bucklin' down too," Holly drawls. "No drinkin', no fightin', no news in the *Star*. You're keepin' him on the straight and narrow, Al."

"He has been surprisingly . . . good lately." It's the truth. He hasn't brought a woman back to the bus since their night on the pier. She hasn't seen Nikki since then either.

"Then why on earth are you avoidin' him?"

"Oh, I don't know." Alabama bites her lip, readying herself for Holly's strangled outburst. Then she takes the plunge and the words topple out in one fast ramble. "Maybe it's because we slept together?"

Holly gasps. "Alabama Grace, what?"

"We slept together last week. He took me boot shopping, and it just happened. And then Brian—he gave me some pompous lecture about how I was ruinin' my chances and Griff's and I . . . I let it get to me, Holly."

An incensed sputter from Holly. So loud, Alabama has to

pull the receiver away from her ear. "That slimy little snake. Send him back home and I will put a boot so far up his ass I'll knock his block off."

"I know." Alabama groans. "I hate lettin' that little weasel scare me off."

"So don't. You're still gonna get the money. You might as well be gettin' a little more from Griff while you can too."

"Holly!" Alabama can practically see her best friend's lascivious eyebrow rise over the phone.

"Well," she hedges. "I'm just sayin'." A beat, then, "Was it good?"

"Oh, yeah." Alabama's face goes warm, her palms clammy. She tries to focus on the conversation at hand and not the memory of Griff's lips kissing on every inch of her body. "Like cold ice cream on a hot summer day," she adds stupidly.

"Then you gotta get that back. Cold ice cream on a summer day? Who passes that up?" Holly makes a sound of disgust. "Fuck Brian. You can't let him control you. That's the exact same thing you were trying to get out of with Six String. So here's what you do. You do Griff on the sly. You pretend Daddy Forester's around and you're back in Clover, humpin' in the shadows. You were good at that."

Alabama scowls at the phone. "Thanks a lot." The thought of bringing her father into this has her dry-heaving. No doubt Griff would feel the same way. While her father never flat out hated on Griff, she knew he wasn't Griff's biggest fan.

"Stop feelin' guilty, Alabama, and give in. It ain't your fault no more. You made mistakes, but you owned them. Maybe Griff is trying to too." When Alabama's silent, Holly goes on. "You were crazy about him. You loved him."

"It can't be love," Alabama says softly. "It definitely isn't for him, and even if it were for me . . . I have to know why he left Clover." She closes her eyes, a pang of hurt in her heart. "I just want an answer."

"I know you do. I know you want all the facts. I know you need 'em."

Alabama nods. She does. She needs them like air. Griff left her without a goodbye. She's carried the betrayal of that all these long years. Having her questions finally answered would put an end to the wondering, would let her process her pain. It's as simple and as complicated as that.

Holly's serious voice takes a turn for the tempting. "No one's sayin' go in deep. Just dip in a toe, you know?"

Alabama laughs. "I regret tellin' you a thing."

"You have to live your life. Have fun. See where it goes. You're not supposed to be a nun, Al."

Alabama laughs. "Maybe I could get that outfit on the roster."

"Hot damn."

Heavy boot steps in the hall, a pounding on the door. "We got ten minutes till the stage, Alabama," Brian bellows.

"Got it," she calls out cheerily, giving her door the finger.

"Wait, wait, wait!" Holly shrieks. "You gonna sing your new song?"

"Gonna try."

Holly snaps an air-kiss in her ear. "Give 'em some sass tonight, Al."

Alabama laughs and hangs up the phone. It's close to showtime, and she still hasn't decided on anything to wear. As her eyes scour the room, they land on a corner chair where her boots sit, still in their bag. She hasn't worn them since her night out with Griff. She's still wearing her torturous heels, one of her stubborn ideas to show Griff that he means nothing.

Which is probably hurting her more than him.

That one night they spent together, Griff had her remembering who she was—wild and free. Not the bitter and competitive bitch Six String churned out. She had a taste of freedom and she wants that same feeling back again.

She wants to be that Alabama.

From the closet, she pulls a pair of torn jeans and a lacey tank top. She dresses fast, slips on her boots, combs fingers through her hair. She puts on the barest of makeup, dark cat eyeliner, and pink gloss. Her freckles stand out like constellations across a pale sky.

She catches her breath when she sees her reflection in the mirror. The old Alabama stares back at her. Not the one Nashville made. That girl from Clover. Who loved the music. Who had every bright dream and impossible hope in the goddamn world.

A smile spreads across Alabama's face.

She can do this.

Kick-start her life.

Alabama's ten songs in before the audience starts shouting for Griff. She considers herself lucky; usually they barely let her make it through the first five.

Glancing over her shoulder, she slices a hand across her throat, telling Coop, the bassist, to cut the pulsing bass line to "High Heels, Higher Expectations."

The band quiets, but the audience doesn't. Beer bottles clatter as they roll around onstage, but Alabama ignores it all. She swivels an eye across the audience. The crowd is big, the biggest one she's seen yet.

"I know, I know," Alabama drawls into the microphone. "Y'all hate the song." Her voice drops to a conspiratorial whisper as she leans in closer to the mic. "Well, if I'm honest about it, I hate it too. But y'all gotta let me get through a few shit singles before you start demandin' blood."

That gets her a few chuckles and the semi-silence of the crowd.

Unhooking the mic, she crosses the stage and swaps out her electric guitar for an acoustic.

Into the mic, she asks, "You want Griff?" A few nods, sharp

whistles float her way. Then she sharpens her voice, pins her eyes to a buffalo-plaid-clad redneck in the corner booth. "Well, you ain't gettin' him. So shut up and listen."

Alabama strums a few chords. "This is a new song I wrote two nights ago. I actually had a conversation with a friend recently who showed me the light a bit. You know, I, uh, forgot how much I love songwritin' and then I got on the bus and it kind of reminded me why I was here." She laughs lightly into the mic. "It's about those people out there who don't get us or like us, or want to change us or dismiss us. And . . . hell, I don't know why I'm still talkin'. I'm just gonna play. Here goes . . ."

She takes a few minutes to gather her bearings, to put on a brave face. She's shaking in her boots, but this is for all the marbles. Screw Six String. Screw Brian. She's gonna do this the way she should've done this in the first place—her way.

It only took her a few days to craft the song—"Wild Card"— from a word Griff had tossed around during their chat on the pier. It bubbled up in her, working its way into a brash callout of the country music industry, of the men who run it and the women who dare to compete with the boys. She even took an old melody from a song she and Griff wrote and reworked it into a ballsy yet hopeful ballad.

Alabama gets close to the mic.

Then, channeling the old country sound she used to play before Six String got their hooks into her, she swings her arm in the air and brings it down. The guitar's twang rings out sharp and clear. The audience stills.

And Alabama sings.

> You came to the stage and found me lookin' sad
> A hoodwink in your eye, a wild card in your hand,
> You said, girl, all you gotta do is play the boys' game
> And for a small price of your soul you can have the same
> Because
> I'm a wild card, wild card, baby
> I'm a wild card, wild card, baby

> I'm your wild card . . .
> I made a deal with the devil just to stay afloat
> And not only did you sink yours, you sank my boat
> But you weren't finished, you moved on
> Leavin' me to be the only one still left with what I've done
> Because
> I'm a wild card, wild card, baby
> I'm a wild card, wild card, baby
> I was your wild card . . .

As she belts out the lyrics, she sees nothing, hears nothing, feels nothing except the strings beneath her fingers, her own voice in her ears, her heartbeat in her palms. Her whole body's drunk on the music. The slow country-blues anthem of her song. It's like a drug, chasing away her numbness, channeling her anger, calming her rocky soul.

> I went through hell for you
> And for myself, I had to fight to stay true
> Because one thing that's different between you and me
> When I come back I'll be better than I'll ever be
> Because
> I'm my wild card, wild card, baby
> I'm my wild card, wild card, baby
> I'm not your wild card, never . . .

When the song is finished, she opens her eyes. As the daze lifts, as sound rushes back, she hears wild boot stomps, shrieking whistles, raucous applause.

Her chest heaves as she drinks in air, drinks in the applause meant for her. Smiling, she stares into the bright lights and scours the clapping crowd.

That's when her heart hitches in her chest.

Griff.

He's sitting alone at the far end of the bar, on the outskirts of the audience, nursing a beer. His expression nearly has her knees buckling. Awe. Sheer awe and pride shine in his eyes.

His reaction has her shivering. Has her hearkening back to Clover, his constant support, him snapping his fingers and saying, "That's the stuff, Al, that's it."

When Alabama smiles, he tugs the brim of his trucker hat down, and an acknowledgment of something unsaid, a promise not yet claimed, passes between them.

She raises a hand and points out into the audience. The spotlight drifts and finally settles on Griff. A cocky smile on his face, he tips his beer to the crowd. "Well," she drawls into the mic, over the hoots and cheers. "You're in luck. You want Griff Greyson, you got him."

With a confident swagger, Griff crosses the bar. He scales the stage like a pro, a beer bottle held loose in his hands as he strides toward Alabama.

She smiles at him, eyes bright as she passes him the mic. Her heartbeat pumps double-time as their fingers brush, every nerve ending on fire, Griff's eyes locked on her face.

"Good luck," she says.

She doesn't stick around to hear his reply, and as she turns on her heel to make her exit, she can feel his gaze burning a hole into her back as the audience screams his name.

They're not the only ones who want Griff Greyson.

chapter
FIFTEEN

EXCITEMENT FLIPS GRIFF'S STOMACH AS HE FINISHES his encore. For the last two hours, his mind's been on Alabama. And now that his song and dance routine is over and done with, he's got nothing else on his mind except finding her.

He leans into the mic, tipping his beer to the crowd. Then he's exiting the stage. Brian's there to meet him, a bottle of water in his hands.

Coop claps him on the back as he passes him. "Damn, Greyson. You were on fire tonight!"

On fire is right. On fire to get the hell offstage and get to Alabama.

Brian swings an arm around his shoulders, pulling him away from the exit. "We're goin' out."

Griff scowls. Ever since Alabama's set foot on the bus, Brian's been trying to herd him in a different direction. Usually he'd be all in. Not tonight. Not anymore.

"So go," Griff says, his eyes scanning backstage, wondering if Alabama stayed for his set—hoping she did.

As if he can read his mind, Brian frowns. "She ain't here, man. She's on the bus and that's where she should stay because we got plans."

Griff follows Brian's eyes. Two giggling blondes wait in the shadows, the angling of their bodies telling him they're ready to boost his ego and then some.

"*You* got plans," Griff shoots back. "Take 'em and have yourself a grand ol' time, Bri."

Brian makes a little huff of annoyance and Griff can't help but bark out a laugh. He knows he's acting like a horny teenage boy, but goddamn. The look Alabama gave him as she was leaving the stage—that dangerous, flirty smile.

He lets out an internal groan. Thinking about it has him hardening. He doesn't know what the hell it means, but he's damn sure gonna find out.

With that, he thunders down the stairs and exits into the alleyway. The bus, parked feet away, shines like a beacon.

Tonight, he saw the real Alabama. Confident, wild, free. A fucking powerhouse. He's never been so proud of her.

She's been ignoring him for a week straight, giving him the runaround like no woman ever has. The more she pulls away, the further over the edge he goes. He's never been so frustrated and simultaneously turned on in his entire life. But he ain't giving up. He ain't backing down. If he has his way, he's bringing that woman back to his bed tonight. The sex wrecked him. He hasn't been able to sleep with her next door to him, to breathe with her scent floating through the hallway of the bus. His dick, his sanity, his heart needs her.

Tonight, he's finding out the reason for her cold shoulder.

On the bus, he quickly scans the living room. "Al?" he calls to radio silence. He checks her room and for good measure checks his. Then he heads to the writing room. A tug in his soul tells him she's there.

He's right.

When he swings the door open, he sees the outline of Alabama sitting on the long black couch in the dim light.

"What're you doin' sittin' in the dark, sweetheart?"

"I'm not in the dark." Her light voice floats. The room's lit up as she flicks on a lamp. Her strawberry-red lips part. "Not anymore."

He steps into the room, shuts the door. "You know, I just

had the best damn set of my life," he says, twisting the signet ring on his finger. "Because of you."

Her eyes gleam. "I had a pretty good set too."

"I know. I heard." He raises a brow. "I know where you got that song too."

"I used your line," she says, glancing down at her notebook. "I didn't think you'd mind."

"It's good, Al," he says, his heart damn near busting out of his chest. "Fuckin' great. They loved you."

She smiles, absorbing his words, her long lashes dark against her cheek.

Griff moves to the couch and sits beside her. Then, risking life and limb, he reaches out to take the notebook from her lap. Though her body tenses, she lets him. Lets him read what she's been working on.

"I just started it," she offers when his eyes light on one song in particular. "It's not much, just a scribblin'."

"You're right," he says, having to push the words past the rock in his throat. He doesn't even have to ask, he knows it in his bones. Her song—it's about them. "But it's somethin'. I see where you're going with it."

Her eyes sparking with competition, she hands him her pen. "Let's see what you got, Greyson."

His heart double-times its rhythm.

He pens a line after hers. Alabama reads it, scribbles, crosses out words, adds her own. Then she writes a few lines and passes it back to Griff. They work in silence, every so often nodding, murmuring appreciation, their bodies curved into each other as they work, heads dipped in solidarity, in concentration.

It's how it used to be.

How it always should have been.

Griff can't tear his gaze from Alabama's face. She's so passionate, so laser-focused, so goddamn beautiful. He wants to sweep her up in his arms and holler out loud, tell her he's all in, he is hers and there ain't one damn thing she can do about it.

Alabama leans back on the couch and evaluates the piece-meal song they put together. "It's rough, but it could be something." She smiles at the notebook. "We'll make songwriters out of us yet."

He stares at her, suddenly dry-mouthed. His heart feels like it's going to stop beating any damn second.

At his silence, she glances up. "What is it?"

He clears his throat. "You've been avoidin' me." But there's no accusation in his words. Only a plea for her to talk to him.

She drops her eyes. "I know."

Griff reaches out to cup her cheek, nearly groaning at the feel of her after a weeklong absence. "Why're you hidin' from me, Al? What'd I do, sweetheart?"

He waits for her to answer him, when suddenly, there's a very warm, very wet mouth on his.

Alabama, her plump red lips crushing his, loops her arms around his neck. The feel of her curves, her breasts pressed against his chest, has Griff letting loose a primal growl. He kisses her back, hungry and wanting, murmuring her name like some dirty reprimand.

With a gasp, Alabama breaks the kiss, but Griff doesn't let her go. Oh, hell no. He holds her tight against him, his gaze riveted on her face as Alabama settles back in his arms. She bites her lip, her expression shamefaced. "I know I've been avoidin' you. I'm sorry," she says. "I got spooked."

He frowns. "By what?"

She looks away from him. "By nothin'."

He wants to press her further but decides not to push it. "You're confusin' as hell, woman."

She tips her head back, exposing the creamy curve of her throat, and laughs. "I aim to please, Greyson."

"I want to do this, Al. Play with you onstage. Sing. Write songs." He pins his eyes to hers. Every card of his is on the table. Hiding them never helped him anyway. "We should be doin' us."

Before she can protest, he goes on. "I know I made mistakes.

I ain't been the best kinda man in the past. But I'm gonna be the best man for you. I won't hurt you."

"Griff." She shakes her head. "Don't make promises you can't keep."

"I mean it." He plunges a hand into all that silky red hair and, palming her neck, pulls her toward him. "I told you, I'm done with all that, Alabama. The drinkin'. The girls."

Curling into his chest, she gives a lazy, content smile. "Hmm. Just like that?"

"Just like that."

"I'll believe it when I see it."

"Oh, you will," he vows. She'll see it and then some. He's never been as serious in his life about something as this. Proving to Alabama that he won't fuck this up. Earning this second chance. Making it work. For good this time.

For-fucking-ever.

He leans in and kisses her slim shoulder. Her creamy skin is cool on his lips and he feels himself hardening. He moves down her throat, pressing a kiss to her pulse.

Alabama tilts her head to the ceiling as Griff's hand slips up her shirt to cup her full breast. Her slender body rumbles out a throaty sigh. "If we do this—which we shouldn't—"

"Which we should," he grumbles between kisses.

Another sigh. "We have to keep it professional." Hearing him groan in distaste, she frowns and pulls back. She places two fingers beneath his chin, raising his face up to meet her eyes. "I mean it, Griff. I worked so hard for this and I don't ever want to go back—"

"I understand."

His tone is serious because her eyes are worried. She's been working so damn hard to fix her reputation and the last thing he wants to do is hurt her. Ruining things for her ain't an option.

"No one can know about us. None of . . ." Her eyes flutter as he lightly twists her nipple through the lace of her bra. "Of this, onstage."

"So what you're telling me is only in the shadows?"

"Griff . . ."

Her head falls back as he drags the cup of her bra down to expose one perfect, pink nipple.

He grins. "Sounds illicit. I like it."

A half truth. He wants nothing more than to show Alabama off to the world, but he's willing to wait for her. It's her pace, her choice, and he'll follow her blind down that path wherever it leads.

Hooking an arm around her slim waist, he pins her to his chest and reclines back onto the couch. Alabama, on top of him, pushes herself up to look at him. "We keep it casual, too," she says. "No stayin' overnight. Or hangin' out together. Nothin' serious. We can't be serious . . ."

He gawks at her. "Goddamn, woman, you got some demands, don't you?"

She nips at his lips. "And you'll go along with all of them."

"Gladly," he murmurs. His dick aching with want, he presses himself against her.

Alabama gasps, then shivers at his hardness. "You're a horndog, Griff."

"A horndog for you. Only you." He groans when he feels Alabama's hand sliding down his thighs.

Alabama unzips his jeans. "You've been good."

"So damn good," he says breathlessly. He can't help his throbbing cock, the drop of his jaw, the pant of his breath, when he sees where this is headed. "I told you, Al, the only one I've been touchin' these days is me, myself and I."

"Really."

He moans when she wraps a hand around his cock and strokes.

"You," he whispers, devouring her mouth. "Is who I want."

Alabama's laugh rings out. "Good lord, Griff. What're we doing? Neckin' in shadows like we used to when we were teenagers? Hidin' from the adults? Hand jobs and blow jobs?"

Griff grins and presses a kiss to her lips. "Sweetheart, that's goddamn right."

Her eyes flash appreciatively. Griff settles back and closes his eyes, losing himself in the sensation as Alabama slips down his legs and takes him in her mouth.

Just like the good ol' days.

chapter
SIXTEEN

ALABAMA PUTS DOWN HER PHONE AND WATCHES GRIFF swagger into the breakfast nook. She's unable to keep the smile off her face at the heated look he gives her. They haven't been able to tear their eyes, their lips, their skin away from each other. For the last week, Alabama's been living on fumes, hustle, and Griff. Every night he joins her onstage at the end of her set to sing a song or two. The one safe way they can be together without attracting any unnecessary attention.

"Mornin', sweetheart." Griff scratches his belly, giving her an eyeful of lean, toned stomach. He pops a Keurig pod into the machine, presses the LCD screen and waits for it to brew. "You sleep okay last night?"

She scoffs. If what they did last night was considered sleep, then she must've had a full night's rest. Although the yawn that's escaping her lips says otherwise.

Griff grins. "You know, you'd get more rest if you stayed over."

Her scowl deepens at the smug look on his handsome face. She finally snuck out of his room last night around two a.m., much to Griff's chagrin.

"I meant what I said." She shrugs her shoulders. "No sleepovers."

"Suit yourself." He nods at her buzzing phone. "What's the news?"

She picks up her phone and scrolls through. "Holly says hi. Daddy is on a tear about the weather. They said frost and there's still sun. And . . ." She arches a brow, excitement coursing through her body. "The *Nashville Star* reviewed us."

His expression darkens. "Alabama, that is the last thing I want to hear this early." Picking up his coffee, he slips into the horseshoe booth beside her.

"Griff, it's eleven a.m."

"Okay, okay." He groans and rubs his face. "Who do I gotta kill?"

She laughs, swats his arm. "No one. Yet." She scoots closer to him, only to be stopped when Griff sticks a broad hand between them.

A cocky smile plays on his face. "Is this the approved two-foot distance?"

She glares his way, not liking the rules thrown back in her face. She could give in, just grip the front of his white T-shirt and yank him in for a kiss. She knows it would please Freddie, her and Griff taking up since their fans love them, but she still can't do it. The main thing stopping her—her reputation. Slowly, she's been regaining some of the traction she lost. In the press. With her fans. Her father. Her and Griff, they have to keep up appearances as long as they can. If not, she could lose everything she's gained.

Knocking her shoulder to his, Alabama scoots away from him. Griff's eyes flash with annoyance, a red-hot yearning to keep her close. But if he can call her bluff, she'll damn sure call his. "You want to hear it or not?"

He gestures for her to go on.

"First the headline: *Two Bad Acts Clean Up Good.*" When Griff nods, she continues. "Turning over a new leaf? Maybe not a good leaf per se, but it's new, different and we like it. Alabama Forester, the so-called pop-country princess, who's had her issues in the press, and with men, has changed. She's shed the glamour and the glitz and joined country-rocker Griff Greyson on his 'Straight to Hell' tour as his opening act. And while she occasionally sings the achingly saccharine track, she's blossoming onstage with a new sound and new songs. With honest clarity, she sings songs about heartbreak, love and loss. She also shines when she's joined by Greyson. The duo is engaging and charismatic, with Forester's raw, ballad-like country croon mixing perfectly with Greyson's rowdy rocker attitude. This is a different Alabama Forester than we've seen in the past and we hope she's here to stay."

She looks back up at Griff. His golden eyes shine with pride and she smiles. "For once the *Star* ain't shittin' all over me."

A grumpy look settles over Griff's face, and he wraps a hand around his coffee. "They never shoulda in the first place."

She glances back at her screen and smiles again, her cloud nine high still hovering around her fringes.

It all feels too good to be true—the review in the *Star*, reconnecting with Griff, the ease with which her songs are coming to her—but she won't fight it. She's learning to embrace what the universe is giving her and trying not to worry so much about it all blowing up in her face.

"You two ready for the show tonight?"

Alabama jumps at the sound of Brian's monotone bleat. "Jesus," she breathes, pressing a hand to her heart. "You scared the hell out of me."

"You're lurkin', Brian," Griff drawls. "Gotta get a new act."

He is. He's always lurking. Ever since Brian's sleazy threat, Alabama's kept a wary distance, but she feels his eyes on her. She hates knowing that he's watching her, that he's trying to control her and Griff both, that he's judging her for doing whatever it is she's doing with Griff.

Brian, leaning back against the kitchenette, surveys the two of them. Alabama fights to keep a neutral face, especially when she feels Griff's hand slide beneath her the skirt of her sweater dress. A covert cop-a-feel from Brian's prying eyes.

Damn you, Griff.

Alabama stifles a moan as Griff's large palm wraps around her thigh and squeezes.

"Freddie's flying in from London," Brian offers. "Since we're doing two nights in Baton Rouge, we're booked at an Extended Stay. It's got a pool," he adds uselessly.

"Can't wait," Griff says dryly. "Sign me up for water aerobics." He stretches lazily in the booth, his eyes landing on Alabama. "Two nights, huh?"

She turns toward him. His eyes have that mischievous glint she knows means trouble. "What're you thinkin', Greyson?"

"I'm thinkin' we do the show together."

"What?" Her eyes widen. Excitement bubbles in her chest like a fountain. "The entire show?"

"The whole damn show." He grins. "You read the review. They fuckin' love us."

"That's not how it works, Griff." Brian's scowling. His face is so red it looks as if he'll start frothing at the mouth any second. "They're payin' to see you, not her."

"They like her," Griff says, his smile fading slightly. Dangerously.

Alabama bites her lip, wishing she weren't suddenly in the middle of a war zone.

Brian shakes his head. "Yeah, well, *she* ain't your sound. You're changin' too much, too fast. You're gonna piss off your fans."

Griff holds up a hand. "Bri—"

But Brian continues. "Not to mention Freddie won't like it. Hell, I don't like it."

"Fuck you and fuck Freddie," Griff snarls. "I'll do what I goddamn want."

Brian shuts his mouth.

Griff's attention snaps back to Alabama, the look in his eyes soft, tender. "But it's up to you."

Alabama's heart flares with pride at Griff's take-charge attitude. The music means something to him again. Not to mention it gives her a slice of joy to openly defy Brian. To know

Brian's riled up, but there's nothing he can do about it because Griff's the boss.

Without batting an eye, Griff's hand slowly slides up the inside of her thigh beneath her dress. "What do you say, sweetheart?" His calloused fingertips trace and tease the lace edge of her panties. "Should we do this thing or what?"

"Yeah," she agrees, near breathless. Her head barely feels on, but she gives a bobblehead nod, her cheeks flushing at the heat pulsing through her like a heartbeat. "Let's do it."

Alabama exits the hotel in a blazing glow of sinking sunlight. Raising a hand to her eyes, she searches the grounds for Griff. Ever since they arrived in Baton Rouge, she's been avoiding Brian, who looked like he wanted to sit her down and give her a good talking-to. Despite having Griff's support, her nerves are shot and she wonders if she's doing the right thing. Wonders if Brian will cause trouble. Wonders if she can keep whatever she and Griff are doing under the radar.

Playing a full set with Griff? Good Lord, how's she going to keep her hands off him?

After circling the pool several times, Alabama finally finds Griff down in the courtyard. She lets out a sigh when she approaches him. "You're in the fountain, Griff."

Griff smirks from his spot in the grungy water. He lowers his aviators to let his gaze glide up her entire body. He's barechested, reclining against the edge of the fountain, a beer in his hands, a cigarette dangling from his lips, and while he looks all kinds of country trash, Alabama can't deny he also looks sexy as hell. All she wants to do is climb in next to him, press up against him and brand every tattoo he owns to her body.

A cocky grin fills his face. "It ain't the pool?"

A smile dances on her lips. "No. It ain't."

"What can I say? It's hot."

"It is," she says, her eyes on his tan, rippled stomach. "It is hot."

Even in late November, the sun in Louisiana has them both sweating like it's the middle of July.

He lifts his beer to the horizon and Alabama sees a photographer scuttle behind a fence. "Gotta keep up the act. Give 'em their picture."

She slips off her shoes. "You don't, though," she says, sitting down on the lip of the fountain to dip her feet in. "You kinda dropped that act six shows ago. And I'll let you in on a little secret." She lowers her voice an octave. "They like you better this way."

The way they scream his name, fill tiny cramped bars just for a chance to see him, gives her such an immense sense of pride. He's finally doing what he always wanted to do—his way.

"The way you used to act, Griff—that ain't you. As much as singin' like Britney Spears wasn't me."

He turns his head to stare into the sunset, the muscle in his jaw tight.

Her stomach flips, a hard thought occurring to her just then. Maybe he misses it. Maybe he's bored. Maybe he wants to go back to his drunk-as-a-skunk womanizing ways. The thought stings. But she reminds herself this is a casual, no-strings-attached deal. When she took this job, she thought she had her priorities figured out—get the money, get out, make a new start. And now . . .

Now she doesn't know what she wants.

She leans forward, resting her elbows on her knees. "We bitin' off more than we can chew, Greyson?"

He hits her with a frown and sits up. "Why're you talkin' like that?"

"I don't know. I just . . ." She trails off when Griff pushes himself toward her, dipping his head to kiss the inside of her knee. His scruff tickles her and goose bumps break out over her skin.

She moves her legs, stopping him with a hand to his shoulder. "Someone could see us."

"So?"

Biting her lip, Alabama dangles her hands in the water, out of view of the photographers. His hands swim toward hers beneath the water. He captures her hand, slipping it into his, weaving their fingers together like perfectly linked pieces. "What we singin' tonight, Alabama?" His expression turns sly. "'Burn Me'? Or maybe 'Find You Again'?"

Her heart radiates pride. In the last week, she and Griff have cranked out more songs than she can count. They're not all keepers, but the ones that are are something special.

She laughs. "We definitely ain't singin' 'Find You Again.'"

They've written most of the song they started the night Griff came to her in the writing room. The only thing it's missing is an ending.

His face clouds up. "Why the hell not?"

"It's not ready, Griff."

"Bullshit." His eyes hold on hers. She's pissing him off. "It's perfect and you know it."

"It ain't perfect. There's no endin'," she shoots back. "And you know it."

As they stare at each other, a cold hard truth wells up in her, making her heart tumble down into her toes. The song isn't done, has no ending, because she and Griff never did. Never will. Her and Griff—they're just a flash-in-the-pan moment. Finishing the song makes it—makes them—real. And she can't make it real. Not when she's vowed to keep this casual. Not when she still doesn't have an answer for why he left her all those years ago.

Alabama won't let herself go there, won't let herself hope. If she hopes, she loses. Even a song can't be trusted, because trusting only leads to trouble. A lifetime of regret and the worst mistakes a person can make.

"Hey." Griff's soft voice breaks the spell of her thoughts. "You're right. We'll sing whatever you want. You pick it."

She swallows and forces a smile. "Okay."

Griff reaches for her, gently taking her wrist in his fingers. "I'm sorry, Al," he says, his face contrite.

Too contrite.

She eyes him suspiciously. "Really?"

"I am, I really am, sweetheart. I mean, I just need to tell you one little thing—"

Alabama yelps as Griff tugs her onto his lap and splashes her down into the water. She sputters and lands a punch to his shoulder. "You asshole!"

A gut-busting laugh rips from Griff.

Untangling herself from him, she pushes up on her knees, pushes Griff away from her. She looks down at her clothes and groans. "You're lucky I ain't dressed."

He's still laughing as she climbs out of the fountain, dripping wet like some drowned rat. "You're a shit, Greyson," she says, squeezing water from the ends of her hair.

"You love it."

The scoff that'd normally be on her lips falls flat. Off in the distance, a flash of blond hair, the soft shuffle of footsteps. She stares at the gate bordering the hotel and a shiver slinks down her spine.

She opens her mouth to tell Griff but instantly forgets what she was planning to say. Because he's looking at her with those primal eyes that tell her he's gonna devour her mouth pretty damn quick.

Alabama sidles away from him, shimmying her hips in a way she knows drives Griff crazy. "Get outta there. We got a show to do. And I gotta get ready."

He stands, water rolling off his muscles. "Need any help dryin' off?"

She glances over her shoulder and wags a finger. "You lack many proper morals, Greyson."

His eyes flash, and then he's out of the fountain, prowling her way.

She gives him an evil grin and walks fast toward her hotel room, feeling Griff following behind her, feeling his body burning with wild desire.

Alabama doesn't know what the hell they're doing anymore, only that she likes it. Only that she wants it to last as long as it can.

chapter
SEVENTEEN

GRIFF KICKS OFF THE CREOLE BALLROOM WITH HIS signature country-rock song, "Roast 'Em Smokey." His fingers burn the guitar strings as he sizzles out a frenetic electric chord. Behind him, his band pumps out licks like fireworks.

> Hey, when ol' Smokey took the stage the crowd was hushed and somber
> They could tell it was that old cowboy's last and final number
> Ol' Smoke shifted in his boots and raised his fist up to the sky
> Said who the hell am I playin' for, all this is just do or die
> Then he let loose that guitar and threw it off the stage
> And that night the outlaw legend of Roast 'Em Smokey was made . . .

When the song's over, he hands his guitar to Scotty and steps back to the mic.

"I know you're wonderin' where she is," he says to the crowd. He saw the look of disappointment on their faces, the craning of necks, when Alabama failed to come out for the opening act and instead it was Griff. It never fails to thrill him—they want Alabama as much as he does. "Hell, I'm wonderin' where she is. You don't think she left me high and dry, do you?" He glances offstage, craning his neck in exaggerated confusion. "Alabama, you back there?"

Freddie's in the audience; he's gotta give her a good show.

Hoots from the crowd and Griff holds up a hand. His smile cocky, he wiggles his eyebrows. "I'm goin' back there. No apologies for what happens next." To Scotty he says, "Let it rip, boys."

The intro riff to "Ring of Fire" follows Griff as he ducks backstage.

He finds Alabama waiting in the shadows, all long legs and wild red hair. His balls clench at the sight of her. She's smoking hot and he already knows he's gonna lose his goddamn mind tonight. She cocks her head, amused. "I think you went in for the wrong profession. Stand-up is more your gig."

He moves for her, fast. They're on each other instantly, hungry as teenagers, as stupid as them too. But he can't help himself. He's so damn hot for Alabama, for this woman who has him on his knees every night, who won't sleep in his bed, who barely believes that he's turned over a new leaf, and he still doesn't care. He'd go to bat for her and then some. Show her until the end of his days that she's the one he wants.

His hands on her waist, his lips on her mouth, Griff walks her backward. He slams her up against the wall, gripping her thigh to drag her leg up around him. There, in the shadows, he kisses her roughly, heated, feasting on her strawberry-red mouth, her soft tongue, the curve of her pale white throat.

A rustle in the dark, fast, retreating footsteps.

Alabama breaks away from him with a gasp. "Someone's there," she says, stiffening in his arms.

"No one's there," he whispers. She relaxes, arcs into him, opening her mouth once again for his. He leans down, devouring it.

The music gets louder, more insistent, the band's cue to get his ass back onstage.

"C'mon," he growls, snatching her hand and pulling her alongside him. It's habit, instinctual to keep her close, to have her near him always. But when they reach the stage, Alabama stops. Griff's stomach drops, reality sideswiping him like a bus, as she extracts her hand from his.

In her eyes, apologies as she straightens her dress, wipes her lips.

"Okay," she says. "Ready."

They walk out. Together. The touch of her hand still burning a hole in his.

Instantly, an uproar. Deafening.

The crowd loses its mind when Alabama walks onstage, and all Griff can do is grin.

Alabama can command the stage like no one else. She's so confident, so cool, so goddamn sexy. Even in the shitty bar with its shitty acoustics, Alabama is a shining light. A fucking powerhouse. And that fucking body. Griff knows he should keep it professional, but still, he can't help his eyes roving over her as she steps up to the mic.

She's a vision to watch. A far cry from the broken-down woman he found waitressing at Mill's Tavern.

Jesus, he's obsessed.

"I think they've been waitin' for you, Alabama," he says into the mic, casting a lingering glance at her.

"Well, hell, let's not keep them waitin' any longer," she says in her trademark Texas drawl. She gives a little shimmy, Griff gives a hoot, and then they kick off their tried-and-true cover of Waylon Jennings' "Mama Tried." Alabama gives the song her own little boost, more folk-country than rock and roll. That combined with Griff's rollicking style has the crowd howling.

When they switch to a raw acoustic number—"Burn Me"—a song they wrote last week, Griff's unable to tear his eyes away from Alabama as they sing. Nothing between them but the lyrics, raging and passionate. The song is all contagious energy and heartbreak. Sparks crackle between them. Alabama can fight it all she wants, but if Griff feels it, everyone can.

Griff grips the mic and belts out, "Maybe you wouldn't remember me. Maybe you had another man in Tennessee. But then you were lookin', walkin' my way. And I knew that night, damn, girl, we were goin' astray . . ."

Beneath darkened lashes, Alabama lasers her gray gaze to his as together they croon, "You gonna burn me, like a match to a flame. You're gonna tell me that you ain't playin' these games. But I see the tricks that you're hidin' under your sleeve. And even though I know you're gonna burn me, baby, burn me, I'm still the fool who wants to believe . . ."

His sound—this sound—is miles from the brash country-rock his fans might expect, but he doesn't give two shits if they like it or not. He hasn't had this much fun in a long damn while. This is what he wants, what he's been missing for so long. Passion. A straight-up love for the music. Music he could only create with—

The thought hits him like buckshot: the music's never mattered to him because it wasn't with Alabama.

That's why he never took it seriously.

Because all along, all this time, it's needed her.

He's needed her.

He glances up, dazed and reeling, to find Alabama smiling at him, beaming like the sun as her powerful vocals ring out across the stage. "Maybe it's the whiskey or the song. Maybe it's that promise about how you'd never do me wrong . . ."

Sweat trails down his face as he stares at her. And as he turns his head to the blinding bright lights of the swaying crowd, he sees that they love her. In that moment, a bone-deep realization nearly knocks him to his knees. He don't got a chance against this. This storm that's coming. The truth he's been trying to ward off ever since she set foot on the bus.

He loves her too.

Still does.

Always has.

He tried to fight it, worried he'd hurt her, drag her into his shit, his messy problems, but he can't deny it anymore. He knows it's not fair; he left her once and now he wants her back, but he's never stopped loving her. She was always the one. And now that he's found her again, he's gotta make her see that. Because one thing's for certain—he ain't gonna let her go again.

After the show, Griff and Alabama escape down the back stairwell, slamming out into the alley where the bus waits.

Alabama stops in her tracks, a hand going to her mouth when she sees the lines of jammed people waiting for them. "Holy shit," she murmurs, turning toward Griff.

He grins. "They're here for you."

She stares, a pink flush spreading on her cheeks.

"They are," he says with pride. "Soak it up, sweetheart."

Her eyes glow. The way she's looking at him twists his stomach and Griff has to fight the urge to take her in his arms and kiss her right there in front of everyone.

"What're you waitin' for?" he says. "Get over there and sign some autographs."

She does. They linger for thirty minutes, Alabama signing autographs and posing for photos, while Griff shakes hands and signs ball caps, beer cans and babies. Brian stands around, taking in the scene, ushering people through the line like cattle.

When they're finished, Griff follows Alabama to the bus. As they walk up the stairs, Griff, his body shielding hers from prying eyes, slips his palm on the curve of her ass. Her laugh is delighted, and his cock stirs.

"I feel bad," Alabama says when they're in the lounge. "There's still a line out there as long as the Nile."

"Don't feel bad," Griff says, reaching out to wrap his arm around her waist. "Feel me." He pulls her into him, burying his face in her hair. "I can't stay away from you," he whispers. They're sweaty and hot and all he wants to do is get sweatier and hotter with Alabama.

She arcs a devilish brow. "Who said I want you to, Greyson?"

The sound of his name on her lips is damn near Pavlovian and he's unable to help himself. He tugs her in and kisses her deep, their tongues tangling together, Griff's hands plunging into her red hair.

But before they get any further, the door opens and Brian strides in.

Griff curses at the interruption.

Alabama stiffens slightly and moves out of Griff's arms.

"Freddie's on her way," Brian announces, propping open the door halfway for their manager's entrance. The buzz of the outside crowd drifts into the bus. "She'll brief us on the tour, then we'll head back to the hotel." He cuts a sharp glance at Griff. "Look at you. She's already got you in those claws."

Griff waves off his cousin's words. The last thing he's worried about is Brian and his shitty opinions. "Make yourself useful and get us a beer."

For once in his life, Brian ignores him. He takes a step forward, arms crossed, face red. This time, he stares down Alabama. "You just couldn't do it, could you?"

Alabama turns her body toward Brian, facing him fully. Her eyes blaze. "What I do is none of your business. Understand that."

Griff frowns, not liking Brian's slimy tone, the implication that he's already had a little chat with Alabama. If Brian's the reason for Alabama getting spooked, his cousin better learn how to run. Fast.

Griff rips a hand through his hair, wanting a goddamned explanation. "What the fuck are you two talkin' about?"

But he's ignored by both Alabama and Brian. They're staring each other down like two guard dogs.

"I warned you to leave Griff alone."

Alabama gets in his face and hisses, "You don't own me, Brian. And no matter what you think, you don't own Griff."

Brian lets out a bitter laugh. "Don't know what I expected from Alabama Forester. But it certainly ain't hands-to-yourself."

Griff turns his head sharply to look at Brian. "Careful," he warns. His voice low and venomous. "Watch how you talk to her."

Brian shakes his head, his nostrils flaring. "You ready to wear that ball and chain, Griff? You two take up now, she's gonna ruin you. It's easy to fix, man, all you gotta do is drop her. Go back to your old sound, your old life. I know you want that. You miss it. The way you're actin' around her—she ain't worth it." He holds Griff's gaze. "We both know why she's here, anyway."

Griff freezes, raging inside, knowing Brian's calling out Griff's bet, the real reason Alabama's been hired by CMI.

Griff meets his cousin's eyes, and it's all he can do not to go fucking nuclear. Christ help him, he wants to swing a fist right now. So damn bad. But he looses a breath, controlling himself. Through gritted teeth, he tells Brian, "What Alabama and I do is our business. Not like I owe you a goddamn explanation."

But Brian can't take the hint to shut the fuck up. He goes on, his eyes on Alabama, his expression one of disgust. "I don't understand, Griff. I don't understand why you're dirtyin' your hands with a little slut like her."

A soft gasp comes from Alabama.

Griff's head snaps to her. His heart clenches at the sight of her teary eyes, her expression hurt, so broken it already has him balling a fist.

No one makes her cry. Fucking no one.

His temper rising, Griff takes a step toward Brian. "I am gonna whip your ass."

Alabama puts a hand on his chest. "You don't have to defend my honor, Griff," she says, her voice shaky.

"Why not?" he growls, placing a hand over hers. "Someone has to."

A smirk snakes across Brian's face. He juts his chin at Griff. "Don't buy the act. She is what they say she is. Trash. Makin' her mark on every man in Nash—"

Griff interjects with a sharp right hook.

Brian staggers back against the wall and then Griff swings

again, knocking him out the open door. Brian sprawls down the stairs and Griff goes after him. They grapple in the parking lot. The crowd outside erupts into chaos at the scene. Cameras flash. Griff barely feels Alabama's hand on his arm, trying to pull him away, talk him down, but he can't be restrained. He won't be.

Another sharp right sends Brian to the ground. His cousin stares up at Griff, wiping blood from his lips.

Griff levels him with a steely eye. "Pack up your shit. I want you off the bus. Tonight."

That's when Griff raises his eyes to the crowd.

They're staring, dumbstruck, cameras flashing, and he realizes what he's done. He started a fight, the one thing he explicitly promised Freddie he wouldn't do.

Griff's stomach plummets.

He just tanked the tour.

He lost Alabama her money.

His heart thundering in his ears, he whips around to apologize, to tell Alabama that he's the worst variety of asshole.

Alabama's staring at him, her teary eyes as big as dinner plates.

But before he can say a word, she's throwing arms around his neck and kissing him like crazy. He tenses, only for a moment, and then leans into her just as fierce. Though he feels the flashbulbs popping around them, the snap of cameras, the excited voices and hushed whispers, he tunes it all out and tunes into Alabama. Red-hot desire rushes through him and he drinks her in, gripping her tight by the hips as they kiss and kiss.

Finally, she pulls back from him with a wrenching gasp.

He grips her by the elbows, confused. "Al, what the fuck?"

A smile cracks her face, her expression joyous and flushed. She holds on to him just as tight. "No one's ever done anything like that for me before." She swallows. "No one."

Griff's chest tightens, and he cups her cheek. "The way he was talkin' to you, I wasn't havin' that. I couldn't—"

"Get inside the bus," a knifelike voice says, the sharp sound of high heels echoing in the small space of the alley. Suddenly Freddie's in front of them, a snarl on her lips. "Now."

Alabama sits beside Griff on the black leather couch, their hands entwined, ready to get their ass reamed by Freddie, who stands over them, her face unreadable. But Alabama's uncaring, because she only has eyes for Griff.

She's shaken by what he's just done for her. In front of everyone, he defended her. He wrecked his own chance at his comeback to put Brian in his place. She wants to be pissed that he just torpedoed the tour, her chance at financial freedom from Six String, but she isn't. She's never found something so damn hot.

When she looks at him, she sees the Griff she knows. That kid from the past who always stuck up for the underdog. A kind man. Caring. Protective. Someone she can lean on, who has her back always.

Not only is she struck by what he's just done, she can't believe what *she's* just done. She kissed him in front of everyone. In front of the cameras, the fans, the world. Strangely, panic hasn't hit her yet. Her reputation's taken harder knocks than this. And she's been honest. For once in her life, she's putting her true self out there. What she wants, how she sings, and most importantly, who she's with.

"You fought, Griff," Freddie explains calmly, like they both weren't there. "You swung a fist. And that fist connected with Brian. With your tour manager."

"Yeah. I sure as hell did. I punched Brian in the fuckin' face," Griff retorts, his expression boiling with annoyance.

Alabama sighs. "Griff, the body's already cold, you don't have to stick another knife in it and watch it bleed."

Griff drags a hand through his hair. "Hell, I ain't sorry."

Freddie sits on the short end of the couch and crosses her slim ankles. She turns to Griff. "Tell me what happened."

Griff's teeth clench, his grip on Alabama's hand tightening. "Brian called Alabama something I ain't repeatin'. And I ain't havin' that." That's when he looks at her, pain and regret etched across his face. "I'm sorry, Al. I snapped. I know I ruined things—"

"No," Alabama says, her heart threatening to drumbeat its way out of her chest. "Don't apologize." She looks at Freddie. "If anyone's to blame, it's me."

Griff starts in his seat next to her. "*Alabama.*"

She ignores his sharp tone, keeping her eyes on Freddie. "It is. I take full responsibility. I brought all this to the tour." She inhales. Griff's shaking his head, his tawny eyes dark and stormy. "Send me home, fire me, but give Griff another chance."

"Goddamnit, no," Griff says, sounding so pissed off and worried that it steals her breath for a moment. "I got all the fault in this. There ain't nothin' Alabama did that warrants sendin' her home. Not one damn thing."

As Freddie sits silent, a curl of unease burrows deep in Alabama's stomach, but she stamps it down. She's doing the right thing. No matter what happens to her.

Freddie evaluates the two of them with a decisive eye. "How very sweet," she finally says. "A united front."

Alabama sits there, her hand clasped with Griff's, feeling like she's back in her daddy's house, ready to get the dressing-down of the century.

Freddie pins her gaze to Alabama. "Brian called you a slut, is that right, Alabama?"

She doesn't flinch. "Yes. That's correct."

"And Griff was defending you."

"He was."

Freddie's sharp swivels to Griff. "The label explicitly specified you don't fight. But they said nothing about working out hurt feelings within the band. And Brian . . . your cousin, he has tended to be a—"

"Sleazebag," Alabama interjects.

Griff chuckles.

Freddie stares. If there's a hint of a smile on her lips, Alabama can't discern it. The woman's locked tighter than Fort Knox. "Yes. Well. You said it smashingly, Alabama. I always thought he was a bit dodgy."

Alabama and Griff glance at each other, confused. Griff makes a gesture of impatience. "What're you sellin', Freddie?"

"It's what we in the business call a loophole. The label won't put you down, Griff. Not for this." She stands, smoothing a non-existent wrinkle from her skirt. "Seeing as how I didn't come all the way out here to witness two hotheaded males butt heads like baboons, I now have good news." Freddie smiles. "Things are looking good for you, Griff. And you, Alabama." She pauses for effect. Then, "The tour's sold out."

Alabama's mind whirls; she's shell-shocked by the news. She squeezes Griff's hand. "That's . . . amazing."

Griff's gaping. "Since when?"

Freddie flaps a hand. "Don't look a gift horse in the mouth, Griff. The remaining two weeks you're on tour, we're switching venues. Bigger, bolder, less beer-splattered venues." Before either of them can react, she goes on. "And I come bearing more good news. A winter tour. Europe."

It's Alabama's turn for her jaw to drop. Holy shit. Holly's gonna go crazy.

"Fuck," Griff says, equally stunned.

"You've done well, Griff. And there is one more thing." Freddie swirls a finger around Alabama and Griff. "The press will want to know—are you two an item?"

For a heartbeat, silence.

Beside her, Griff's gone still. Alabama's very aware he's waiting for her to answer. He's made it clear where he stands, and now it's her turn to decide.

But is this really what she wants? To give her and Griff another shot? Can she trust that the man who left her once won't leave her again?

Alabama tries to control her emotions, tries to tell herself that what's between her and Griff is still casual, that her feelings aren't deep and dangerous and all kinds of conflicting.

She looks up at Freddie. "Yes," she says quickly. Then amends, "We're sleepin' together."

"I see," Freddie says.

Griff stares at her, his Adam's apple bobbing. She can see he doesn't agree with how Alabama's phrased it, but he finally turns to Freddie, confirming what Alabama's said. "That's right."

"Very good," she says tartly. "I'll alert the social media manager and fill in for Brian until we find a replacement." Then Freddie's eyes alight on Griff. "We're pleased, Griff. You've done everything we've asked you to." Her lips curve in a twisting, knowing smile. "And then some."

Beside Alabama, Griff's spine goes stiff, his face paling considerably.

With a nod, Freddie exits the bus.

For a long moment, Griff and Alabama stare at each other speechless, processing the whirlwind of information laid on them.

Then the bus rumbles to life, jolting them into action.

Griff exhales and sits back against the couch, slapping his hands on the knees of his jeans. Alabama lets out a bright burst of laughter and collapses against him, burying her face in his chest. When she lifts her face, she's met by Griff's sweet kiss.

"So we're sleepin' together?" he says, arching a brow when they finally pull away.

Alabama smooths her fingers over the rings he wears. The metal cool and cutting. "Let's just stick to what we decided."

His eyes flash. "And what's that?"

"Casual."

"Casual, huh?" His eyes scan hers, as if seeking something else. As if disagreeing with her completely.

She nods. "Casual."

After a few moments of silence, she curls her neck against his shoulder. "Well, that didn't last long."

Griff snorts. "What? Brian's career?"

"No. Keeping our—whatever this is—under wraps."

"I'm sorry—"

"Don't be." She gives him a stern look. "I kissed *you*, Griff. It's out. And now . . . now let's see where all these bad decisions go." She tries for a cavalier shrug. "No strings attached."

"What if I want those strings?" Griff asks.

She drops her eyes.

She's torn. She knows he wants more from her, but there's still a piece of her that's fearful. She can't give herself over completely until she has an answer about why he left Clover. She knows she should just ask him, stop the hints, stop dancing around the issue, but she's stubborn. And she's still hurting. She won't beg for it. She wants him to give it up. Willingly.

But that doesn't mean she won't do this, only that she isn't all in.

It can't be love.

It just can't.

"Let's just . . . play it by ear, okay?" She presses a kiss to his lips before they can turn into a scowl. "What you did tonight . . . it meant so much, Griff."

He brushes a gentle thumb across her cheek, a look of primal protection flickering in his eyes. "I'm your man, Alabama. Ain't no one talkin' to you like that. Ever."

Your man.

Alabama shivers at the words, hating herself for how much she wants them to be true.

The whine of the bus brakes chases away her cobweb of thoughts. Her gaze on the window, on the neon glow of the hotel sign, she says, "We're here."

But Griff doesn't move. "I'm tired of sleepin' alone, sweet-heart." He holds her gaze, his expression shameless. "Stay with me tonight."

Her lips part to say no, but she can't. She can't refuse him anymore. "Yes," she says, a rush of heat blooming across her face, in her heart. "Yes."

chapter
EIGHTEEN

"READY FOR A LITTLE HAIR OF THE DOG?" Griff swaggers.

Alabama chuckles. "Think you can handle day drinkin'?"

He scoffs. "Hell, I ain't that old."

They link hands and walk down the cobblestone street to Galveston's Strand Historic District. Griff and Alabama have another day off before the last week of their tour kicks off in their home state of Texas. In their downtime, they take in Galveston. It feels like a vacation, eating BBQ, visiting the Old Quarter Café to see where Townes Van Zandt used to play, and buying novelty T-shirts at cheesy tourist traps.

It's been two weeks since Alabama and Griff's public kiss. Ever since then it feels as if her entire universe has opened up. The media only has kind things to say, and while her father hasn't returned her call about the winter tour, Alabama feels only relief. She's back on top. With her music, with Griff, with the *Nashville Star*. Her own terms, without apology, without shame. And soon, she'll have enough money to pay off her legal bills. It all has her feeling vibrant and unstoppable.

Griff tugs her to a stop outside an old bar with crumbling shutters and lit torches. Alabama lifts her face, shielding her eyes against the late afternoon sun.

"The Old Church," she says, raising a brow at the name. "Isn't that sacrilege?"

Griff's smile is devilish. "You're with me, ain't you?"

She lightly slaps a palm against his chest. Then grips the front of his shirt and pulls him along with her. "C'mon, Greyson."

They duck into the bar. It's dim and noisy. The lounge furnished with plush leather seating and curved booths. At the far end of the room, pool tables, darts and high-tops take up most of the space.

They weave in and out of the bustling crowd, searching for a table. That's when Alabama freezes in her boots.

It's Luke Kincaid.

He's at a pool table, surrounded by the rest of the Brothers Kincaid, his brother, Seth, and best friend, Jace. Next to Luke— his wife, Sal. As Alabama scans the group, she sees they wear the fatigue that comes with a tour. Just like Alabama and Griff, they're here blowing off some steam on their day off. The last thing she wants to do is ruin it.

She pivots to Griff. "Let's get out of here."

"No way," he says, staring past her. "We ain't runnin.'"

Alabama's stomach twists. The dark grin on Griff's face says it all. Says he's looking for trouble. "Don't you dare," she hisses, grasping Griff's hand.

"Sorry, sweetheart." His lip curls, his eyes still on Luke. "'Bout time I gave that guy a piece of my mind."

With that, he stalks across the bar, leaving Alabama behind him.

"Damn you, Griff," Alabama swears in exasperation. She hustles after him, but he's already pulling up alongside the pool table.

"Hey, Kincaid," Griff says and Luke glances up. "Fancy meetin' you here."

Luke's dark eyes widen at the unannounced guest, the beer bottle dropping from his lips. His gaze flickers to Alabama, his expression shadowed with uncertainty.

"Greyson," Luke answers easily. "How you doin', Alabama?"

"Oh, we're great." Alabama gives Luke a *forgive-me* smile. "I'm sorry for the interruption." Her hand shoots out to squeeze

Griff's arm, viselike, hoping he gets the message to exit the chat. "He's mostly tame."

Sal, at the other end of the pool table, smiles at her like there's no trace of the past between them.

Seth keeps a close watch on his brother and Griff, his blue eyes blazing.

Alabama remembers last seeing Sal and Seth in a hotel room, where she explained the role she played in Mort setting up Luke. It had been awkward and uncomfortable, but she owed Sal that explanation.

Griff pretends to scour the crowd. "You here with Mort Stein?" he asks carelessly. Alabama closes her eyes, wanting to drop through the floor. Though it's no secret there's no love lost between Griff and the Brothers Kincaid, she's not thrilled he's planning to hassle Luke. A man who doesn't deserve his wrath. A man who's been nothing but kind to her when she tried to wreck his world.

Luke stiffens, and his bandmates drift to his side, their stances tense.

"No," Luke says evenly. "I ain't here with Mort. I broke it off, and you know that, Greyson."

"Worry about your own career," Seth snaps. "If you still got one."

"Oh, yeah, you," Griff says to Seth with a sneer. "Left me high and dry in Florida." He juts his chin at Jace. "The both of you. Never recovered from that tour."

"From what I understand, you don't need a lot of help tankin' tours," Seth mutters.

Jace snickers.

Sal, her face neutral, approaches them.

Luke extends a hand behind him as if stopping Sal from getting closer. His expression says if Griff starts a fight with his wife here, Luke will end him.

"You got somethin' to say, Greyson, or you want to get the hell out of my face and leave me and my wife alone?"

"You gotta a lot of nerve doin' what you did to Alabama," Griff growls.

Luke looks unhappy. "Alabama and I don't have no issue. We settled it last year and she knows it."

"Maybe so," Griff needles. "Maybe now it's you and me who have the issue."

Jace's face screws up. "Piss off, Greyson."

Alabama rolls her eyes, a rush of heat hitting her face. "Good Lord, Griff, behave." She swivels regretful eyes to Luke. "I'm so sorry about this." She takes Griff's arm. "Let's go."

Luke's jaw clenches. "I'd take her advice if I were you."

Alabama's stomach rolls. Because she's staring at a man who's getting pissed. It's a sight. Luke Kincaid, the easygoing front-man of the Brothers Kincaid, angry. But she gets his anger. His wife's here and she's been through some shit. The last thing Sal needs is some gigantic asshole like Griff hassling her husband. She wouldn't blame Luke for swinging a fist.

Griff draws himself up to full height. "And if I don't?"

Seth tenses next to Luke.

A husky voice breaks the tension. "Don't be the *start-fights-in-a-bar* guy. No one likes that guy."

Blinking, Griff glances down at the petite dark-haired woman in front of him. Sal stares up at Griff, her large green eyes calm and unafraid, a pleasant smile on her pretty face.

Griff's face reddens with sudden embarrassment and Alabama has to smother a smile at the quick shaming Sal's bestowed upon him.

"Listen to her," Alabama says, her eyes meeting Sal's. She crosses her arms, the two women putting up a united front. "Be nice, or leave, Griff."

Griff's jaw unclenches. He and Luke hold each other uneasily in their stare and then their bodies relax.

"You're right," Griff says, the admission a grit of regret. "I didn't mean to come up in here and start shit." He runs a hand across his jaw and nods at Sal. "I'm sorry, ma'am."

Luke wraps an arm around Sal's shoulder. "It ain't a problem."

"You could join us," Sal offers. "If you want."

Jace chalks his pool cue. "Always got room for one more."

Sal's eyes metronome between Griff and Luke. Then, looking as if she's decided her husband won't lay Griff out, she says, "You want to take a trip to the bar with me, Alabama?"

"Good Lord, that's a hard yes," Alabama replies, shooting Griff a dagger-eyed stare. "I need a stiff drink after that."

Griff winces, his expression all apologies.

Stepping around Luke, Sal presses close to Seth. "Play nice," she says.

Seth scoffs but socks her arm affectionately. "I'm always nice."

Alabama gives Griff one last look of warning, and then she and Sal head toward the bar, leaving the boys behind them.

Griff winces as Alabama walks away from him. The over-the-shoulder glare she shoots him burns as red as her hair.

Fuck.

He lets out a long breath, his fists unclenching as he comes down from his hotheaded asshole antics.

He doesn't know what his fucking problem is. You think he would've learned with Brian. But the minute he saw Kincaid, some primitive caveman reaction took over his goddamn senses. It made him crazy. Made him possessed with a need to defend Alabama, even though deep down, he knows it ain't the guy's fault.

At least all of it.

"You gonna play or not?"

Griff looks over to see Seth Kincaid glowering at him. Before Griff can reply, Seth flings the pool cue his way, catching him off guard and hitting him hard in the stomach.

Annoyance simmers, but Griff swallows back his retort, not wanting to break another promise to Alabama. Besides, he's got no right to get pissed when he's the one who came in fists swinging.

Luke's brow furrows. He shoots his brother a warning glance. "You heard Sal."

Seth shrugs. "He started it." Then, after a last evaluating look at Griff, he and Jace rack up the balls.

Staking the end of the pool cue in the ground, Griff eyes Luke. "I fucked up," he says. It's as close to an apology as he can give Luke Kincaid. "Tryin' to start something with your wife here. It ain't a good look for me."

Jace and Seth scoff in unison.

"Same look as I remember," Seth mutters from across the pool table. "Startin' fights like an asshole."

"Pretty much par for the course," Jace agrees, lowering his cue to break the balls.

Luke sighs and shakes his head. He turns to Griff and makes a *help-yourself* gesture to a bucket of beers on a corner high-top. "Already forgotten."

Griff pulls a sweaty bottle of Shiner Bock from the bucket. "You on tour?" he asks, searching for a topic of conversation that's common ground for both him and Luke. It's the only explanation for their random run-in. Trust goddamn bad luck to put him on the same path as the Brothers Kincaid.

"Yeah." Luke takes a swig of his beer. "We played last night at the American Airlines Center in Dallas." He lifts his eyes. "And you were at . . . ?"

"Willie's Crab Shack," Griff grunts.

A snort comes from Seth. But he keeps his mouth shut and takes his shot, knocking a striped ball into the corner pocket.

Griff leans back against the wall and assesses Luke. "You know, I heard your last album. Can't say it impressed me." He can't resist goading Kincaid.

An amused chuckle rolls off Luke's lips. "Oh, yeah? I could

say the same thing about yours. Think I saw it down at the bargain bin at Wal-Mart."

Both men stare at each other for a long beat and then slow smiles spread across their faces.

Griff bursts into a gut-busting laugh. "Alright, I'm owned, Kincaid."

Luke shrugs. "You made it easy, man."

As Luke steps up to take his shot, trading bullshit banter with Jace and Seth, Griff searches the crowd for Alabama. She stands at the bar, in animated conversation with Sal, and a rush of shame hits Griff fast and hard. If Sal can be cool toward Alabama, he ought to be able to pull his head out of his own ass and act like a decent human being.

For a couple of hours at least.

Sipping his beer, Griff takes a second to evaluate Luke's wife. Sal's small and slender with dark hair and startling green eyes. A petite powerhouse who put him in his place faster than any man could.

That's when a faint memory drifts into Griff's brain. He frowns, remembering the *Nashville Star* headlines he had either scoffed at or discounted.

Sal. She's the reason Jace and Seth left his tour. All this time he'd been thinking they were assholes who blew him off, when in reality, they had found Sal in Florida. She had been in a plane crash, kidnapped, and returned to Luke with no memory.

Shit.

A rock's wedged itself in his throat. So tight he wonders if he'll ever get it loose.

He's a world-class prick.

"Your wife," Griff says in a quiet voice when Luke strides back to him. "How's she doin'?"

Luke's face creases with surprise at the question. Like he hadn't expected Griff to remember, or care. That thought has him feeling like shit all over again. Then Luke's expression softens. "She's doin' great. Thanks."

"Her memory," Griff ventures carefully. "She ever get it back?"

"Bits and pieces. But not really."

He grimaces. "Goddamn, Kincaid. I'm sorry to hear it."

"It's okay. We're takin' it day by day." Luke nods slow, the tight pain in his voice hitting Griff square in the gut. He can't imagine what the guy's been through. If something like that ever happened to Alabama . . .

He'd be a fucking goner.

He takes a quick swig of beer to drown out the chilling thought.

Luke's expression grows serious. "Listen. About Mort Stein . . ."

Griff holds up a hand. "You don't gotta explain."

"No, I do." Luke's mouth twists in an adamant white line. "That son of a bitch is a spineless asshole that should have had his legs broken."

Griff nods, echoing Luke's assessment. "I won't argue with that."

"And for what it's worth, I *am* sorry." Luke scrubs a tired hand down his face. "The press crucifyin' Alabama like they've done is bullshit."

"It is," Griff says bluntly. "She don't deserve any of it."

"I know. The whole situation's a clusterfuck and she got the brunt of it. Hell, if it were Sal . . ." Luke breaks off and glances back toward where Sal sits at the bar. "I don't blame you for bein' pissed. For wantin' to do everything you could to protect her." The catch in his voice tells Griff the guy's haunted. Something Griff can relate to pretty damn well.

Griff's chest grows tight. "Yeah. I would."

As his eyes land on Alabama, all the air in his lungs leaves him. He loves her. So damn much. And he can feel her. Keeping her heart on lockdown, holding herself back, all because the one thing she needs—an explanation about Clover—Griff won't give her.

Her words from days ago still ring in his head. *Let's just stick to what we decided . . . casual.*

But goddamn, for Griff it's anything but casual.

Which means he's got to tell her. He's got to be honest about everything. Why he left Clover. About the real reason she's on this tour. Most importantly that he loves her. That he can't live without her for another second.

He's wasted enough fucking time as it is.

Griff starts when he realizes Luke's giving him a wry stare.

Chuckling, Luke raises his beer, tilting its lip toward Alabama. "Never thought I'd see it, Greyson."

He slicks a hand through his hair, embarrassed at being caught gawking at Alabama like some lovesick fool. "That obvious?"

Luke shrugs. "Pretty obvious."

"My whole damn world right there," he tells Luke, taking a sip of his beer.

"Hey, Greyson!"

The sharp drawl has Griff looking up. Seth Kincaid, his arms out, his face creased with annoyance. "You gonna play pool or dick around all night tellin' your life story?"

Griff spins his cue. There's a swagger in his step as he approaches the table. "Twenty bucks says I kick your ass, Kincaid."

Luke smiles. "It's on."

Alabama sits on a barstool next to Sal, nervous but trying not to show it. Here's a woman whose husband she kissed to help Mort Stein sink his claws into him, and she's been nothing but gracious to her. Sal should hate Alabama for tearing her world apart, and instead she's sitting beside her with a smile on her face.

Sal shifts in her seat, her chocolate-brown hair swinging as she glances at Alabama. "I bet you're thinking right about now, in all the bars, in all of Texas, why'd I have to walk into this one," she jokes.

"No, it's not that. It's just . . ." Alabama takes a breath, takes a gulp of her martini to ease her nerves. "You remember me, right?"

Laughing, Sal opens her palm, accepting the vodka soda the bartender slides her way. "Of course I do." She brushes her dark hair away from her face. "We don't despise you, Alabama." Her pretty face clouds up. "No matter what those stupid newspapers say."

Stirring her martini, Alabama glances back over her shoulder at Luke and Griff, who are deep in conversation. So far there've been no thrown fists, no swinging pool cues.

"It definitely ain't my favorite coincidence," Alabama admits. "But it looks like they're keepin' the peace." She gives Sal an apologetic smile. "Again, I'm sorry about Griff."

"It's okay. I get why he'd be upset." A hint of a smile plays on her face, telling Alabama she's seen the news about the two of them.

"It's better coverage than I'm used to gettin'."

Sal makes a face. "I'm sorry. The *Star* is trash and the people who write for them garbage." Her face clouds, no doubt remembering the headlines that dogged her after she returned home to Luke. But then she gives Alabama a serene smile. "You're on tour with Griff now. How's that going?"

A slow, sudden flush creeps across Alabama's neck. "It's good. Real good."

"Well, you *sound* good. I saw a clip of 'Wild Card' on CMT." She sips her drink, her green eyes dancing. "It's a great song."

Alabama smiles at the compliment, Sal's kind words like a salve.

"How about you?" Alabama asks. "How are you doin'?" She knows the question holds a ton of weight. Until six months ago, Sal was missing, presumed dead in a plane crash. But when she was found, she had lost her memory and remembered nothing and no one—not even Luke.

"I'm doing well. I'm actually taking classes to recertify as a paramedic." Sal frowns and gives a quick, wondering shake of her head. "It's strange. It's like muscle memory. All of my training's coming back, easily—surprise, surprise—so soon I'll be cleared to go back to work."

"But other than that, your memory still hasn't returned?" Alabama asks, her gaze meeting Sal's.

"No." Sal tilts her dark head and gives a well-practiced shrug that tells Alabama she's very used to answering the question. "This is just my life now and I'm perfectly okay with that."

They're interrupted by the bartender, asking if they want another round. "Might as well," Sal says, lifting her glass and swirling around its remnants like a cyclone before draining it dry.

Her tone is grim, and Alabama looks at her curiously. Sal drops her eyes, her cheeks turning pink. "Luke and I—we're trying to get pregnant. But it hasn't happened yet." Her voice catches on the last sentence. "I had a miscarriage before the plane crash . . . and we've had one more since then."

"Oh Lord," Alabama presses a hand to her heart. "I'm so sorry, Sal."

"It's okay." Squaring her shoulders, Sal straightens up on the barstool. Her face clears out, something resolute taking over the grief in her expression. "I've been lucky with a lot of second chances in life, so I'm trying not to let it all get to me, you know?"

"Yeah," Alabama says softly. "I do."

At the drop of their drinks on the bar top, Alabama glances at Sal. "Want to go kick Griff's ass in pool?" she asks, wanting to steer the conversation away from the hard topic.

Sal grins. "Let's go show 'em how it's done."

One game of pool turns to two turns to three, and before Alabama knows it the afternoon's turned to early evening. When they finally pour out of the bar, around eight o'clock, Griff's slapping a twenty-dollar bill in Luke's hand and Seth's cackling his glee at the stars.

Alabama and Griff cross the parking lot and slow, stopping

to say goodbye to the group. The air is sticky and hot with humidity. A big, beautiful December moon brightens the sky. Griff, wrapping an arm around Alabama's shoulders, points his fingers at Luke. "Never thought I'd see the day, Kincaid."

Luke nods at him. "I'd have to say the same about you, Greyson." He looks at Alabama, his dark eyes warm and serious. "You let me know if I need to issue a statement or something. Get the *Star* off your back."

"I appreciate that, Luke." She gives Griff a smile, and he squeezes her tight against him. "But I'm a big girl. I think everything's gonna be peachy."

Sal flutters her fingers. "See y'all back in Nashville."

Alabama's heart swells. To her, Sal's words carry redemption, normality, forgiveness. She watches Luke and the group part, only to be approached by an eager crowd of people seeking autographs. A feeling of contentment elevates her soul. A feeling that everything's going to be okay.

"Hey," Griff says, stopping Alabama in the middle of the parking lot. "You ain't too mad at me, are you?" He stares at her, his expression so hangdog and contrite that Alabama can't even play pissed.

"Nah," she says, sliding a hand up his chest. "Besides, you surprised me. Playin' nice with Luke Kincaid." She arches a brow. "Who'da thought?"

Griff glowers. "Ah, hell," he says. "He can play a good game of pool. But I still don't like the guy."

Alabama laughs. "Uh-huh. Nice try, Greyson."

That's when, from somewhere behind her, Alabama hears soft footsteps whisking across the cement. The hair on the back of her neck prickles. She studies the parking lot.

Seth and Sal Kincaid, laughing about something.

Jace and Luke, scrawling autographs on the back of a fan's T-shirt.

Still, a chill runs down her spine. It's the same eerie feeling she had at the fountain, backstage in Baton Rouge, this entire tour.

She leans into Griff, her eyes watching the shadows. "Someone's there, Griff."

"It's the *Star*," he growls, surveying the buildings around them like he'll personally detonate them himself. When his gaze lands back on Alabama, a wolfish grin appears on his face. "They want a show, hell, let's give 'em one."

He grasps the nape of her neck and hauls her into his muscled chest for a crushing kiss. His lips, hot on hers, have Alabama tangling her fingers in Griff's hair, contouring her body to his.

At first, her only thought is the surrounding cameras, tomorrow's headline, and then as Griff deepens the kiss, she lets it all go. She gives in, gives the kiss her all as a slight thrill sweeps her up. The thrill of the tabloids watching, the thrill of controlling her own narrative, has her heart sparking. She devours Griff's lips, her body burning up with hungry need.

With a sucking gasp, they pull away.

Griff stares at her, fire and lust blazing in his eyes. "Front-page news."

She laughs breathlessly and links her hand with his.

"C'mon, you ol' renegade," Alabama teases, taking a few steps off to the side. But Griff stays where he is, shouting something at Luke, and his hand leaves hers, breaking their connection.

That's when, out of the corner of her eye, she sees a flash of blond.

Alabama's body goes rigid.

Nikki's emerging from behind a parked car, twenty feet from Griff, who doesn't see her. She takes jerky steps toward him, her face twisted up into a look of something terrible, something violent and angry.

What Alabama sees next has her heart lurching.

A gun dangles in Nikki's right hand.

It all happens so fast.

Nikki raises and aims the gun. At Griff's chest.

"No!" Alabama cries, her ragged scream upsetting the night. And then she's running, flying through the air.

Not Griff, is all Alabama can think. *No no no please not him.* She sees it in Nikki's face—she means to kill him. And Alabama will be damned if she lets Griff gets hurt. She can't lose him. Not now. Not again.

The shot rings out.

Without hesitation, Alabama throws herself in front of Griff.

She barely glimpses his golden eyes widening in horror before she flattens herself against him. Before the bullet slams into her shoulder with red-hot ferocity.

The world topsy-turvies as she and Griff fall backwards to the ground.

She lies draped over him, her ears ringing, her eyes disbelieving as the world explodes into chaos. Luke Kincaid throwing his arms around his wife, shielding her with his body, as a second and third shot whiz through the air.

Then silence.

Griff, his breathing ragged, cradles the back of Alabama's head and lifts her body up with his own. He turns her over in his lap and then she's staring up into his wild eyes.

"*Nonononono . . .*" His voice comes fever-pitched and frantic as his eyes scan her body, her arm. "*Fuck*," he swears. "Fuck! Christ! Oh Jesus Christ, sweetheart, what'd you do?"

Alabama's vision clears and she sucks in a terrible gasp. Pain, needlelike and prickling, radiates in her left shoulder.

She swallows, wanting to reassure him, wanting that awful look off his face. "I'm okay, Griff. It's just a scratch."

"Goddamnit, it ain't just a scratch, it's . . ." He breaks off, his face lined with frustration and despair. He whips his head up. "We need an ambulance! Now!"

Then his eyes are on hers again, his pupils so dilated all she can see is just a faint ring of gold.

"You gotta stay with me, Alabama, you hear me?" His entire body trembles as he cradles her in his arms.

She tries to nod, but her neck just falls back over the fulcrum of Griff's arm. Her vision blurs, images going fuzzy as she tries to focus.

Then there's a rustle of movement, and then there's Sal Kincaid.

The woman's skirting the ground, keeping herself low, ignoring her husband's vicious curse. She lands beside them with a soft exhale. "Lay her down and keep her still," she instructs Griff, her face grim with worry.

The world tilts as Alabama's placed on the hard cement, Griff looking tortured at not being able to keep her in his arms. But he doesn't leave her side. He grasps her hand and holds it tight.

Sal snaps her fingers. "Let me have your jacket, Seth." A pair of cowboy boots move in Alabama's periphery, and then Sal has a thin piece of plaid fabric in her hands. Folding it into a square, she clamps the pad over the bullet hole in her arm.

Alabama hisses a pain-filled gasp.

Sal, her green eyes fixed on Alabama, gives her a small smile. "You're going to be okay, Alabama. I'm going to check for more wounds, just in case, alright?"

Alabama nods, nods, nods, but she can't stop shaking. Can't stop the pain that keeps slicing through her arm with laser-like precision. It doesn't feel like a bullet. It feels like fire, like molten lava streaming down her arm. Oh Lord. It hurts something fierce.

Alabama dares a glance at her arm and instantly wishes she hadn't. Bright red blood seeps through Sal's fingers, through the thin cloth covering her shoulder. A sudden rush of nausea overtakes her and she whimpers.

"Look at me," Griff commands hoarsely. "Not at that. You hear me? Eyes on me, Al."

He squeezes her hand, only she can't squeeze it back.

For a moment, her eyes lock with Griff's. The pain and sorrow tightening his handsome face has her wanting to say everything to him, has her wanting to tell him what she's always known, what she's been putting off, but there's no time.

She's sinking. Her pulse is a rush in her ears, her mind emptying as her body goes hot and cold all over. And then she feels herself going limp, her eyes rolling back in her head, as she finally, mercifully, slips into the encroaching darkness.

Griff's heart stops when Alabama's hand slips from his grasp. All he can do is watch in horror as she trembles and then goes still and limp on the hard ground.

The shuttering of her eyes, the roll back to whites is enough to end him.

She's gone, she's gone, she's gone . . .

"No!" Griff shouts. His entire body jolts like he's been electrified. Frantic, he tries to gather her in his arms like he can fucking reach into her chest and start her heart himself, but Sal stops him with a calm hand to his shoulder.

"She's in shock," Sal explains, giving Griff a sad look of sympathy at where his mind has gone. "But I can't be sure an artery wasn't hit. She needs medical treatment immediately."

She raises her worried eyes to Luke, who hovers nearby on his cell phone. Kincaid stares at his wife as she works, his voice a numb monotone as he relays information into the phone.

Griff's gut clenches. When he turns his attention back to Alabama, the air rushes out of him.

Her blood. It's everywhere.

On the ground mixing with her hair, on Griff's shirt, on his hands. Hands that won't stop shaking, because her blood isn't stopping. It flows like a river, seeping through the makeshift bandage on her arm, through Sal's clamped fingers.

He squeezes Alabama's hand, dying for her to squeeze back, to show him she's still here with him. She's got to be.

Please, God. Griff dips his head, his eyes on Alabama's gray face. On her still-rising chest, her breathing shallow and ragged.

The sight of her unmoving and unconscious fills Griff with a dread he's never known. He can't lose her. Not again.

The sudden flash of a camera has Griff whipping his head up. *Motherfuckers.*

Rage and fury gnaw at his nerves and he wants to launch himself to his feet, to find the lurking photographer and rip him to shreds. But he can't. He can't do any of that because he can't leave Alabama. He could kill someone, most likely himself if this doesn't end like it needs to, if this doesn't end with Alabama's heart pumping strong and her eyes opening.

Another flash has Griff at his absolute breaking point.

He's never felt so fucking powerless in his life. Powerless to stop the blood, to protect Alabama, to take her pain and make it his.

"Goddamnnit, stop," he says, his body shaking with raw agony. His fists curl against the knees of his jeans. "Please, just fuckin' stop. Leave her alone. Leave her the fuck alone."

Leaning down, he tries to wrap his arms around Alabama, to shield her from any further photos, but that's when two pairs of legs and boots settle in front of him. He looks up to see Jace and Seth, their bodies providing a cover for Alabama from the photographers.

All Griff can do is nod his thanks, his throat so tight from emotion he can't even get the words out.

The scream of a siren pierces the night air.

Griff's head snaps up. "Fuckin' finally," he bites out, the anxiety in his chest building when he sees the red and blue lights of the ambulance.

All he can do is stand there, fists knotted, numb and helpless as the paramedics work on Alabama. He wants to fight to be by her side, to know what's happening, to demand they fucking fix her, but he knows that won't help Alabama any. He has to wait. Has to wait and see if his life means anything to him anymore.

As he watches Alabama get lifted onto the stretcher, he hears a sharp, shrill voice.

Nikki.

She's in cuffs, being led to a police cruiser by a female cop.

Fury grips Griff in a blind rage.

With two fast boot-stomping strides, he crosses that parking lot. Nikki looks up. When she sees who it is, she flinches, trying to move closer to the police officer for protection.

"Sir," the cop says. "I'm afraid I have to ask you to back up . . ."

Griff gets close, ignoring the cop. His body shakes with an absolute feral rage, a feeling primitive and protective. He meets the terrified eyes of Nikki, who's trembling against the cop's hold. "You're lucky you're a woman."

He says it calmly and quietly, but it has all the effect of an atom bomb.

Nikki pales and glances down at the ground. But Griff stands his ground, staring at her. He means it. If Nikki were a man, he'd beat him to death where he stands. Without hesitation, with relish. Griff doesn't give a shit that the bullet was meant for him. It hit the woman he loves. The woman he finally found again, and if she's taken from him . . . if he loses her because of this . . . because of him . . .

"You're lucky," he repeats, teeth gritted, fists clenched.

A sharp whistle has him turning.

Luke Kincaid's pointing at the ambulance where Alabama's being loaded up. "You're gonna want to get on that, Greyson," he shouts. "Now."

Griff turns and rushes across the parking lot.

She has to be okay. She has to.

chapter
NINETEEN

*S*HE'S HURT AND IT'S HIS FAULT. *AGAIN.*

Griff sits in a hard hospital chair across from Luke and Sal Kincaid. All three of them wait for news on Alabama, but no one speaks.

Griff's falling apart. Why the hell won't anyone tell him what's going on? The next person who comes through that door without word on Alabama better be ready for a swinging fist. It's been two hours, and all he's done is sit here, helpless as fuck, letting the hours tick by, letting every phone call go ignored. Most of them from Freddie. But the tour's the least of his fucking worries.

All he can think about is Alabama.

His mind won't stop running circles around him with guilt. From going to every single what-if in the damn book. What if he treated Nikki better? What if he never put Alabama on that bus? And worse, the one that hits the hardest: what if she doesn't make it?

Leaning forward, he buries his face in his hands.

Jesus, please let her be okay. His life won't mean anything without her.

At the thought, he shudders. Fuck, he's a fool. A goddamn idiot. For not telling her he loved her. For ever letting her go in the first place.

Sure, he's been a shitty person, a failure of a man, but Christ, please don't let him deserve this. Let lightning strike him down, let him never sing another song again, but not this. Not his Alabama.

She's hurt and it's his fault. Again.

"You know what they're going to do, don't you?" a soft voice says and Griff raises his head.

Sal's curled up against Luke, his arm wrapped tight around her waist. Her clothes are covered in dried blood, her face pale, but her green eyes bright. She looks exhausted but still kicking. "They're going to clean it out, stitch her up and send her home in a day or so." She nods, her smile encouraging. "I know there was a lot of blood, but . . . Alabama's tough. She'll make it."

"She saved my life," he says, his voice rough with tears. His throat knots and he closes his eyes briefly. "If she ain't okay . . ."

He breaks off, the memory of the sound the bullet made as it slammed into Alabama too awful for words. He'd heard the gunshot, so sharp it sounded like lightning. He saw Alabama, a blur of movement as she flew across the space between them. And then he felt her, slamming herself into him to take both of them to the ground.

At first, his conscious brain couldn't understand what was happening. It was only seconds later when he felt warm blood, felt Alabama shuddering and going limp against his chest that he realized what she had done.

What had possessed her to do that?

She had taken his bullet. Had shielded his body with her own.

He swipes a hand across his face, tears stinging the back of his eyes. Once, he might have tried to hide his emotions, to beat back the tears, but he can't. The wall he's built is down. Only Alabama could get him on his knees. Make him crumble.

Luke winces in sympathy. "I've been there, man. You gotta hang in the best you can." His eyes brush to Sal and he pulls her in closer.

"Mr. Greyson?"

Griff stiffens at the sight of the doctor stepping into the waiting room. Poker-faced, eyes unreadable behind his dark glasses, he approaches Griff, a tablet in his hands.

Fear grabs Griff by the jugular.

He launches to his feet, barely able to hear over the roaring in his head. "Tell me," he croaks, and he barely recognizes his voice. "Tell me good news, doc. Tell me my whole world ain't over."

"You want good news, you got it."

The doctor smiles and Griff has to reach out and hold the wall to stay standing. "The bullet entered the shoulder and punched through clean. Frankly, she's lucky. No arteries were hit, which is a miracle in itself. She lost a lot of blood, and she'll need physical therapy for that arm, but she'll make a full recovery."

Griff closes his eyes, a sudden rush of relief sweeping him up. "Thank God."

"We've cauterized the bleeding, stitched it up and are treating her with antibiotics and IV fluids," the doctor says. "We'll want to keep her here under twenty-four-hour observation, but then she'll be fine to go home. She'll be in a sling for a while, so best to limit any strenuous activity."

Griff meets the doctor's eyes, a surge of emotion welling up in him. "Thank you," he says, reaching out to shake his hand. "Thank you so damn much."

The doctor nods. "She's sleeping right now, but you can see her whenever you're ready."

With that, the doctor exits the waiting room and ducks into another patient's room.

Blowing out a relieved breath, Griff turns to Sal, who's now standing. A smile lights up her face.

"Hell, you were right," he says.

Before she can say a word, Griff pulls Sal into a bone-crushing hug and lifts her up off her feet. "Shit," he laughs when he breaks their hug and eases her down. "I'm gonna name our babies after you."

She laughs in response, the color on her cheeks darkening.

Next, Griff extends a grateful hand to Luke. "I owe you, man. Many bottles of whiskey."

Luke shakes his hand. "Look me up when you get back to

Nashville." He gives Griff a knowing look. "And if you wanna stay sane, don't read the papers tomorrow."

Sal squeezes Griff's arm. "Give Alabama our best." After a long last look at him, she takes Luke's hand. "We're here if you need anything."

Griff watches them disappear down the hall before he turns and makes his way to Alabama's hospital room. For a long second, he stands there, steeling himself to go in, and then finally, he opens the door.

He nearly goes down to his knees.

Alabama—his strong, independent Alabama—looks more fragile than he's ever seen her. Hooked up to a myriad of beeping machines, an IV drips into her arm. She's asleep, her long red hair fanned across the pillow. Her dark, delicate lashes resting against her pale cheeks. Her chest, the slow rise and fall of it, is better than any sight Griff's ever seen. Every breath she takes means he takes one as well.

But her arm.

As Griff creeps closer, he winces at the painful sight. Alabama's left shoulder is wrapped in layers and layers of tight, white bandages. It rests in a sling and lies limp and immobilized and across her chest.

The image slices through his brain like a scalpel, churning his gut and turning the blood in his veins to antifreeze.

It's too close. Too close to Clover. Too close to that girl lying in that hospital bed, battered and bruised, Griff going to see her, to tell her he loved her, that he was sorry for the accident, and knowing in a few short months, he'd be leaving.

He'd leave her like a fucking coward, and he wouldn't look back.

She could've died. She could've died and it would have been his fault. Again.

The words echo into his heart and twist his soul in two.

And then Griff collapses to his knees. Soft, silent tears

obscure his vision. But he lets them fall. He won't wipe them away and he won't stop himself.

He deserves this.

He hasn't cried since he left Clover—not even when his own mother died—hasn't cried since that night on the Ridge where he and Alabama hung upside down in that battered Jeep and he knew beyond any doubt that she was hurt.

That he had hurt her.

And now he's here again. Alabama unconscious in a hospital bed, and all he can think is that he did this to her. He got her hurt, again, because of the shitty person he is, because of his goddamn selfish past.

Kneeling beside the bed, Griff gathers Alabama's slack hand in his. He leans forward, pressing his lips to her fingers, to the pulse in her wrist. He's never felt anything more precious. He's got to tell her. He can't waste another moment.

He almost lost his second chance before he had it.

The painful truth has a shuddering sob rocketing out of him, but he makes himself say the words, what he's felt for damn near his entire life.

"I love you," he says in a barely audible whisper. He closes his eyes and buries his face against her knuckles. "I love you so goddamn much, Alabama."

Alabama's eyes open. She squints in the dim sunlight, scouring her surroundings. There are cords curled around her hand, the beep and whir of machines, vases of colorful flowers, and at the end of the bed, the strangest sight she's ever encountered.

Griff Greyson.

He's slumped facedown on her lap, the lower half of his body in a metal chair beside her bed. One arm tucked beneath his chest, the other outstretched above his head, clasping her hand in his.

A faint smile tugs at her mouth. If the *Star* could see their tough outlaw now . . .

Extending her good arm, she runs her hand through Griff's dirty-blond hair. As she takes him in, her heart halts. In sleep, he looks like a very vulnerable, very exhausted little boy. Alabama closes her eyes as she smooths a palm down the cheek of his scruffy beard, the very feel of him like a beacon of comfort.

Even after everything that happened, he's still here. He hasn't left her. Not even during the ambulance ride. Alabama has a vague recollection of him being there, of his voice, gravel-tough yet wet, talking to her over the scream of the siren, demanding she be okay, telling her he was sorry, so damn sorry.

Alabama shifts in bed, groaning at the painful ache in her arm. Her father had described being shot as pouring hot sauce on a wound, and now she knows what he meant. Gingerly, curiously, she fingers the strap of her sling, the bandage wrapped tight around her shoulder and bicep.

"Careful. You don't want to pull a stitch."

The voice has her turning her head to see Griff sitting up and watching her with a sharp-eyed gaze. He looks tired, like an exhausted husk of a man.

She swallows, clears her scratchy throat and says, "Griff."

"How you feelin'?" he asks, settling himself back in the chair but still remaining close to her side. He takes her hand in his again, stroking a gentle thumb across her knuckles.

"Okay, I guess. Kind of numb. Dreamy." Alabama smiles faintly and makes eyes at her IV. "You're missin' out on whatever they got me hooked up to."

He chuckles. Then his face turns serious, his eyes falling on her arm. "The doctor says you're gonna be okay. You got some stitches, and you'll be hurtin' for a while, but now all you need is rest."

"Hmm." She leans her head back against the pillow. "Lucky me."

At this, his eyes flash in anger. "You're goddamn right, you're lucky."

Suddenly, Griff stands and starts pacing like a caged animal. His anger, his frustration, his worry, radiates and all Alabama can do is watch in stunned silence.

"Griff, what—"

He whirls around, ripping a hand through his hair. "You could have been killed. You damn near were."

Her mouth goes dry.

She drops her eyes as heat floods her cheeks. She knows. Knows she's stupid, knows she could've died. And yet, the minute she saw the gun, she knew what she was doing. Protecting Griff. The thought of a life without him . . .

She couldn't lose him. She knows this with every bone in her aching body.

Alabama grits her teeth and tries to sit up. "I was scared. I was scared for you, Griff."

His mouth tightens. "*You* were scared?" He thrashes his head, looking like he wants to shake her awake. "Damn it, Alabama. If that bullet had been two inches to the right—I could have lost you. What were you thinkin'? What in the almighty fuck were you thinkin'?"

Too pissed off to hold it back any longer, she holds Griff's burning stare and fires back, "I was thinkin' I love you, you damn idiot."

Griff's eyes widen.

He stands so still she can't be sure he's breathing.

But the words are out. So she whispers again, "I love you."

Alabama looks away, her heart in her throat. She's angry at herself for giving in, for not keeping it casual when she said she would keep it casual, for still not having her answer about Clover. But when she saw the gun, she knew. She knew what she felt for Griff, and now, she can't deny it any longer.

Her chest tightens as Griff seats himself on the edge of the bed, right beside her hip.

"Al," he begins, gathering himself.

She cuts him off, squeezing her eyes shut against the tears that threaten to fall. "You don't have to do this, Griff. You don't have to say it back just because I'm in a hospital bed."

As soon as the words are out of her mouth, she regrets it.

The harsh hitch of his breath tells him she's hurt him.

"Look at me," he demands. "Now."

She does.

Alabama meets Griff's lionlike eyes, his haunted and haggard expression.

Then Griff reaches out and gently takes her hand. "I love you, Alabama," he says in a voice so fierce it leaves no room for doubt. Unwavering love shines bright in his eyes. "I should have told you weeks ago. I still love you. I never stopped. And I was a damn fool for givin' you up."

Heat flares in her heart. Tears stream down her face. His words terrify her, but they also fill her with hope, with light. And suddenly, the past doesn't matter. Why is she worrying about what went wrong instead of what she can have again? For once, she knows what she wants. And that's Griff.

Still holding his gaze, Alabama's response is to reach for him with her good arm.

Griff answers her, his muscular arms wrapping around her to hold her close, yet loose. He's careful not to disrupt the bandages, to put her in more pain. And yet, she craves his bruising grip. The warmth, the hardness of his body. It's what she needs to feel that she is really still alive.

Griff buries his face in her hair, his exhale tremulous.

When he pulls back, he sweeps his mouth against hers. The kiss is near-reverent, as soft and as tender as anything Alabama's ever felt. He cups her face in his hand. "I love you," he breathes against her mouth, a blessed murmur, a promise against her lips.

And then Alabama has her mouth on his, her good arm

twining around his neck. The kiss is sparking and lit and Alabama can feel it electrifying her all the way to her toes. To her soul.

At her needy little moan, Griff rips away from her, his breathing uneven. "Easy," he says, raising his hands in front of himself like he's worried he'll hurt her. "We got time, sweetheart."

Alabama pulls back, staring at him through heavy lashes. She reaches out to touch Griff's scarred cheek. "For bein' such a tough guy, you sure melt real quick."

He grins but says nothing, instead helping her settle back against the pillow. Warm and numb and content, she lays back down, watching as Griff adjusts the blanket over her lap, his laser-sharp gaze taking her in. "I want you to get some sleep, Al." His lips thin out when he sees her unspoken protest. "I'm serious. You need rest."

She does. She needs rest. She needs—

Alabama gasps. Griff immediately grabs her elbow. "What's wrong?" he asks, his expression one of panic.

She looks up at him. "The tour."

Griff groans. A dark look passes over his face and he drags a hand through his hair. "Don't with the tour."

"We only had one more week."

She sighs, disappointment washing over her. It kills her she won't get to finish it out.

"Alabama, that is the last thing on my mind right now." Once Griff seems to decide she's appropriately tucked in—so tight she can barely move—he sits on the edge of the bed again, next to her shoulder. He traces a finger across the apple of her cheek. "It can wait, sweetheart."

"It doesn't have to, though," she says earnestly. "You can keep it goin' without me."

Griff frowns. "Let's get one thing fuckin' straight. I ain't leavin' your side, Al. I go where you go. And I sure as hell ain't doin' the tour without you."

Alabama's cheeks redden, shaken by the intensity of Griff's declaration.

But then reality settles around her like a lead weight.

She shakes her head and rubs a palm over her tired eyes. "I can't go back to Nashville, Griff. I can't be there. Especially after this . . ."

For a long moment, the air leaves her lungs. She doesn't feel ready, doesn't feel steady enough to face the shitshow of media waiting for her.

Griff tenses and she can see him thinking the exact same thing. Nashville will trap her. She'll have no peace, no silence, no safety.

And that's when Alabama's hit by a powerful need to go back home. To go back to Holly, to her father, to Clover and its quiet country.

So Alabama says softly, "I have to go home, Griff."

Home.

The minute she says it, tears well in her eyes. And maybe it's the drugs or being shot, but she's reminded that she and Griff don't have a home. Not them, not really. They had a bus and a bed and a song and that was it. And Alabama has Griff, only she's not expecting him to go with her. She knows where he stands on his hometown and would never ask that of him.

"Home," he echoes, his voice faint and faraway.

Then he's scooping up her hand and pressing a kiss to her wrist. She shivers as his lips brush against her heartbeat. "I'll take you home, Al," he says without an ounce of hesitation, and her eyes widen in surprise. "We're goin' back to Clover."

chapter
TWENTY

RIFF STOPS FOR GAS IN SOME ONE-HORSE TEXAS TOWN where the motto is "Blessed by Big Hearts and Bigger Hats." He and Alabama are about an hour from Clover. The next tour stop had been Austin, so naturally, Alabama had insisted they drive through their home state. *It'll be fun*, she had said. He scowls as he sticks the gas nozzle in the tank. Well, it sure as shit hasn't been fun for her. The ride's been agony.

Though she's kept a brave face, Griff can read her clear as day. She's faking it, pretending she's okay when she's feeling like hell. It's only been two days since the hospital and Alabama's acting like she could rope any bull in Texas. Which is another reason he's going where she's going. To watch over her. To keep her safe. To keep her in goddamn bed.

He glances up, watching as Alabama exits the convenience store, a plastic sack held loose in her hand. Her bad shoulder's swaddled in a layer of bandages and hung in a sling that wraps around her shoulder and chest.

Alabama greets him with a grin. "I got some goodies."

He hustles over to her and gently helps her inside the rental truck. Boosting himself up on the step, he leans over and buckles her seat belt, making sure she's strapped in nice and tight. When he's finished, he tightens the gas cap, hops into the driver's seat and points them east. Then they're zipping down the freeway.

Beside him, Alabama unpacks the sack. "Raisinets, Funyuns, Cheetos. All prime road trip food."

He raises a brow, nodding at the tabloids she's trying to hide, still tucked away in the sack. "And what's that? Prime reading material?" A guilty expression crosses her face at being caught. "They upset you," he growls, "I'm gonna be pretty fuckin' pissed."

They're gonna upset him too.

The last thing he wants to see is another photo of Alabama in the paper, crumpled in his arms. He doesn't care what he told Alabama about fighting. If he ever runs into the photographer who snapped the photo of her at her most vulnerable, he's gonna put a fist through his face.

She waves him off and pulls out a magazine. "Let me live, Griff." He watches as she tries to open it one-handed and fails miserably. Her face crinkles in frustration as the pages stick together.

He smirks. "Yeah, well, you need me to open it, so how about you just wait till we're in Clover?"

"Fine." She sticks her tongue out at him. "Killjoy." She tosses the tabloids on the dash, the headlines reflected back at him in the glass.

Clenching his jaw, Griff closes his eyes for a brief second. He can't shake the images of blood gushing from Alabama's arm, the slap of the bullet hitting her flesh, the shutter of her gray eyes.

And the blood. There was so much goddamn blood.

The memory of Alabama literally shielding him with her body is one he'll never forget. He'll never want to either.

"Griff?"

The sound of Alabama's soft drawl calls him back. Shaking himself out of his daze, he turns to find her staring at him, her pretty brow furrowed. "Are you alright?"

"Fine. Don't you worry about me," he says, sweeping his gaze over her.

She's tucking herself back into the seat, looking extremely un-Alabama-like in black leggings, a loose sweatshirt that hangs off a shoulder, and sneakers. She's fresh-faced, her red hair piled high in a messy bun, but to Griff, he's never seen a woman more beautiful. He's never seen one as tired either.

Of fucking course she's tired. She's doing a cross-country jaunt when she should be resting in bed. But that's Alabama. The strongest person he knows. He loves her strength—but, at times, it also frustrates the hell out of him.

He watches her with anxious eyes as she opens the glove box and shakes a pain pill out into her palm. She dry-swallows it, then shifts in the seat, trying to get comfortable.

"You hurtin'?" Griff knows she'd rather stick it out than admit she's in pain.

"Good Lord, Griff, I'm fine." She lets out a deep drawl of a sigh. "Can we just not do this? You worryin' about me. Holly's gonna henpeck me to death enough when we get back to Clover as it is."

"So you want me to what? Put you to work? Maybe get you sloppin' stables?"

"That's more like it." Her face brightens. "Your mom's house. Now that could be a project."

He glances quick at her, his frown deepening. She doesn't sound like she's joking. In fact, she sounds like she's pretty damn serious. Well, Griff is serious too. Serious about getting her back to his house and letting her heal. She's barely been out of the hospital two days and already she's talking about home renovations.

"You try to lift anything more than a book," Griff warns, "and you're gettin' hogtied to the bed."

"Hmm." Her lips quirk. "Sounds like something you'd like."

Griff grits his teeth at the flexing of his dick. "Oh no. You ain't baitin' me. We get back to Clover, you're stayin' in bed. Alone."

She smiles, humor sparking in her eyes. "We'll see about that."

The way she's looking at him—he damn near got her killed and all she can do is make eyes at him.

Goddamn.

Her *I love you* wrecked him. He's wanted those words for

so long, and now that he has them, he's scared shitless. Not because of what they mean, but because of what he's done to her.

She's hurt and it's his fault. Again.

"You nervous?" she asks, startling him from his thoughts. "To go back home?"

He grins. "I went back to get you, didn't I?"

"For more than twenty-four hours, Griff. You know, you actually have to see people now." She tucks a stray lock of hair behind her ear. "Daddy knows you're comin' home. He wanted me to stay with him, but I told him I'm stayin' with you." Her gray eyes search out his as if reading him for regret. "If that's still okay."

"More than," he says, forcing the words out from the knot in his throat.

"I'm twenty-nine years old," Alabama says hotly. The apples of her cheeks turn an adorable shade of pink, and Griff fights the urge to pull over, take her in his arms and kiss her senseless. "I should be able to not regress to a child the minute I set foot in my hometown."

He chuckles, returning his gaze to the road.

"I told him I didn't want there to be problems—"

He cuts her a look. "And there won't be."

He means it. Though seeing Alabama's father isn't high on his list of priorities, telling her about the past isn't either. Especially not now. He knows she needs it to move on with him, but all he wants her to do is recover her strength. Though it's just stitches and a sling, Griff knows the emotional wounds will go much deeper. He's gonna be there for her. To give her anything she asks.

And if there's one thing he's damn certain of, he ain't running again. So he's gonna take whatever shit Newton is gonna throw down, take it for Alabama, and only this time he ain't leaving with his tail tucked between his legs. He's leaving with Alabama. With the woman he loves held tight by his side.

The way it should have been in the first place.

Alabama gives a wistful little sigh. He glances over at her in time to see the sign for Austin fly by.

"Don't be doin' that," he warns.

He's already got a call scheduled with Freddie for later today to figure out the rest of the tour schedule. Not like he'd tell Alabama that. Not yet.

Her glance is exasperated. "I can still sing, Griff."

"I know you can, and we're gonna do that, just after you rest."

"Yeah, yeah." She rolls her eyes but smiles at him. "You're a pain in my ass, Greyson." She shifts in her seat, too fast, and winces at the pain spearing through her shoulder.

"Feeling's mutual," he says, trying to keep his voice cool, but his gaze lingers, worried. Watchful.

After a second, Alabama curls back in the seat and closes her eyes.

Griff exhales a breath and steers the truck toward Clover. His knuckles, white on the wheel, tell him what he needs to do. Face everything he's been running from. Face the past so he can have a future with the woman he loves.

Alabama wakes to the slowing of the truck, the feel of movement that tells her they're off the freeway and on a small-town dusty dirt road. Blinking away sleep, she turns her face to the window, to the familiar scenery. They're half an hour from Clover. She can gauge the distance by the corn silos sitting tall on the horizon. She always used them to count down the time. At the bounce of the railroad tracks, the sharp jostle of her arm, she lets out a pained moan.

"Hey." Alabama turns her head to find Griff staring at her. His lionlike eyes are soft, clouded with concern. "How you feelin'?"

She stretches in the seat the best she can. "Sore. Stiff." She flashes Griff a smile. "I'll survive."

He looks back at the road, his face focused and granite-tough.

Alabama eyes Griff's handsome profile and wonders.

He's been so strong for her, so kind, so damn beautiful—helping her with anything she needs, giving her whatever she's asked for. Sunlight catches the scar on his cheek, glossy and ragged, but she smiles. She loves that scar. Loves everything about him, including his reckless streak, his roving hands, his fierce and loyal protection of her.

And still, doubt needles her heart.

She needs help, but Griff doesn't have to give it. He should be on tour instead of going back to Clover to play house with her. Soon, they'll be turned loose in the real world. They'll be in Clover, where every good and bad reminder of the past will be unearthed.

Coming home could bring out the old wounds in Griff.

He could run. Again.

She has to be real about this. About them. Sure, they have five shows left—but what are they to each other? Despite the confessions of love, no one's made promises; no one's talked about the future.

She dares a quick glance at Griff. She loves him. She knows that without a doubt. But is she a fool? Is she making the same mistake all over again?

Griff, feeling her gaze on him, glances over. "Somethin' on your mind, sweetheart?"

She takes a breath and opens her mouth. "I know it's too late, we're here, but . . . you still have time to turn back." His brow furrows and she goes on. "I didn't give you much choice in the hospital. You don't have to do this. You don't owe me anything. Least of all takin' care of me when you could be on the road."

His lips thin out, a cloud of a storm darkening his face. He's angry. Pissed off if she had to use a better word. "That ain't what this is."

"Griff—"

"Look, if you think I'm gonna drop you off in your dad's front yard you got another thing comin.'"

The words come out like gunfire, and Alabama sits back, abashed. Griff keeps his eyes glued to the road, his knuckles white on the wheel.

Then he takes a breath and looks her way again. He holds her stare, fire blazing in his eyes. "I love you, Al. Okay? You hear me? You get that through your stubborn skull and fast."

Alabama smiles faintly. "You're just sayin' that because I took a bullet for you."

Griff curses at her but reaches out to squeeze her thigh. His touch is warm, comforting, and she's surprised to feel hot tears beading her eyes. Not wanting Griff to see and worry, she turns her face to the window. They're on Main Street, coming up on the town square.

Clearing her throat, forcing away memories of the gunshot, Alabama taps the glass. She eyes the carved statue of Griff the town erected when his first album went platinum. "There you are . . ."

He makes a sound of disgust and increases their speed.

Soon, they're on Lonestar Road, pulling into the drive of Griff's house. The For Sale sign hangs at a crooked angle, the shutters have seen better days, the grass is dry and dead, but it's all still there. All is as Alabama remembers, and the lead weight in her stomach is replaced by one of hope.

Home.

Alabama brightens, seeing a friendly sight. Holly, her curly blond hair wrapped in a red bandanna, sits on the front porch. She stands when Griff cuts the engine, throwing up her arms to crow, "Well, lookie what we got here! The big city slickers comin' home to roost."

Exiting the truck, Griff walks around to the passenger side and opens the door. Instead of helping her out, he slips his arms beneath her, cradling her close.

Alabama flushes, looping her good arm around his neck.

"I can walk, Griff," she says as he carries her to the porch steps. "My legs ain't broken."

With a grunt that tells her he doesn't care, he gently sets her down next to Holly. Alabama wobbles but steadies once Holly pulls her into a loose hug. "My baby, my precious gem, my poor little shot princess."

Griff grimaces at Holly's words. But all he says is, "Watch her arm."

Smiling, Alabama pulls back. Holly, unsure where her hands should go, because normally she'd be all over Alabama with the eagerness of a puppy, clasps them to her chest. "You gave me a fright, Al," she says, tears in her eyes.

"I know." She squeezes Holly's arm. "Gotta keep you on your toes."

Hope held high in her chest, Alabama scans the yard for another familiar face. Holly, following her gaze, says in the lowest of low voices, "Your daddy ain't comin', Al."

Her mouth goes dry. "Oh."

A harsh, angry swear blasts from Griff.

Holly bites her lip, her face etched with sympathy. "He'll be by, he's just . . . you know, station stuff."

Alabama forces a lean smile. "Right. Station stuff."

Holly turns her owl-eyed gaze to Griff. "How is she?"

"You know, the usual," Griff replies, his voice gruff. "Stubborn, not listenin' to orders, in pain and hidin' it."

"Oh, so the famous Alabama trifecta."

Alabama rolls her eyes. "I'm right here, y'all. I can hear you."

Holly waves her off. "Bed's all made up," she tells Griff in a take-charge tone that tells Alabama she and Griff have been plotting. "Everything's dusty but slightly livable inside. So what's next, Grumps?"

Griff scowls, then starts, "The bags."

When Alabama makes a move to follow, Griff blocks her with his body. His face red and flustered, he wears a mildly pained expression. "You—just stop. I'll get 'em. Rest, that's what you're doin.'" He looks at Holly. "Permission granted to tie her to the damn bed if you have to."

Holly gives a salute and grasps Alabama's good shoulder. "You see? We're both going to be tyrants. You have no choice in the matter."

As she's steered inside by Holly, Alabama glances over her shoulder at Griff as he strides across the lawn to the truck.

Happy.

Despite everything that's happened, she's happy.

chapter
TWENTY-ONE

LABAMA SIPS THE TEA HOLLY'S MADE AND SWIVELS her eyes around the bedroom. The curtains are open, letting in a flood of sunlight, and while the house is a crumbling mess, it's clean and sparkling.

Even just a little love and care has its old bones singing.

She shifts against the pillows propping her up into a rigid sitting position. Lying down kills, so it looks like she'll have to get used to sleeping like an animatronic robot.

Holly comes sashaying through the door, Alabama's belongings in hand. She tosses the suitcase on a chair, tosses the tabloids across the bed. "There," she says, her lips curving in a faint smile. "It's like old times, trashy gossip rags and girl talk."

Alabama toasts her with her tea. "Only with chamomile instead of alcohol."

A wiggle of Holly's eyebrows. "I can spike it."

Alabama chuckles. "And rile Griff up even more? Let's do it."

With a laugh, Holly climbs onto the bed and flips open a magazine. "Did you see these yet?" She flashes an apologetic smile. "I kinda peeked."

Alabama's eyebrows get higher and higher as she scans the headlines.

Ripped from the Lyrics of a Country Song!
Alabama Forester Gunned Down by Crazed Stalker

"And this one?" Holly pretends to gag at the cover of the *Nashville Star*. In her most dramatic voice, she reads: "Other Woman Alabama Forester Takes Bullet for Sal Kincaid."

Alabama shrugs. "Drama sells."

Holly wrinkles her nose. "All about Sal."

"Come on," Alabama says. While she appreciates her best friend's fierce defense of her, she knows Sal doesn't deserve the wrath. "All they wanna do is pit us against each other." She shakes her head and sets her cup of tea down on the tray. "Sal saved my life. Honestly, she's probably the one person who's stood up the most for me in the press."

Holly winces and glances down at the magazine. "Well, shit, don't I feel like an asshole."

A rustle of pages, and then, carefully, softly, Holly asks, "What about this photo?"

Alabama's stomach dips.

The photo's heartbreaking.

Still, she can't pull her gaze away from the image of a distraught-looking Griff crumpled on the ground, his arms wrapped around Alabama.

But it's his face that has tears springing to her eyes.

His face contorted into an expression she's only seen once before in her life. That night on the Ridge.

"It's awful," Alabama whispers, suddenly chilled, suddenly hating how their tragedy's been captured on camera for the entire world to see. "It's an awful photo."

A tear slips down her face, and then another.

Holly stares at her. "It says a lot, don't you think?"

Alabama wipes her cheek and drops her eyes. Her friend's asking her what's up, calling her on her tears, on that photo, and she won't let her get away with a bullshit answer.

Raising her eyes, Alabama licks her lips. "I did it on purpose."

Holly's brows lower as her gaze narrows. "You did what on purpose?"

"Getting shot." She winces, whispers. "I took the bullet for Griff."

"*Alabama Grace*." Holly looks horrified.

"And before you say it, I know. I know I could've died. I

know my arm could be fucked up, maybe forever, but I don't care." Groaning, Alabama buries her face in her hand. "I love him. God help me, I love him. I'm an idiot, but I do."

When she raises her face, Holly's pursing her lips, a lecture on the tip of her tongue. But before Holly can say a word, Alabama pins her with a look. "I couldn't stand the thought of him hurt. I—I didn't think. I just reacted."

"Why am I not surprised?" Holly throws up her arms in frustration. "Alabama Forester's motto from the dawn of time."

The sound that comes out of Alabama is a gut-busting laugh. She holds her arm tight against herself, trying to keep it still. "Stop," she says, hitting Holly with her foot. "You're gonna make me bust a stitch."

She wipes her eyes, tears and laughter intermingling. She hadn't realized how badly she needed this. A friend. Confession. A tough talking-to.

"Everything okay in here?" a rough voice says from the hallway.

Alabama glances up to see Griff hanging in the doorway, tattooed arms crossed, biceps bulging. He wears a deep frown that says he sees her tears, sees the magazines on the bed and isn't a fan of any of it.

"Honest to God, Griff, you're hoverin'," she says, exasperated. The last five minutes, she's heard him prowling around in the hall like some mangy tomcat.

His scowl deepens. "I don't hover. I do, however, care, and if she gets you worked up . . ." His firm tone tells her he's about five minutes away from booting Holly and the magazines out the front door.

Holly rolls her eyes, waves a placating hand at Griff. "Okay, okay. Five minutes, then I'll am-scray, grump-ay."

Griff scowls at Holly but then lasers his gaze to Alabama. Heat flares in her cheeks at his cocky half-smile. At the spark of love burning bright behind his golden eyes.

After Griff disappears, Holly turns to Alabama. "Tell me everything."

So Alabama takes a breath and does just that.

Griff ambles down the hall, scowling at the giggles that follow him. He's being overbearing, but hell if he knows how to be anything else. Alabama ain't one to sit still, not for a minute. So it's up to him to keep her off her feet and relaxing.

He comes to a stop at the foot of the stairs, running a finger down the banister to find it free of dust. He thanks his lucky stars that Holly came through for him. That Alabama didn't have to come back to a pigsty of a run-down shack.

But it could still be better. He knows the old house and his mom deserve more.

A low vibration has Griff slipping his cell phone from his pocket. "What?"

"Hello there."

Griff fights a groan when he hears Freddie's abrasive accent. He's been so caught up in worrying about Alabama, he's forgotten about their scheduled phone call. They haven't spoken since the hospital, since Griff called to tell her Alabama had been shot, that Nikki was in jail, that he was dangerously close to losing his mind.

Pausing midstride, he sighs and leans back against the wall. "I've only got a minute, Freddie." He glances at the door, keeping one ear out for Alabama.

"Alabama." The click-click-click of Freddie's nails sound over the line. "Tell me, Griff, when will she be ready to play?"

"Are you fuckin' serious?" His fist curls around the phone, hot anger lashing his spine.

"Ah yes, formalities first. How is she doing?"

"You don't care, Freddie, so don't piss me off by askin'."

"Yes, unfortunately, I can't care because my first order of

business is business. Your business, Griff. The tour was hot and now it's not. We need to reschedule ASAP to secure sponsors for the winter tour. If not, we lose our chance."

Needling his brow, Griff shoves off the wall and enters the kitchen. Spying Alabama's purse on the counter, he rummages around for her pain pills, finally finding the brown-yellow bottle buried at the bottom. Freddie goes on. "Luckily, the photo is keeping you in the public eye at least." There's a devilish smile in her voice. "Dare I say, you look convincing."

Griff slams a fist on the counter. "I'm gonna tell you one last time, it ain't a goddamn act." He's pissed. He needs Freddie to hear him, to get it through her bird brain that nothing he feels for Alabama is fake. That the bet he made don't mean shit. That she's his and he ain't letting her go again.

Freddie's snort is curt, disbelieving.

"Do you hear me?" he says, his tone taking on a tender edge of seriousness. "I love that woman. She's my priority and I want you to understand that. Fuckin' fast, Freddie, because now you're really pissin' me off."

There's a pause, so long that at first, Griff almost thinks the line's gone dead.

Then, "Very well," she says, her voice harder than it was. Any trace of levity gone. "I understand completely."

Griff frowns.

"Two weeks."

"Two weeks? You're fuckin'—"

"Get her ready. If she can't handle the terms, perhaps she shouldn't be paid."

Griff sucks in a breath. "You're a cold bitch, Freddie."

"I could say the same thing about you."

At the sound of footsteps behind him, Griff ends the call without a goodbye and glances back over his shoulder. It's Holly. She enters the kitchen, her sharp brown eyes on the pill bottle in his hands.

"Never thought I'd see the day you'd be playin' nursemaid," she quips, adjusting the tangled bracelets on her wrists.

Griff keeps a neutral face and crosses his arms. "Yeah, well, it's for Alabama."

Her voice steady, she walks toward him. "She took a bullet for you, Griff."

The reminder sinks its fangs into his throat. "I know." He swallows thickly, aware of Holly's accusing eyes burning a hole through him. "I ain't happy about it."

"She is, though. And do you know why? Because she loves you."

Emotion hits him quick and fast, and all he can do is nod. "I love her too."

She stops inches from him. "Then don't hurt her."

"I won't." His voice is like gravel; he can barely get the promise out.

But Holly isn't done. "Don't lead her on if you ain't serious. She needs this new start. If you ain't plannin' to be a part of that, walk away. Let her have this, without you, and move on. You both move on."

Griff's stomach clenches at the thought of another man in Alabama's bed, taking her out at night, writing her a love song.

"I ain't walkin' away," he says in a low voice. "I did it once, never again."

Holly stares at him, her eyes calculating, like she's a human lie detector, then she lifts her chin and grins.

"Good. Because she's hurtin' right now, but you know what? She's the happiest I've ever seen her." Holly jabs a finger in his chest. "That's because of you. So, you know. I'm rootin' for you, Griff. Even if you are a scoundrel."

He snorts. "Thanks for the vote of confidence."

Adjusting her bag on her shoulder, Holly takes three quick strides to the front door. Griff follows her into the hall.

She pauses, hand on the doorknob, and glances back over

her shoulder. "Don't forget—I work in a kitchen. I know how to swing a fryin' pan." Her eyes glitter. "If you hurt her, I'll kill you."

He nods and then says, "Thanks. For doin' what you could to clean up the house."

"You're welcome." She tucks a lock of her curly hair behind her ear and juts her chin. Her gold cross earrings sparkle in the light of the sun. "Now if you'll excuse me, I have a deputy sheriff to go scream at."

The door shuts with a soft click and Griff's left there with his heart thundering in his ears. He breathes out, lacing a palm across the back of his neck and bowing his head to the cool wood of the front door.

She's hurt and it's his fault. Again.

Letting out a frustrated growl, Griff squeezes his eyes shut against the mantra tattooed onto his brain.

"Fuck," he mutters. Holly's message came through loud and clear. Alabama's a good woman. And Griff Greyson sure as hell doesn't deserve a good woman.

Alabama trusts him, and all he's done is lie to her again and again.

"Hey."

Alabama's soft drawl hits Griff's ears and he jolts. He turns around to see her standing in the hall wearing a faint smile. "I was lookin' for those."

Coming back to the present, Griff glances down to see the pill bottle practically strangled in his right hand. "Shit," he says, feeling like a prick. Her face is pale, her smile laced with pain.

He swallows. "I was meanin' to bring them to you."

"Holly talkin' your ear off?"

Griff exhales and walks toward her. "Somethin' like that."

When Alabama tilts her head, copper strands of her hair spill around her shoulders. Griff freezes. The flash of red has his heart lurching, has him remembering her blood on his hands, her blood pooling beneath her—

"Griff?"

He blinks himself awake.

She frowns for a moment, her gray eyes searching out his face. "Everything okay?"

"Besides the hole in your arm?" He slips an arm around her waist to pull her in close. "It's great."

For a moment, he lets his gaze sweep over her, guilt and sorrow flooding him. She'll have a scar for the rest of her life. Her shoulder might never work like it should. He runs a gentle hand down the strap of her sling, checking to make sure it's not too loose.

"How about you let me change that bandage, then I'll order a pizza?"

"Ah, the glamorous life of a country singer."

Griff laughs. "For you, sweetheart, I'll take it. Any day, every day."

With a happy little sigh, Alabama leans into him, resting her cheek against his shoulder. He palms the side of her face and traces a thumb across her cheekbone. In his arms, she feels so precious, so infinitely his that for a long second, he can't breathe. All he can do is just hold on to her as tightly as he can. "I'm glad you're here, Al."

She snuggles against him, her heart pulsing in sync with his. "Me too."

chapter
TWENTY-TWO

ALABAMA WAKES TO A BRUTAL, NEEDLING PAIN running down her arm. A pain that has her swearing so viciously it'd even have Griff raising a brow. As her eyes adjust, she takes in the blue moonlight streaming through the open window. The world is silent around her, the only sound the rush of the wind through the cornfield, the chirring of insects in the night.

She flinches as she adjusts her uncomfortable position. Sleeping sitting up is a pain in her ass. She eyes the nightstand, where her pain medication sits. Briefly, she considers taking another pill, but she hates the way they make her mind foggy. As she tries once again to sit up straight, she's hit by another hiss of pain. She grabs at her throbbing arm, at the fresh bandage Griff applied hours earlier.

Breathing through the ache, she glances over, where beside her, Griff sleeps easy. He's on his stomach, arms hooked beneath his pillow. Smiling, she reaches out, running her fingers along his spine, the curve of his muscled back. He's so damn sexy. Her bad boy with a dirty mouth.

She closes her eyes at the rush of love swelling in her. She couldn't do this without him.

She knows she could wake Griff, have him help her into a more comfortable sleeping position, but she wants to let him rest. He's been fussing all day, settling them in, helping her in and out of the shower, getting her dressed.

Either way, it's too late now. She's wide awake, restless and hurting. So much for counting sheep. Slowly, so as not to jostle her arm, she slips out of bed.

Naked, her hair trailing down her breasts, she softly pads down the hall. Between Holly and Griff's fussing, she's barely had time to scope out the house.

Griff's mama's house is as she remembers it, although it's seen better days.

A majority of the doors are shut, like they're trying to keep out the past. The curved banister that leads up to the second floor is shedding its paint. She picks off a few faded pink flecks with her nails. Red, she thinks. It used to be red.

Alabama drifts through the house like a ghost, taking it all in with a nostalgic eye. The under-the-stairs closet where she and Griff would sneak kisses. The round kitchen table where Mrs. Greyson would fix them peanut butter and jelly while she listened to their out-of-tune songs. The small powder room where she got her first period and Mrs. Greyson smuggled her a pad and wisely showed her the ways of a woman.

Alabama chuckles at the memory.

The house sings her a song, and she's listening. Everything needs—no, wants—a good sanding down, a fresh coat of paint, a skilled hand.

She stops in the parlor. Slanted lines of moonlight fall through the dusty blinds, casting their beams across Alabama's naked form. She crouches beside the record player and, one-handed, selects a record. She sets the needle down and lets it spin. She stands there in the dark and closes her eyes, listening to Patsy Cline's melancholy melody.

As she does, tears unexpectedly fill her eyes.

She tries to stop, tries to force her gaze on the window, but she can't bury it anymore. She hasn't cried, hasn't allowed herself to feel the force of her actions since she got shot.

Alabama closes her eyes. She sobs quietly, her entire body racking. Each breath she takes is a shudder that has her shoulder aching. But she embraces that pain. She could've died, and she didn't. She's still ticking and loving Griff. The thought makes her want to grab onto life with both hands. Makes her want to live to her wildest.

"Midnight stroll?"

Griff's low growl at her back has her pulse ratcheting up several notches.

She glances over her shoulder to see him standing in the long corridor. His brow cocked, his eyes appreciative and roving.

Wiping quick at her face, she turns toward him. "Couldn't sleep."

At the sight of her tears, the devilish smile disappears from his face. Instantly, his eyes cloud with worry and he moves toward her, inhabiting her space in the best possible way. He's so close she can feel the heat of his body, the concern emanating from him.

He cups her face, his rings tangling in her hair. His gaze captures hers. "What can I do?"

The question unmoors her in its sincerity, in his primal determination to give her anything she needs. "Just this," Alabama says, slipping her good arm around his waist. His hand moves from her face to the small of her back. As they begin to sway, Griff dips his forehead to hers and closes his eyes. Slow and steady they move, the music swirling the air, their breaths like a pulse between them.

It's quiet for so long until Griff lets out an anguished gasp. "You could have died." The words, tortured, wrench from his lips.

Alabama leans into him, his strong body giving her the support she needs.

Finally, she speaks. "I know. But I didn't."

She opens her eyes, staring at him. Moonlight glances off his cheekbone, his scar, his chiseled bearded jaw, his wet eyes.

Her heart soars, content and sure.

Nothing she's done with Griff is a mistake. She ran blind into the path of a bullet. She could have left this earth without him, taken his spot because she loved him, and she would have never regretted it.

Never.

A head rush of love and lust hit her all at once. A desperation to make up for what she could have lost.

Alabama's hand drifts to Griff's chest, and she places a palm over his heart. Slowly, she moves it up his chest, over his shoulder to mold around the nape of his neck.

And then she kisses him. Kisses him like their love's never been a thing of the past, like he is everything she needs, like that bullet never left that gun.

Griff's kiss is gentle, light-years away from the savage kisses she's used to. It's the kiss she wants. Needs.

She needs Griff in absolutely the worst way, at absolutely the worst time. Except for gentle touches that tell her he's there, he hasn't touched her in damn near three days. Crazy is what she's going.

With a growl, Griff breaks the kiss. Panting, he tugs her gently away from him.

She bites her lip and leans in to nip at his shoulder. "I'm lonesome, Griff."

His eyes flash. "Sweetheart, you ain't ready for this." The voice that comes out of him is a rough drawl which only turns her on more.

"You're worryin' too much . . ." A sweep of her lips against his. "And you're not doing enough of this."

"Damn it. I don't want to hurt you."

Though he's keeping her at a distance, his body is stiff and rigid with want. It's taking all he has to keep hands to himself. She sees it. Hell, she can *feel* it. He's rock-hard, his erection jutting impatiently.

"You won't." She stares at him with hooded eyes. "Stayin' away from me hurts worse."

His expression tells her she's killing him. Well, hell, the

feeling's mutual. Griff stands in front of her, bare-chested and muscled, looking so damn sexy, she feels like a burnin' fuse.

With a tortured groan, he kisses her again, this time ravaging her mouth roughly. Griff's kiss is like an echo, like a scream into her soul telling her how much he needs her.

At Alabama's needy moan, he backs her up against the wall. His body molds to hers as he lifts her in his arms. Alabama wraps her long legs around his waist, her good arm around his neck. Griff lifts her in his arms, carefully cradling her as he slickly slides into her.

Alabama gasps softly at the sensation. She's already wet, pulsing with heat. She tilts her hips back to accept him deeper and his own moan answers hers, guttural and primal.

Alabama closes her eyes. Tonight, there's no pain. There's only her and Griff.

Her protector. Her man.

And he's wrecking her. In the best possible way.

Instead of rutting like some lovesick teenager in heat, Griff's thrusts are slow, almost wavelike in their intensity. As Alabama's rhythmically lifted in his powerful arms, she can't help but let herself go limp beneath him and let him take charge. Let him show her what they have.

It's a claiming, a connection, an understanding that they are here together, they have chosen this path again, and they will give it their best shot.

Her vision blurs with tears. She wants this. Wants him. Wants everything with him.

They pant. Long, languid breaths mingle between them. She tips her head back against the wall, her hair spilling over her shoulders as Griff kisses her throat. His lips are hot, better than a sunburn in summer, and she whimpers in pleasure.

"Griff," she begs as she trembles in his arms. "Please . . ." The slow wave building in her stomach, her toes, down below threatens to come crashing down.

She can't hold on much longer.

"I love you." He buries his face in her hair and whispers, "I love you so goddamn much, Alabama."

Alabama threads her fingers through his hair and arches into him. "I love you."

Once more, he captures her mouth and with one last thrust, they both go together. Alabama cries out in ecstasy, the feeling like peace. Like a rush of sunlight after the rain.

And then Griff's gathering her close as Alabama collapses in his arms.

There's nothing else to say. Tonight, in this house, she has every second chance she could ever want in this crazy life of hers. She only hopes Griff feels the same.

chapter
TWENTY-THREE

G RIFF'S UP BEFORE ALABAMA. THE TEXAS MORNING brings with it a violent sunrise of red and gold. Across the field, birds chirp their melodies, the weeping willows swish in the crisp morning breeze.

He keeps quiet, drawing the curtains and dressing quickly. When he pulls a light blanket over Alabama's body, she lets out a small moan. He gives her a long look, watching as she stirs slightly before settling back into her uncomfortable sitting-up position. He dips to kiss her brow, then silently exits the bedroom, wanting her to rest as long as she can.

He trudges to the kitchen, intent on whipping up some breakfast. Alabama's been subsisting on junk food and Jell-O and he's hell-bent on getting a home-cooked meal into her stomach. A low chuckle rolls out of Griff at the thought of him cooking. The last time he handled a frying pan, he was threatening to knock the block off Beau Dallas.

He stops in the middle of the kitchen and glances around. It's sparse. A jar of honey sits on the shelf. A grocery store tray of cinnamon rolls brought over by Holly. In the fridge, bacon and a tub of butter. He'll have to make a trip to the store later and get them all the fixings.

At least there's coffee. While he grinds and measures the beans, the memory of last night hangs heavy in his mind. Alabama standing in the foyer wearing nothing but her long red hair. Her lips, tasting like milk and honey, her soft, needy moans, her long nails, dug deep into his shoulder, hard enough to draw blood.

A shiver runs down his spine. Fucking Christ, that X-rated look in her eyes when she takes what she wants. It's one of the things he loves about her. That she's unabashedly ready, willing and as able as him to call the shots.

Even though Griff can't help but consider it his life's mission to give Alabama anything she wants—in or out of bed.

Griff scowls at the military salute his dick's snapped to and adjusts himself. His brain on horndog hyperspeed. Like he's a goddamn teenager all over again.

Baseball, he thinks, letting out a rough breath to cool off. *Smooth jazz. Banking statements.*

As the coffee machine bubbles its last brew, his eyes brush to the doorway, watching for Alabama. He's eager to see her. Last night was something else. The sex was different than anything he's ever had with her. Slow, a claiming, a release. An admittance they were both lucky to be alive. He knows he loves her, has known for so damn long now, but he wants more.

He wants forever.

Griff grabs two mugs from the cabinet and by the time he's pouring himself out a steaming cup of coffee, the scent of coconut and sunlight fills his nose. He glances up to find Alabama entering the kitchen.

He pushes his cup of coffee toward her and pours another cup for himself. "Hey, good mornin'."

"Mornin' to you," she says, her drawl soft and lilting as she joins him at the counter.

"You sleep okay?" he asks, his eyes scanning her. She's still in the silk pajama pants and yellow tank top Griff changed her into last night after their midnight meetup. Her feet are bare, her face bleary from sleep.

"Hmm. Like a robot." Smiling, she brushes hair from her face and extends her good arm out above her head in a stretch. "How long have you been up?"

"Long enough to make coffee."

"So the perfect amount of time." She clasps her hand around the mug and brings it to her lips for a long sip.

"There's no milk," Griff offers. "Our only options for breakfast are butter or bacon. I'll take a trip to the store later." He makes sure to put the emphasis on him. Alabama exerting herself ain't an option.

Alabama smiles and lifts her cup. "I don't need anything right now, just this." A look of warm affection crosses her gorgeous face. "Just you. C'mon. Let's sit."

They take their coffees and move to the small round table in the bay window nook. Alabama winces as she lowers herself into a chair, Griff's stomach tightening at the pain in her grimace.

For a long second, she stares out the window at the dusty dirt drive, then her gaze jumps to Griff. "Have you heard anything about the tour?"

Griff shifts in the chair. "Freddie called me yesterday."

"And you're just now telling me this?" She raises an eyebrow. "Well?"

He sighs, unhappy with the terms Freddie's laid down. "We got two weeks."

"I can work with that."

He frowns. "Al—"

"You forget I still need the money, Griff." She looks down at her coffee, pulling the mug against her chest.

He opens his mouth to tell her he'll write her a goddamn check right now. That he'll do his damnedest to give her anything she needs, that her troubles are his, but then he checks himself. She'd rip up that check so fast he'd feel it in his balls. Alabama taking handouts ain't her style.

"I know," he says. "I just don't like the thought of you pushin' yourself."

"I may not be able to play a guitar, but I can sure as hell sing." She looks to the window again, then turns a wry eye his way. "So two weeks. We could do a lot in two weeks."

His eyes narrow at the mischievous tone in her voice. "You're plotting."

"Not plotting." She sets her coffee on the table. "So listen, last night I was thinkin'—"

Griff smirks. "Thinkin', huh? I don't recall much thinkin' goin' on."

Her lips twitch at the corners. "You know, before the whole sex-in-the-hallway plot twist."

"Oh, that." A cavalier shrug, a sip of his coffee. "Completely forgot it even happened."

Her eyes widen in mock offense. "How dare you, Griff Greyson. I give you my best in my delicate condition and you forget?"

She goes to kick him, but Griff catches up her bare foot and rests it in his lap. Smiling, Alabama settles back in her chair and goes on. "We could fix up the house. This house," she says when Griff raises a brow. She leans forward, her eyes bright and sparkling. "This house has stories, Griff. Our stories. Della's. We should treat it right, make it pretty. Maybe it will finally sell, maybe it won't, but I think it deserves it. Your mom deserves it."

Griff sits silent for a long moment. His breath's held tight in his chest. The kindness, the selflessness of her words stuns him. For years, his mother's death left him lost, left him angry. He's been haunted by not going home, for failing to do the right thing over and over again. Alabama knows that. And here she is offering to help him put the pieces of his past back together again. To give him another chance to be the man his mama always knew he was.

Goddamn, if he didn't love her already, this would cement it.

His throat bobs. "Mom would like that."

Alabama's smile rivals the sun. "Then let's do it." When Griff's worried eyes land on her arm, she wags a finger. "I can still paint a fence, Griff. Stop worryin' and let's have some fun."

He laughs. "Okay, okay. You convinced me."

"Good. Now we just gotta—" The smile drops off her lips as Alabama's eyes flash open.

Griff follows her wide-eyed gaze to the window. Shit.

Newton Forester's police cruiser sits in the drive. Alabama's father, barrel-chested and belly-heavy, exits the car, his gun and badge glinting in the sunlight.

Alabama's face is a mess of nerves. Bracing a hand on the table, she winces as she struggles to push herself up. Griff's beside her, slipping an arm through hers. "Not so fast," he warns. "You pull a stitch I'm takin' you to Doc Hinton."

She gives him a look. "He's a vet, Griff."

"Exactly."

A sharp rap sounds. Alabama flashes him a harried glance before hurrying to the door. Her face full of hope and excitement, she takes a breath, smooths her hair behind her ears, and then swings it open.

"Daddy, hi," she says.

Newton stands on the doorstep, stiff and unreadable, a plastic sack tucked under his arm. His eyes examine Alabama, a sudden softness crossing his face, but it disappears when he sees Griff standing behind Alabama in the hall.

"Alabama Grace," Newton booms. "I heard you were hangin' around these parts. How you been?"

"I'm good." Her smile's wobbly. "How about comin' in?"

Newton gives a rumble of affirmation and steps inside, moving past Griff without acknowledgment.

"We were just havin' coffee," Alabama offers, shutting the door. She steps forward, leading Newton down the hall into the kitchen. "You want a cup?"

"Might as well."

Griff's stomach knots up as Newton scans the ancient house, the contents of the bare kitchen. He can already hear the man bitching down at the station about the run-down conditions his daughter's living in.

"I'll get it," Griff says, intercepting Alabama before she can start bustling around. He pours a cup and slides it across the counter to Newton, who sets the plastic sack down.

"Looks to be in the eighties today." Newton sips his coffee slow and stares out the bay window. "A real scorcher."

Taking that to be directed at him, Griff looks out the window and says, "Hot for this time of year."

"Almanac's wrong," Newton grouses. "Every damn year. I got winter vegetables dyin' on me."

Speaking of dying, Griff is. A slow death at the pained attempt to make small talk. But he forces himself to be nice. He can feel Alabama looking between the two men she loves and aching for them to get along.

Griff clears his throat. "How's the department treatin' you, Newton?"

"Can't complain. More paperwork than I care to fill out." Newton's eyes skim over Alabama. "You bein' kind to that arm?"

"I am." Her smile is bright. "Griff's takin' great care of me."

"Glad to hear it."

Newton's clipped tone tells Griff he is not, in fact, glad to hear it. And that tells Griff exactly where he stands with Newton. The same spot he was in when he left Clover twelve years ago. To Newton, he's still the same damn dumb kid who hurt his daughter.

Griff's chest tightens and he stares down at the rings on his fingers.

Not like there's much difference today.

"You want some breakfast?" Alabama asks, trying to keep her dad for a while. "We don't have much, but we could whip up some bacon."

"Nothin' for me," Newton says, holding up a meaty paw. "I gotta git. But before I do . . ." He rustles around in the plastic sack and pulls out a bundle of letters wrapped with a rubber band. "I brought you some things."

Alabama pales, disbelief clouding her expression. "You brought me . . ."

"Your bills," Newton interjects. "They've been stacking up ever since you ran back to Nashville. Think you'll be payin' them soon?"

As if remembering all of her money troubles, Alabama presses her lips together and nods, but Griff sees the tears filling her eyes. "I will."

Her voice, a hushed whisper, has Griff's heart detonating.

Griff looks at Newton, a slice of anger welling in him. Anger that Newton's so damn stubborn he'd rather throw Alabama's mistakes back in her face than actually care about his daughter.

"I have to use the bathroom," Alabama whispers, blinking back tears. "Excuse me."

With that, she pushes past her father, the soft shuffle of her footsteps disappearing down the hall.

Griff slams a hand on the counter. "You're a damn fool, you know that?"

Fuck the fact that it's Alabama's father; it's Griff's goddamn house and Newton Forester coming in here to insult Alabama ain't happening. "You're gonna push her away. For good one of these days."

Newton eyes him evenly, unmoved. "She's gotta learn actions have consequences."

"Consequences?" His teeth clench. "How about you say fuck your consequences and instead care about what happens to her? That's all she wants. She wants you to be a father and not a damn cop."

"I've cared for Alabama her entire life," Newton grinds out, going red in the face. "Which is more than I can say for you."

The knife of guilt twists.

A flash of red, of blood corkscrews his vision.

But Griff shakes it away. He isn't stopping. He draws himself up and clenches his fists. "And whose fault is that? I was a kid. I ran when you told me to." He shakes his head in disgust, at himself, at Newton. And he makes a decision. "I ain't doin' it no more. She deserves to know the truth."

"And how's that gonna treat her?" Griff's surprised when the old man's eyes suddenly fill with tears. "All you been doin' your entire life is lettin' her down," he says, jamming a finger in Griff's direction. "You shoulda stayed away from her. You shoulda let her be. Now look what's happened to her."

The accusation's a punch to the gut and Griff stiffens.

She's hurt and it's his fault. Again.

With those last cutting words, Newton turns and storms out of the house. The clatter of the screen door sounds so much like a bullet that Griff jumps. He tries to breathe, tries to come down off the words hurled at him, but guilt's dug its roots in deep and won't let go.

Every word Newton said was true. Alabama's been nothing but a gift to him; she got him out of that dark place he'd been sinking, knocked some sense into him, and what did he do?

He got her fucking shot.

He let her down.

That thought has any resolve to tell her the truth evaporating like early-morning mist. If she learned the truth . . . she'd leave him. It was in their cards. She'd do to Griff what he did to her because the past in Clover—it sticks.

And there's not a damn thing he can do to escape it.

chapter
TWENTY-FOUR

ALABAMA TURNS A CORNER IN AISLE FOUR OF BOB'S True Value and finds Griff staring at a row of hammers. From a distance, she evaluates him. Ever since her father left the house, Griff's been edgy and quiet. Even now, his face is dark and serious. He's a million miles away from her and she doesn't know what it'll take to rope him back.

She walks down the aisle and comes to stand beside him, slipping her hand into his. "Must be some serious hammer decisions."

He tenses beside her and then squeezes her hand. "I'm about done here."

"I'm sorry, Griff."

At that, he turns to look at her, his brow furrowed. "What're you talkin' about?"

"My dad, he wasn't very nice to you."

He grunts. "He wasn't very nice *to you*, Al."

"He's just tryin' to make sure I take care of myself."

Griff shakes his head, his face darkening. "Stop makin' excuses for him." He lets go of her hand abruptly to drift away from her, his eyes still scanning the tools in front of him.

She frowns and follows. She's not letting him off the hook that easily. "What's goin' on, Greyson?"

He looks at her, his jaw clenched. "Let's just say your dad makes some good points."

Heat courses through her. Of course, her father would have

had a little chat with Griff. She nods in understanding. "He said somethin' to you."

"Hell, I can't blame the man," Griff says in a defeated voice. "His only daughter got shot. *You* got shot, Alabama. *I* got you shot."

Her throat tightens. The faraway look in his eyes tells her he's lost in the night of the accident. All these years later, he's still blaming himself for their past. It's the only reason why her father's words have hit so hard.

"You didn't get me shot," she says carefully.

"I sure as hell did. I got you roped up in all the shit I've been doin' and it got you hurt." He rips a hand through his hair. "I should have never tracked you down for this tour, Al."

Her heart pounds out a shaky rhythm. She doesn't know what this conversation means—only that she won't let him blame himself. She meets his stare with a determined one of her own. "Yes, you should have."

His gaze moves away from her, a muscle clenching in his jaw.

"Listen to me," she says sternly. "You gave me a chance, Griff. You trusted me because of my voice. You never pegged me like the papers. You let me be myself and you knew who I was. And that means everything to me."

Griff closes his eyes, his expression paling.

Alabama takes a step toward him. "Are you having second thoughts about us? I know we didn't promise each other anything, so if you don't want me here—"

His breath is sharp, and briefly, a look of panic crosses his face. "I ain't sayin' that. I'm sayin' I got you hurt again and I fuckin' hate myself for it." His throat bobs. "I'm not a good man for you, Alabama."

The fear of losing him curdles her stomach. She takes a step toward him, her hand outstretched, her voice steady, despite her hammering heart.

Griff may be wild and reckless, but she trusts him. She found him again; he's hers, the only one she wants in this hard old world. She knows that he'll always be the one she comes back to, misses at night, wants inside her, and for that reason she's got to hold on.

She won't let go again.

"Yes, you are," she says softly. "I said it before and I'll say it again. You are the best man for me, Griff."

He stares at her. "Are you sure about that?" he asks hoarsely.

"As sure as the songs we sing." She holds his gaze. "Each night. Every night. All the damn time."

That's when his eyes come alive. Desperate, hungry. Griff strides back to her, his boots heavy and pounding, and ever so gently, he wraps her in his arms. His lips sweeping against her ear, he whispers, "I'm an asshole. I'm sorry." He takes her face in his hands, bringing her gaze to his. "I love you, Al. I want you here with me and I'm sorry, but Christ, your dad is a prick."

Alabama lets out a laugh of relief. "I can't believe we just had this conversation at Bob's True Value."

A slow chuckle comes from Griff, and then he's pulling away. The look in his eyes tells Alabama he's back in the present, back with her. "Are we okay?" His voice is husky with emotion.

She presses a kiss to his lips. "Better than."

He grins, grabs her hand. "C'mon. Let's pick a hammer and get the hell out of here."

On the drive home, a Texas thunderstorm rolls in, drenching all of Alabama's plans to swing a hammer and get to work. So she and Griff set to work putting away the groceries and hardware supplies.

After a simple dinner of tomato soup and grilled cheese sandwiches, Alabama curls up on the couch, watching as Griff lights a fire in the crumbling fireplace. When the flames are strong and kicking, Griff disappears. He returns with his guitar and Alabama's notebook.

He places it in her lap and seats himself beside her on the floral couch.

"Since we ain't workin' on the house, what do you say we finish that song we've been playin'?" he asks, his eyes on her.

Her insides warm, and she sees this is Griff's way of showing her he's still serious. About them, their tour and the music.

Dipping his head, Griff strums his guitar. His voice, gritty and brooding, rings out as he sings what they've written so far. Alabama listens, tapping out a beat on her notebook with her pen. Her ears pick up on the harmony, the pulse of the strings, the meaning lurking behind the lyrics.

> You left me with the pieces of my heart in my hands
> My tough-talkin' cowboy, you rolled out of town with your band
> All I had was your whisper, your Texas goodbye
> Aw, baby, crazy in my mind, tears in my eye
>
> I don't reckon it'll get better
> Go back to the way it was back then
> Because the cold hard truth is that
> Baby, you broke my heart and never will I find you again …
>
> Then time passed and we were on the corner of Broadway
> You caught my eye and you turned my way
> Told me I was lookin' good and it's been so long
> And then you bit your lip and said
> Sweetheart, for years I've been so damn wrong
>
> I want to reckon it could get better
> Go back to the way it was back then
> Because the cold hard truth is that
> Baby, you broke my heart but maybe I could find you again …

"The sound's good," she offers when Griff's stops singing. "I like what you did with the chord change on that second half."

He arcs a brow, knowing her. Knowing where she's going with this. "But?"

She hesitates, her eyes on the last verse. "But the end still ain't workin'."

"That's where you come in."

"But you agree, right?"

His golden eyes are thoughtful. "I do. But hell if I know the endin' to a story fifteen years in the makin'."

Alabama runs a hand over her notebook. "Maybe there's no endin'. Maybe it just keeps goin' and not even the universe can end it."

"I tend to like that explanation."

She smiles. "Either way, I love the song. It's so close."

Griff sets a broad hand on her bare thigh. "That smile looks good on you, Al."

She inclines her head. "You ever wonder if we could have made it as the Copper Hounds?"

His eyes widen, and then he grins. "You know, I don't know about that." He tugs at the end of his scruff. "I would've hoped so."

"Me too." She chews on the thought. "We could do it."

He cuts her a sharp look. "What're you talkin' about?"

"We're good together. Everyone says it. Even the *Star*. After the winter tour, we—we could do our own thing for a while. Record the song together. If you want." She flushes, instantly annoyed with herself. Good Lord, she's acting like she just proposed or something.

Griff's staring at her like she's gone crazy, then his face breaks out into a rare overjoyed smile. "Fuck yeah, I want."

"You do?"

"Definitely. Hell, let's do it right now!" He slaps his hands together with such force that Alabama laughs.

"After the winter tour." Alabama sighs impatiently, dropping her head back against the couch. She misses the stage, the spotlight. As long as she has that and Griff, even a busted arm can't get her down. "I can't wait. I want it so damn bad."

"I know you do."

"I need it."

"I know that too."

Alabama glances up at the twang of a guitar. Griff's setting it aside, lowering himself to the rug in front of her. He takes her notebook and places it on the coffee table behind them. Then he wraps his arms around Alabama's waist and buries his face in her abdomen. His hungry, near-reverent shudder has her toes curling. Alabama runs her fingers through his hair and smiles in response.

No one holds her tighter than Griff.

Lifting her shirt, Griff trails fervent kisses across her stomach, her sternum, her breasts. She meets his eyes to find his gaze greedy and wanting.

"Our music," Alabama murmurs, her mind wanting to keep the conversation going, the song playing, even as her body screams at her to not be an idiot. "If we don't practice, we're gonna get rusty and . . . oh . . ."

She closes her eyes as Griff takes her breast in his mouth.

Her grip on his hair tightens.

"I think I know a cure for gettin' rusty."

Pulling away, Griff looks up at her. Cockiness dances in those tawny gold eyes. Knowledge that she is as hot for him as he is for her.

Her body arches, aching, on the couch. "Griff . . ."

"Woman, hush," he says, his smile devilish, before diving back in to devour her once more.

Alabama tips her head back, letting Griff consume her, giving herself over to the moment. This one perfect moment in time where she has everything she's ever wanted.

chapter
TWENTY-FIVE

THE NEXT WEEK PASSES BY IN A SLOW BLUR OF LAZINESS. Long days sleeping in, penning new songs by the fire, watching bad TV, and working on the house. In less than a week, they'll be on a bus to Austin to finish out the last five shows in the tour.

Their time in Clover is ticking down.

And while Griff knows Alabama is anxious to get back on the road, he's enjoyed the time spent in Clover. Though the bad memories aren't gone, they've been replaced. With new memories. With Alabama. With promises of the future.

Lifting his head, Griff glances at Alabama. She's on the opposite end of the couch, her legs tucked beneath Griff's, notebook in hand. He smiles at the small frown lines creasing her brow as she reads the lyrics they wrote this morning.

She's come alive since being here; they both have.

Sensing his eyes on her, she looks up and smiles. "Why do I feel like we haven't moved from this couch?" she asks, giving a little stretch.

"Because we haven't."

She scoffs, her look dubious. "You're forgetting about the thirty pounds of lumber we hauled yesterday, and the cans of paint, and the rototiller we rented."

"You're right," Griff says. "My back won't let me forget it."

She winces, an apology in her eyes. "I'm sorry. You've been doing most of the work."

He pins a stern gaze on her. "Don't think I didn't see you out there tryin' to steer that wheelbarrow one-handed."

She flushes at being caught, then she laughs, reaching down to skim her fingers against his. "C'mon. Let's go fix up those dents in the barn roof. I still need to paint the front door." She wiggles her eyebrows. "We're in the homestretch, Greyson."

He groans. All he wants to do is stay here with Alabama beside him. He hasn't felt this content in ages.

Griff grunts. "You know, your work ethic is not my most favorite thing about you." But he swings his legs off the couch.

Alabama does the same, but she moves too fast and bites back a gasp. Her good hand flies to her sling.

Whip-quick, Griff's there. He kneels in front of her, his eyes scanning her. "You okay?"

Her face is a mess of pain. "Fine," she grits out. She lets out a sigh of frustration. "Never gonna go away, is it?"

Griff's heart clenches at the dejected look on Alabama's face. He aches to take away her pain. She's healing quickly, the stitches long since dissolved. But the doctor warned them both that she was in for a long recovery. Both physically and emotionally. She'll have a scar that'll never fade, and physical therapy to do for her arm. It could be months before she can play a guitar. If ever.

"It'll get better," he says and slides a hand over her knee, giving it a reassuring squeeze. "It'll just take time."

"Yeah." She exhales a long breath, her face determined, courageous. "I'll have to see someone when I get back to Nashville."

Griff nods. "I got some names if you want them."

She looks at him quick, curious. "What do you mean you 'got some names'?"

He clears his throat, hating the look she's giving him. The look that tells him she's caught him being a good guy. He started researching physical therapists the night they got into Clover. He found the best ones in Nashville. No goddamn way was he letting her go to some Joe Schmo off the street.

"Therapists," he says gruffly. "For your arm."

A small smile plays on her lips. "Griff Greyson, you've been doin' research for little ol' me?"

He growls. "Just take the damn recommendation."

Her face turning serious, she leans forward and sweeps her lips across his. "Thank you. I appreciate that. Very much."

His throat constricting, Griff stands and helps Alabama do the same. "You ready to get to work or you just plannin' to bust my balls all day?"

"Hmm. Maybe later."

She tosses him a flirty smile, moving past him, brushing her body against his. Griff's heart twists, every part of him wanting her more than the air he breathes.

Alabama hums as she paints the front door of the house a brilliant ruby red. The one activity she can do well one-armed. She and Griff have been working all afternoon, and while the sun's slowly lowering in the sky, it's still blistering. Texas heat in December is doing them in like nothing else.

She chuckles, thinking about the sheepish look on Griff's face as he admitted he had found her a physical therapist. She doesn't know if she could love a man more. The thought of him taking that on for her is doing all kinds of things to her heart. She's falling hard, falling deep. She wishes her teenage self were here to talk some sense into her, or tell her she's doing the right thing. But the right thing doesn't match the feelings in her heart, or the bond between her and Griff. That crackling, glowing bond that has her hoping for the future. For a piece of home with him.

Even her arm can't get her down. For the first time in a long time, she finds herself looking forward to the what-comes-next. The rest of the tour hangs bright like a guiding light in front of her, but even more, she's eager to record "Find You Again" with

Griff, potentially resurrect the Copper Hounds, pay off the lawyers and finally be free from the shackles of Six String.

She's lucky. She found all this again.

The image of her copper penny shines bright in her mind. And just like that, she wants it. No, she needs it. Needs that small piece of Alabama back. Because now, she wants to show her past self the way forward.

Splotch.

Alabama glances down to see a thick glob of red paint splashed on the inside of her wrist. Thin tendrils snake their way slowly down her arm. "Shit," she swears, noticing there's more on her hands, the front of her plaid shirt stained with red. She growls at her clumsiness but shrugs it off and continues painting.

When she's finished, she steps back and evaluates her handiwork. She smiles. The front door is as dazzling and as happy as Griff's mama herself was. He'll love it.

Glancing over her shoulder, Alabama gives a wistful glance at the For Sale sign swinging in the breeze. It's a mistake, but she's come to think of the house as hers. It seems like such a shame to get rid of it, but whoever buys it will be one very lucky owner.

The sound of Griff's hammer pounding the old tin roof carries across the lawn.

Alabama steps out of the shade of the porch. Across the lawn, Griff works on the barn roof. She smiles. He looks like a sweaty redneck. His shirt off, his ball cap backward. A very sexy, shirtless, sweaty redneck.

Shielding her eyes, she lifts her gaze to the sun. They should have sweet tea like Griff's mom used to make. And tonight, after the house is quiet and the sun is down, wine and whiskey. With a last glance at Griff, she disappears into the house to make them something cool to drink, thoughts of the future blazing a trail of hope through her mind.

Griff pulls a dented section of roof back with the stud welder. He blows out a breath and curses the sun. The unusual heat wave that rolled in has it hot, too damn hot. He oughta be in the house with Alabama. He oughta be in the house with Alabama in bed. A sly grin plays on his face as he thinks about that teasing smile on her face from earlier today. That flirty drawl that always told him she could give as good as Griff.

The sound of the creaky screen door has him glancing over at the main house.

Coming out from underneath the awning of the porch is Alabama. She's smiling, calling up to him, her hands outstretched, her palms—

Griff blinks.

Blood.

Fuck. She's covered in blood.

It's everywhere.

The sound of a gunshot blasts his skull.

The scent of gunpowder overpowers his nostrils.

The air goes out of his lungs, every vein of his filling up with pure terror.

Griff gives a jerk, desperate to get to her, to stop the blood. He scrambles up, too fast, and slips on the slick panels.

Alabama's eyes shoot open.

She runs toward him.

He tumbles off the roof, the air rushing around him as he falls to the ground. He lands hard on his shoulder.

Alabama's panicked voice sounds around him. Ignoring the pain in his arm, he pushes himself up. He grabs her wrist roughly, yanking her into him, and her pleas for him to answer her die off. With fast, frantic hands he wipes at the blood on her shirt, trying to clean it away, trying to staunch the blood. "You're bleedin'," he says. "Alabama, you're bleedin'. We gotta stop it. We gotta stop the blood . . ."

"No, no, no," she says urgently, breaking his grasp to palm his face. "It's not blood, Griff. It's paint. It's paint."

For a long moment, Griff only stares. Shakes.

She forces his eyes to hers and nods. "Do you hear me? It's paint . . . okay? I'm okay, everything's okay. It's just paint."

He blinks, coming back down to earth. His breathing steadies as he realizes that Alabama is beside him. That she is okay.

That none of it was real.

Alabama scoots closer, the sides of their thighs touching. "Are you hurt, Griff?" She pats him down with a shaky hand, her eyes wet, her face worried. "Is anything broken?"

Rolling his neck on his shoulders, he gives a dark laugh. "No. Just fuckin' sore." He lifts his eyes to the roof. "It ain't that far of a drop."

"Easy for you to say." She sits back on her heels. A massive relieved sigh shakes out of her. Tears shine in her eyes. "You scared me to death."

"Hey, don't cry." He reaches out to brush a tear away from her face. "I'm okay, sweetheart."

Her face is wary. "Griff."

He shifts his weight, and Alabama's there, slinging an arm around his waist and helping him stand the best she can.

A curse rips out of him when he puts pressure on his leg. Pain radiates down the back of his hamstring. "Think I pulled a damn muscle."

A tear-choked laugh erupts from Alabama as they both hobble toward the house. "Good Lord, Griff. Two fine messes we are."

Alabama enters the bedroom to find Griff in pajama pants, his hair damp from the shower, wincing as he lowers himself onto the bed. He stares out the window, his face creased and far off.

"What hurts?" she asks softly.

He startles. His face clouds up, angry at himself for worrying her.

"You can't fool me, Greyson." Alabama crosses the room and sets a glass of water on his nightstand. "You're hurtin', so take this." She snaps one of her pain pills in half and gives it to him.

With a smirk, he swallows it down. "I'll be better in the mornin.'"

Alabama places a steady palm on his chest "And until then . . ." Slowly, she presses him back into the bed.

His face screws up into a grump of an expression. "Alabama, I'm fine."

"Well, how 'bout you humor me and let me fuss for once." She fluffs the pillow behind him and covers him with the sheet. When she's finally satisfied he's comfortable, she lets out a long breath and sits beside him. "What happened today, Griff?"

His throat works as he swallows. "I don't know," he says, reaching out to take her hand in his. He turns it over in his palm. Stares hard at it even though the dried paint's been long scrubbed away. "I was lookin' down and all I saw was you covered in blood. I heard the gunshot. I saw it, Al, clear as day." He lets out a dark swear, and when he raises his eyes, Alabama sees the anguish there. "I saw you bleedin.'"

Her stomach nosedives at the mention of the bullet and the blood. But she forces the memory from her mind to focus on Griff. She wants nothing more than to ease his pain, to take away those awful images in his head. Images she has every time she closes her eyes.

Griff goes on, a hollowness to his voice. "I panicked. I wasn't thinkin'. All I knew was that I had to get to you and then—"

He trails off, letting the rest of the sentence go unfinished.

Alabama laughs. "Yeah. And then." She's quiet for a long moment, and then she bites her lip and looks at him. "Looks like we're both gonna need some therapy when we get back to Nashville."

"That's all I want to do," Griff says, not refuting her

suggestion. His hand tightens around hers. "Finish up this damn tour and get back to Nashville." His gaze meets hers. "With you."

The soft look he gives her warms Alabama like the sun.

It's all she wants. A sign, a second chance. A second chance with Griff.

Alabama smiles. "I think that can be arranged."

Then, noticing Griff's eyelids going heavy, the sleeping pill having its desired effect, Alabama stands.

"Where you goin'?" Griff murmurs, not letting go of her hand.

She brushes a lock of hair from his eyes. "I'm gonna let you sleep."

"It's early," he complains.

"It is. And that's why I'm goin' to clean up the kitchen. You, however, are restin.'"

"Are you sure?" He wiggles his brows, his grin sly. "You could come to bed."

She rolls her eyes. "Shut up and go to sleep, Griff."

Griff settles back with a grumble but remains watching her as she opens the windows and dims the light, his face thoughtful, tender. Finally, he says, "My mom would love the house, Al. Thank you."

Alabama's chest squeezes tight. "You're welcome." She dips to press a kiss to his lips and then, remembering her musings on the porch, whispers, "I want my penny back, Greyson."

Griff's grin is dopey with sleep. "Hmmm," he murmurs, his eyelids fighting gravity. "In the dresser . . ."

By the time Alabama straightens up, Griff's asleep. She smiles down at him, his face peaceful and adorably, misleadingly, innocent.

She goes to the dresser and slides out the top drawer. She's rifling around under papers when she finds the penny. Two of them, in fact. Hers and Griff's. A pang of sadness moving through her, she goes to scoop both of them up when her hand knocks something hard and square.

Alabama blinks as she pulls out a small jewelry box yellowed with age. She frowns, puzzled, and opens it.

She gasps.

It's an engagement ring. A silver band with a princess-cut solitaire.

She stares, hands shaking. In that moment, the world falls away, sounds go silent, her vision tunnels, and Alabama's back in that summer.

Her heart pounds furiously in her ears. The ring's hers. She knows it. Or rather, it was supposed to be hers.

Lightheaded, Alabama snaps the case shut and puts it back where she found it. Quietly, she shuts the drawer, gripping the edge of the dresser so that her knees don't give out.

Her eyes fill with tears.

She had thought she was okay. That she could move on without an answer from Griff, that she could forgive the past, but this. The ring—it's Pandora's box. It's the sharp sting of rejection all over again.

Anger and pain swell up in her, the size of a tsunami.

Griff had a ring for her. He planned to propose. So why in the hell did he leave?

Alabama glances over her shoulder at a sleeping Griff. She feels her face, her blood, her heart harden. No more. Whatever he's been hiding is coming out. She has to know.

Tomorrow.

She gets answers tomorrow. One way or another, she'll make Griff talk.

chapter
TWENTY-SIX

GRIFF WAKES THE NEXT MORNING TO AN EMPTY BED. He showers and changes quickly, and then he's exiting the bedroom, a smile on his face after a good night's sleep. He finds Alabama in the kitchen. She's standing behind the counter, a cup of coffee clasped in her hand.

"Hey, good mornin', sweetheart," Griff says, slipping close and bringing her in for a kiss. But Alabama turns her face away and the kiss glances off the side of her lips.

She sets down her mug. "How's your shoulder?"

He wiggles his eyebrows. "Like it never happened."

"That's good."

He surveys Alabama as he pours himself a cup of coffee. Somehow she's got herself dressed for the day, wearing skin-tight blue jeans and a low-cut sweater that show off her gorgeous curves and utterly destroys any ounce of self-control he thought he had left.

"How 'bout we take a trip to Austin today?" Griff asks. "I was thinkin' we get us a hotel. Go out for a nice dinner. Listen to some live music." He palms her bare shoulder, leaning in to kiss her freckles. "Lord knows you've been workin' too hard."

Alabama stiffens at his touch. "Not today, Griff."

With that, she moves out of his space to walk toward the bay window. Her eyes are empty as she stares out at the lawn.

Griff frowns. There's a chill in the air. Alabama's expression more closed off than Fort fucking Knox. They had left things okay last night, or so he thought. Maybe he got carried away talking about the future.

Either way, he's gonna figure it out. Fast.

Griff moves to her side. "Hey, what's goin' on?"

"Nothin,'" comes her curt reply.

He gives her an evaluating glance. She's pale, dark circles lingering beneath her eyes. His heart twists and guilt hits him like a Mack truck. If she ain't taking care of herself, that's on him. She's been working hard as hell to fix his mama's place and it's taking a toll on her.

"You feelin' okay?" he asks, pressing a palm to her forehead.

She shrugs off his hand, her expression unreadable. "I'm fine, Griff."

"You tell me, then," he says, at a loss for what's eating her. "We got the house done. What do we do today?"

Finally, she faces him. Her eyes flash fire. "Let's take a drive."

Before he can respond, she turns on her heel and strides to the hallway. She snatches the keys from the entry table and storms through the screen door without a backwards glance. Griff hurries after her to catch up, watching as she pulls herself into the driver's seat and starts the truck.

"I'm drivin,'" she says when he pauses by the window. "Get in."

He opens his mouth to argue with her, to tell her that driving one-handed is a goddamn stupid idea, but sees that if he does, he runs a good risk of her running him down.

Griff climbs into the passenger seat. Before he can get settled, Alabama's gunning the gas and hauling ass out of the driveway.

He snaps on his seat belt. "Where we goin'?"

"You'll see."

He sits back, unnerved, watching the scenery flash by. Soon the long dirt road leading out of the house turns to paved road as they enter Clover proper.

"Easy," he warns as she plows down Main Street. "It's thirty-five here."

But she doesn't let off the gas. Alabama steers the truck one-handed, a herky-jerky movement that has Griff cringing. "What do you care?" she asks, side-eyeing him. "Aren't you supposed to be a rebel, Griff? Play it fast, play it loose, and not care who you hurt?"

Her words are harsh and Griff sucks in a breath, his hackles rising. "What the fuck's goin' on, Alabama?"

"You tell me." She punches the gas. Griff lurches forward, bracing himself with a palm to the dash, the truck picking up even more speed now that they're off the Main Street drag. "Why did you leave Clover?"

His eyes jerk her way. "Al—"

"No. You ain't gettin' out of this."

She yanks the wheel hard. Instead of turning right and taking the loop around Clover, she goes left. Griff freezes when he sees the paved road. The same paved road that dissolves to gravel and rock in a steep ascent up to the Ridge.

"You're answerin' my question, Griff. Why. Did. You. Leave. Clover?"

Griff's heart is in his throat, but his eyes are on the speedometer. She's going fast, dirt and gravel kicking out like shrapnel. Alabama's hair whipped wild by the wind as she steers them up the steep slope.

To his horror, Griff sees she doesn't have her seat belt on.

He takes a steadying breath. "Pull over, okay, sweetheart? Pull over and I'll tell you everything."

But Alabama isn't listening. She barely hears Griff. Her eyes are fiery, her voice shaking out in a trembling rattle. "I found the ring," she says, and Griff goes cold. "You were gonna propose, and you left. You left me, Griff. Why?"

Fuck.

He wants to throw up. Finding the ring pushed her to her breaking point. It's his fault, he's been ducking, dodging the past, the reason he left, and now, now she's imagining the worst. She's thinking that everything between them is all bullshit.

"Okay," he says, trying to keep a soothing tone. "I'll tell you. I'll you everything. Just slow the hell down."

"Tell me now."

Another lurch as she punches the gas pedal to the floor. The speedometer ticks up to seventy. The truck shudders like it's on its last legs.

Griff's eyes widen when he sees it.

Up ahead, the sandstone cliff waits. The steep outcropping where he rolled the Jeep, where he and Alabama hung upside down for hours until help came.

"I'm waitin'," Alabama shouts over the sound of the wind, the low croon of the radio.

His heart thundering in his ears, Griff bangs on the dash with an open hand. "Goddamn it, Al! You're gonna kill us!"

"Good!" she shoots back. "And then I'll never know and you can go to hell with that on your conscience."

Closer and closer they get to the precipice of the cliff.

Alabama doesn't so much as blink.

"Your father!" Griff blurts, ripping a nervous hand through his hair. "I left Clover because of your father! Fuck."

For an instant, Alabama's disbelieving eyes flash to Griff's. Then she slams on the brakes.

The truck goes into a skid and they're both thrown forward.

Alabama lets out a cry of pain, but Griff's held tight by his seat belt, unable to help her. Gritting his teeth, Griff braces himself against the dash as it spins out, doing a full three-sixty in the middle of the road. He feels the truck lift up on one side and then slam back to the ground with a groaning thud.

His breath coming in heavy punches, Griff sags back against the seat. What he sees next has his heart lurching in his chest.

Alabama.

She's slumped over the steering wheel, unmoving.

He rips off his seat belt and tears toward her. "Alabama?"

Too frantic to care about being gentle, he peels her away from the steering wheel. Desperate to see her face, to make sure she's okay. He cradles her in his arms and stares down at her. Her eyes are closed and there's a small gash on her hairline. "*Alabama*," he grinds out, his heart threatening to give out. He shakes her roughly, desperate for her to answer him.

A violent sob wrenches from her mouth. Then, her eyes flutter open to stare up at him. Hot tears track down her face. "Tell me, please," she whispers, her voice breaking on the words.

"Okay." He takes a resigned breath and kisses her brow. "Okay, sweetheart."

Alabama sits with her back pressed against the driver's-side door. She's silent as she waits for Griff to begin. Her heart pounds like a drum. She's nervous—this is what she wants, what she nearly ran them off the road for, and yet the truth could change everything. It could change them.

It could end them.

Griff rubs his hands together, the knock of his rings like a starter pistol. "I messed up," he says, a ragged hollowness to his voice. "Everything we had, I messed it all up the night of the kegger."

"The night of Johnny's party?" Alabama asks, old memories poking her mind.

Griff nods. "We were celebratin'. Or at least I was." His eyes meet hers, then flick to the windshield. "I had just bought the ring that mornin'. I saved all summer for it, workin' at Hank's Hardware. I wanted it on your finger by the time you went back to school."

The words are like a knife to her heart, and Alabama flinches. But she stays quiet, wanting him to get it out, to go at his own pace.

"So I told Johnny about the ring and we had some beers," Griff says, low-voiced. "I wasn't drunk, but I was drinkin'. And then you pulled up in your daddy's Jeep and—"

"I asked you to drive," Alabama finishes.

He swallows. "I never even thought about sayin' no. I was so damn happy to see you, so fuckin' high from that day, I agreed. I never should have got behind that wheel." He swears and shakes his head, still angry at himself after all these years. "The rollover was my fault. I lost control, and I got you hurt and I have no damn excuse for it."

Alabama frowns, confused. "I know all that, Griff. Except the drinkin' part and . . . well, you were a kid. You were at a party. How does my father fit into any of this?"

Griff's posture stiffens, his fingers curling to a fist on the legs of his jeans. "He told me to leave. And like a damn fool, I listened."

Alabama's stomach flips, the world around her tilting on its axis. "What're you talkin' about?"

Griff runs a hand over the back of his head. "The day after the accident, when I was waitin' to see you, your father came out and said he wanted to talk to me. He told me he knew I had been drinkin' that night, that he had enough to pin me with a DUI." His jaw works the words over, his eyes shiny with tears at the memory. "He said that if you had died it would have been murder."

Alabama covers her mouth. "He said that?"

Griff nods, then goes on. "He told me if I stuck around I'd only keep hurtin' you. He warned me not to wreck your chances in Nashville." He blows out a breath. "I didn't know what to do. I panicked. I thought for sure he'd arrest me. The thought of my mama, the thought of you findin' out what I had done—I couldn't handle it, Al. So I left."

The decade-overdue confession hangs in the air between them like a noose.

Alabama sits silently, taking it all in.

She's never been so shocked, never expected the root of Griff's exit from Clover was that her father had basically blackmailed him into leaving. She wants to call bullshit, to tell Griff he's wrong, but she can't. Because she knows her father. Newton Forester doesn't allow mistakes. Not in his town, and sure as hell not with his daughter.

Griff's eyes glisten and Alabama's heart breaks at the anguish in his face. "I was a coward who let your father chase me away from you. It was my worst damn mistake, Alabama, and I'll never forgive myself for leavin' you."

She wets her lips. "Why didn't you tell me?"

"I shoulda, but I couldn't. I was too damn embarrassed and angry with myself. At Newton, too. He was your daddy. You loved him, you looked up to him. Anytime I ever thought about tellin' you, I had been gone too long. I didn't want to hurt your relationship with your father. I didn't want to take him away from you, too."

A soft sob bursts from Alabama's lips. She presses her lips tightly together and thrashes her head. Wanting to refute his words. Wanting it not to be true. But it is true. Utterly and horribly true. These last twelve years, Griff's been carrying around this guilt. Keeping her father's secret all because he didn't want to hurt her.

A despondent look crosses Griff's face at the sight of her tears. He reaches out to take her hand, then stops himself and makes a fist instead. "I wish I could turn back the fuckin' clock and tell you everything. That I never stopped lovin' you. That I thought I was doin' the right thing by leavin', only it tore me up inside a thousand times over."

He inhales sharply. "I'm so damn sorry, sweetheart. I never wanted to hurt you. But I did. Because I know you needed an explanation and I didn't give it to you."

Alabama sits silent, sits stunned, for so long Griff's unable to stand it.

"Say somethin'. Anything," he pleads. "Tell me I don't deserve you. Tell me I'm a coward. Tell me we're done."

She rubs a palm over her wet eyes, her shoulders trembling violently. "Stop it. Stop it, Griff."

He stares at her, his expression bereft. "Tell me you hate me."

"I can't," she whispers. She swallows down her tears and meets Griff's eyes. "I can't because I love you."

At that, Griff lets out a wild cry. He quickly closes the gap between them, gathering her to his chest. Alabama shakes against him, burying her face in his neck to weep a river. Griff holds her tight, smoothing her hair as she cries.

When her breathing settles and her heart stops its furious racing, Alabama shifts in his arms, tilting her face to look at Griff. At the same sweet boy she loved so many years ago, who's now a beautiful, kind man, haunted by the past, by a need for forgiveness he never thought he'd get.

Griff.

The man she loves.

She had thought his story would be devastating. And it is—because her father was behind him leaving. But Griff had always loved her, had kept the ring all these long years, had been tortured by the truth, had thought for so long that he didn't deserve love, her love, any love.

All these years—he had paid the price to protect Alabama.

Griff brushes away her tears with the pads of his thumbs, his own eyes misty. "What I did—I let you down, Al."

"No," she says fiercely. She's adamant that he hear her. She palms his cheek, her fingers tracing the line of his scar. "No, you didn't. My father did. You were a kid, Griff. You made a mistake." Her expression hardens. "He was the adult. A cop. *He* should have known better."

"I'm still sorry."

"Don't be. I'm glad I know."

"You know what we gotta do now, though?"

"What?"

He leans in, brushing his lips across hers. Though his smile is roguish, his expression is serious. "Make up for all the time we lost."

She smiles. "I thought we were already doing that."

When she leans in to kiss him, Alabama's arm gives a sudden throb and she has to choke back a gasp. She's gonna pay for this; she can already feel her arm screaming at her for being a dumbass idiot.

Griff looks at her shrewdly, like he knows she's trying to hide her pain. He pulls back to check her sling, his touch featherlight. When he looks at her, he's scowling. "I'd say you deserve it for pullin' this goddamn stunt." A flash of anger surges in his eyes. "You could have killed yourself."

Alabama cocks a brow. "It worked, didn't it?"

Griff's snarl tells her she's dangerously close to spending the next week in solitary confinement.

"What d'you say we get on home and get off this goddamn cliff?" Griff puts a hand on the wheel. "And this time I'm fuckin' drivin'."

Her lips curve, but there's no humor in it. "There's just one thing I have to do first."

"What's that?"

She sighs and lifts her gaze to his. "I have to go to my father's."

chapter
TWENTY-SEVEN

ALABAMA SITS SILENTLY, STARING OUT THE windshield as Griff rolls the truck into the driveway of her father's house. Newton's in the yard, red-faced as he digs up weeds from the garden. A hollow aching feeling settles in the pit of her stomach. She has to confront her father. She has to tell him that she knows. That what he's done is unacceptable in so many ways.

"Alabama?"

She looks over at Griff, who's watching her with worry.

"You don't got to do this, you know."

"I do. It's not right what he did. All this time, he—" She breaks off, her faith in her father badly shaken. He's always been her rock, always taught her right from wrong, and for him to do something like this—it's unconscionable.

But she can't let him get away with it. Not anymore. She'll be damned if she lets her father treat Griff like shit. Lets him shame her for her mistakes when he's made some doozies of his own.

Alabama exhales, trying to screw up her courage.

"You want me to come with you?" Griff asks in a low voice.

Her heart swells, knowing that he would, knowing that he'd be beside her every step of the way if she let him. "No." Giving him a half-smile, she reaches for the door handle. "I have to do this myself."

Then she's out and walking on wobbly legs. Her heart pumps frantically in her chest, the winking sun above burning a hole through her defenses.

At the sight of Alabama, her father straightens up, a question on his lips, but Alabama holds up a hand, cutting him off. "This'll only take a second."

She stands in front of him and squares up her body, her nerves. "I know what you did to Griff." Briefly, her father's gaze flicks to the truck then back to her. "I know you threatened him with a DUI. I know you made him leave Clover."

Her father's face goes bright red. Then he huffs. "I'm not doin' this, Alabama Grace."

He turns away from her and heads to the house.

Alabama clenches her jaw and follows, crunching over dried leaves and dirt. "Oh, yes, we most certainly are doin' this." She walks fast after him. The volume of her voice increases. She'll make him hear her. "You made Griff leave, Daddy. For so long I thought he didn't love me, I thought he didn't want me, but it was all you. *You did it.* How could you?"

Her father stops. So abruptly Alabama nearly runs into him.

"I had to," he booms, crossing his meaty arms over his chest. "He was never gonna be good enough for you, Bama."

Red colors her vision and she pulls her good hand to a fist. "But that was my decision, and you took that away. You called the shots when no one asked you to."

"I did what I had to do to protect you."

"Griff was a kid and he messed up. We both did. And so did you."

Her father bristles, but Alabama plows ahead, plows down the sadness to dig deep for her own feelings. "I've been tryin' to be like you my entire life. Be good, play by the rules, keep it honest. And the one time I didn't, when I really needed you after Six String, you could barely look me in the eye. You were so embarrassed by me. Well, guess what? I was embarrassed by myself. But I made a mistake, I owned up to it, and you, my own father, couldn't even stand by me to tell me it was all gonna be okay."

Something like regret crosses her father's face. "Alabama . . ."

"You always taught me to do the right thing, but you didn't.

You should be ashamed of yourself." Alabama's chest tightens and she takes a shaky breath. "And you know what? Griff's been there. He hasn't made me feel bad or less than or worthless for what I did. He believed in me when you didn't."

Her father drops his head, saying nothing.

Alabama's eyes burn. She can't see his face, doesn't need to. She's done. She's said all she has in her, and if he doesn't understand, that's on him.

With that, she turns on her heel and strides fast for the truck.

Once inside, Griff backs out of the drive. When they're out of view of the house, Griff pulls over onto the shoulder of the road and lets the truck idle.

He turns toward her. "Are you okay?"

She stares straight ahead. Every part of her trembling, feeling as if it will burst. Feeling as if she will never be the same again.

"Yes."

"You sure?"

"No." She shakes her head and turns her teary gaze to Griff. At the sight of him moving toward her, already coming for her, his arms outstretched, she bursts into tears.

He has her. He always has.

It's Saturday night and the buzz of neon lights Mill's Tavern. The microphone glitters in the overhead stage lights, and the waitresses sling beers with reckless abandon.

Griff, his guitar strapped around his back, holds open the back door for Alabama. It's their last night in Clover. Tomorrow, bright and early, a bus will pick them up and take them to Austin.

"How's it lookin' in there?" Alabama asks Holly, who's waiting in the wings.

"It's a full house," Holly says as Griff and Alabama follow her down the hall. "All of Clover came out to see y'all rattle the stage." She leads them to a door and opens it with celebratory fanfare. "Ta-da! I made a green room."

Griff smothers a chuckle. The cramped storage room's been made up into a small buffet of food and drinks laid out on packing crates. "Lukewarm beer," he says dryly, peering into a cooler. "Nice touch, Holly."

"The day I treat you like a star is the day I gnaw off my arm," Holly retorts. She claps her hands together. "I'll rally the crowd. You're on in five."

Griff rolls his eyes as Holly makes a quick exit. "Well, she's definitely got the lingo down."

Alabama stares at Griff. "Are we crazy for doin' this?"

"You ain't crazy," he says, giving Alabama a long look. "I, however, may need to rethink my decision." He's seeing people he hasn't seen in a decade. People that know how he's fucked up, that he never came back for his mama's funeral, relatives he's avoided because, well, he's been too ashamed to face his family. To admit he's done everything in his life wrong.

Everything up till now, he thinks, his eyes on Alabama.

"Too late." She scoffs and socks his arm. "You go where I go."

"You're damn right I do." He reaches out and cups the side of her face. When she meets his gaze, his breath catches in his throat. He still can't believe how fucking lucky he is.

All the secrets he's been hiding about the past, they're out now. Alabama heard them and held them. She forgives him. It still has Griff marveling. Has him loving her even more than he ever has. Her unadulterated belief in him, her unswerving ability to back him up, to see him as a good man—it confounds him and leaves him thankful, all at the same time. He's never known a stronger, more remarkable woman than her. And he thanks his lucky, goddamn stars above every damn day that she's his.

Alabama leans into his touch and then ducks her head close to his. Her voice a whisper. "I'm nervous—why am I nervous?"

Griff smiles. Alabama's never nervous playing for a packed crowd, but Clover's different. It's her hometown. She hasn't been on that stage since she and Griff were teenagers picking instruments. That stage is where they got their start, dreamed their dreams. So it's a fitting end to their time in Clover. Alabama just wants to get it right. And Griff wants to be beside her every step of the way.

"You're nervous because we're gonna play our song," Griff says, pulling her into his arms.

The corners of her lips quirk. "You mean our unfinished song."

"Relax." He kisses her brow. "I'll be up there with you."

"I know you will." She links her hand with his. "I got my penny in my pocket."

His fingers tighten around hers. "Same here, sweetheart."

Holly pops her head into the room. "Lovebirds, y'all ready?"

They exit the storage room and cross the floor to the small stage, where they begin setting up. Alabama chuckles as Griff opens his guitar case, laying it out on the lip of the stage to receive tips.

He gives her a wink. "Just like old times." He plugs the guitar into the amp and helps Alabama adjust her mic. Then Griff nods to Holly to show they're ready.

When he looks out into the crowd, he sees them. His Aunt Bonnie. His Uncle Clay. His cousins. They let out a hoot, waving at him with wild abandon. The tension Griff's been holding on to eases. There's no trace of anger or embarrassment in their faces. He raises a hand and gives them a wave back.

Alabama's grinning, clearly delighted on his behalf.

Holly hops onstage to make introductions. "Y'all know 'em. Y'all love 'em. We're so happy to welcome back to the stage, twelve years later, I may add, Alabama Forester and that loveable asshole Griff Greyson!"

Griff shakes his head, but he smiles, finding Alabama's eyes on him.

Scattered applause breaks out in the audience. Beers are raised and whistles are shrieked. The excitement's contagious and a crackle of adrenaline shoots through Griff. He hasn't realized how much he missed the stage. Two weeks away has been too damn long.

Alabama wiggles her brows. "Should we do it?" she asks Griff.

He meets her wild smile with one of his own. "Aw, what the hell."

Into the mic, he says, "We're the Copper Hounds, and you know the drill. Get your voices ready, Clover."

With that, they launch into one of the best sets of their lives. Ten tight songs. Alabama stomps her boots, Griff shreds his strings, their collaboration the most perfect fusing of country, rock and roll and folk. They sing long and loud into the night, Alabama's smooth-silky voice mixing with Griff's gravel grit.

Every song thunderous, every guitar strum heartfelt.

It's their sound. Not the manufactured made-up Griff and Alabama that Nashville taught them to be. Tonight, they're the Copper Hounds, back on the stage that made them.

Back to the lives they wanted.

chapter
TWENTY-EIGHT

FROM THE STAGE WINGS, GRIFF WATCHES ALABAMA adjust her microphone. They're in Oklahoma at an indoor/outdoor concert venue called the Pub Station. It's the last day of soundcheck, their last show on the "Straight to Hell" tour, and Griff's never been so damn happy.

Alabama swirls a finger, telling the band she wants to run through "Find You Again." Griff shakes his head, chuckling. She's been fussing with that damn song ending all week. She's written three different endings and isn't satisfied with any of them. And he loves it. It's their song. He's never been so proud of something he created. The second they're back in Nashville, they're gonna cut it as the Copper Hounds.

With a toss of her red hair, Alabama glances over her shoulder like she can feel Griff's eyes on her. She gives him a wink and then turns back to the music. The sight of her smile sends his pulse racing. Hell, just how strong she's been these last three weeks has him bowing at the altar of Alabama. But he isn't surprised. That's her. She's been shot in the goddamn arm and still she's giving orders, still nailing every one of her sets like a pro, still kicking ass. He's never seen someone so strong, so fucking fierce, so determined to reclaim her song and her image. It turns him on, has his chest bursting with pride. With love.

That feeling ain't gonna go away anytime soon. Not if Griff has anything to say about it.

Alabama hasn't brought up the ring since she took Griff on her terrifying drive to the Ridge. But he's been thinking about it.

Thinking about using it. Soon, too. He didn't tell her he brought it back from Clover with him. The thought of them going separate ways in a few short days has his blood pressure spiking. He doesn't want to be separate from Alabama. Not anymore. He knows it ain't his style, that he'll have his doubters, but fuck everyone who thinks they know him. Let 'em see the real Griff Greyson. He has. The man up on that stage in Clover, singing the best damned songs he had ever written in his life. There was more in him—more grit, gravel and life—than there ever has been. He wants to hold on to that.

He doesn't know if he can ever express what Alabama means to him, but that doesn't mean he ain't gonna try for the rest of his life to prove to her that he deserves her.

From the darkness comes the hiss of his name. "Griff."

Scowling, he turns around to find Freddie standing in front of him in a crisp linen pantsuit. He grins, seeing a light bead of sweat on her forehead. "You look hot, Freddie."

She harrumphs. "I am, indeed, sweating bullets, as they say 'round these parts."

Griff gestures at the surroundings. "You here to scope out the countryside? I hear they're doing two-for-one hayrides down at the county fair."

Her lip curls in disgust. "Absolutely not. I come bearing good news, Griff. Come, walk with me."

With a last glance at Alabama, he follows Freddie back into the shadows of the stage. She glances up at the catwalk, then nods at Griff. "Well, this is very hushed and clandestine, isn't it?"

Griff, impatient to get back to Alabama, hooks his fingers around his belt. "Why're you here, Freddie?"

"I seem to remember a time when you preferred me around. When I was bailing you out of trouble, isn't that right?" She holds his stare for a long second and then flaps a cavalier hand to show she isn't insulted. "The good news is that the overseas tour this winter is a go. We've secured our sponsors, not to mention slightly better accommodations and venues. The last thing we need to decide on is a tour name."

A smile spreads slow across Griff's face. "Hell, that's great. Alabama's gonna be thrilled." He frowns. "But wait, why you havin' this conversation with just me?" He hooks a thumb back toward the stage. "Hang on, I'll go get her."

Freddie holds up a *stop-right-there* hand. "I'm afraid it's just you, Griff."

"Just me what?"

"It's just you on the tour."

He shakes his head like there's water in his ears. "Now wait a goddamn minute. We promised her—"

"There's no promise without a contract," Freddie says. "She'll still get paid for this tour. Don't worry."

Griff's heart jackhammers against his ribs. This ain't happening. It can't. He swallows. "She's the one who should be goin', not me. She's the one proppin' up the show, the songs."

Freddie nods. "She has been. I'm not arguing that. However, this wasn't a charity to boost her image. It was to boost yours. Remember? You and your fans?" Freddie frowns and glances toward the stage where the band is tuning instruments. "She doesn't go. And that's final. She'll understand."

"She won't understand," Griff snaps, his fingers curling into fists at Freddie's dismissive attitude of Alabama. No way in hell will she understand. She's been put through the wringer with managers, with contracts, and to do this to her again, to betray her, it's gonna kill her.

It's killing Griff. In that instant, he knows he's been flat out lied to. CMI had no intention of keeping Alabama for the winter tour. They fucking used her. Just like everyone else. Just like he did.

The thought that Griff himself had a hand in it is like a punch to the stomach.

"You better start talkin', Freddie," he snarls. "Fuckin' fast."

She holds his stare for a beat. Then she says, "A fling, Griff.

That's all it was supposed to be." Freddie's face is cold, closed off. "The plan was to fuck her, not fall for her. We can't have you attached on tour." Freddie tosses her hair. "I am merely protecting my best asset and resorting your priorities."

Griff groans, recognizing his mistake. He gave too much to Freddie on that last conversation in Clover. He didn't hide how he felt about Alabama. Freddie saw it. And she didn't like it.

"You're good," Freddie continues. "You have clout now. You don't need her."

"I do," Griff says, his voice thick with pain. All of his defenses crumbling. His heart aching. "I need her."

Freddie gives him a look reserved for a child. "Griff, I know you feel bad for her, but that's your dick talking. You forget why this whole thing started in the first place. To save your own ass. You wanted this. And you got it."

He did. He had wanted to make the label happy, to avoid getting his ass dropped. It was what he wanted, only now . . . now it's not what he wants at all.

"Look, I don't know what the big fuss is. You didn't want her in the first place. Which reminds me." Freddie digs around in her purse and comes up with a crisp fifty-dollar bill. "I owe you."

He stares in horror as she presses the money in his palm.

"Who can forget our bet?" Freddie utters a merry laugh and Griff's stomach plunges. "'I'll have her in bed in a week.'" Her British accent disappears as she mimics Griff's gruff Texas twang. "I was quite doubtful at the time, but you proved me wrong, you cad."

His throat constricting, he stares at the money in his hand, hating it. Hating himself, hating the cruel bet he made about Alabama. Hating that he's not that guy anymore—that selfish asshole only concerned with himself—because that would make this a hell of a lot easier.

"Oh, don't look so glum, Griff. You did it." Freddie zips her purse. "The tour's nearly over. We have good things in our future, so cheer up."

Griff looks at the ground, numb. Cheer. Right. It's gonna be a cold day in hell before he feels any of that again.

Freddie takes three strides toward the exit, then emits a great, sucking gasp.

Griff raises his face. To his horror, he sees Alabama stepping out of the shadows, the sheet music for "Find You Again" clenched in her hand.

He stiffens, his heart pounding hard.

Alabama, her face a mask of anger, gives Freddie a scorching glare that has her scuttling. The faint *click-clack* of her heels sounds across the cement as she makes a hasty exit.

Then, Alabama lasers her gaze to Griff, and he knows without a doubt that she's heard everything. She's heard the absolute worst.

chapter
TWENTY-NINE

LABAMA STANDS BENEATH THE EAVE, HER HANDS trembling at her sides. The words she's heard from Freddie have stopped her cold. She can't make them compute. Doesn't want to. She doesn't dare breathe; if she breathes, she'll fracture into a thousand sharp pieces capable of slicing anyone who gets in her way.

She meets Griff's eyes. Her heart's a dull roar in her ears. She wets her lips. "Is it true?"

Griff's mouth opens, closes, a pleading expression on his face. "Sweetheart, listen—"

"Don't." Alabama cuts him off with a shake of her head. "Don't call me that." She forces herself to take a step forward. "I want to know if what Freddie said was true. Did you make a bet about me?"

He stares at her like he wants to deny it, but then he nods. "I did. I wasn't thinkin'. And I fucked up. Royally. I hate myself for it." He scrubs a hand down his face. "That guy who made the bet—that ain't me. Not anymore. Back then, I didn't care about anyone but myself. But now—"

"But that didn't stop you from going along with it." She clenches her jaw, her body alternating between hot and cold shivers. "That didn't stop you from fuckin' me."

He rears back like she's slapped him.

Alabama stares at Griff, sick to her stomach. The old familiar pain of betrayal snakes its way through her heart. Everything's been yanked away from her. The tour. Her trust in Griff. Her self-respect.

"So you what? You used me because of Mort? Because you thought that if I was just slutty enough, I'd sell your records?" Her laugh is bitter. "Well, congratulations. You played the part perfectly. You got what you wanted, didn't you? Tour, sales. You must be happy."

"No." His voice is haggard, desperate. "Alabama—"

She shakes her head. "You knew it was important to me, you knew how much I wasn't that person, was fighting to break away from my bad reputation. And yet you used me for those same reasons. How could you? I trusted you, Griff."

She hates the way her voice shakes, the way it gives everything away. She took a chance on him again, loved him again, and what has he done? It was all just a joke to him. She was a joke to him.

Regret blazes in his eyes. "I know. I know." He steps toward her, his hand outstretched. "I'm so sorry, Al. So damn sorry. I don't know how to fix this. But I will. I swear, I'll—"

"Don't bother. You can't fix this. You used me, just like Mort. And for a second time in my life, I'm an idiot." She laughs bitterly. "I'm just another notch on your belt, and you're just the same old Griff. You'll never change."

His entire face shatters. "Don't say that," he whispers. "I love you."

The words hurt worse than the bullet she took for him.

Tears slip down her cheeks, and she lets out a sob. "It's not enough. It doesn't matter anymore."

"The hell it doesn't," he growls.

Anger wells in her, and she curls her fingers into her palm. She can feel herself shutting down, see the headlines, the press camped outside, the stories. And her temper flares, wanting to hurt Griff as much as he's hurt her.

She draws herself up, feeling numb inside. "Think of it this way, Griff. Now we're all wrapped up nice and easy. Your tour fling's over and you're free to sleep your way around Europe."

He stares at her, his expression crushed. "That's bullshit," he flings back. "What we have is fuckin' amazing."

"Had," she says, her heart ripping out of her chest. "What we had."

"Don't." Griff squeezes his eyes shut. "Don't do this."

She stares at him, wanting to throw herself into his arms, to have him hold her close. Instead, she exhales a breath, willing her disobedient heart to ice over. "Here."

She steps forward, holding out the sheet music, but he doesn't—won't—take it.

"The song's yours," Griff says, his voice cracking.

"I don't want the fuckin' song!" she shouts, her voice echoing in the space. "I wanted you, Griff." She's crying now, hot tears tracking down her face. "I wanted you and you fucked it all up. Just like you did in Clover."

With a sob, she whips an arm up and tosses the lyrics into the air. The pages of song flutter around them like fallen doves before slowly whisking to the cement.

She takes a shuddering breath. "I'm done, Griff. I'll finish the show, but I'm flyin' back to Nashville tonight." She kicks at a sheet of paper fluttering on the ground. "Thanks for everything. If I would have known I'd be gettin' fucked over, I woulda stayed with Mort."

Griff's breath is sharp, and he opens his mouth, but she's tearing his gaze from his and spinning around on her heel before he can reply.

She wants nothing from him. No excuses, no apologies. All she wants to do is get away. Before she regrets her decision.

This time, it's her turn to leave. And not look back.

chapter
THIRTY

ALABAMA SCOWLS AT THE TICKER HEADLINE BEING played on the *Nashville Star*—*Secret Source Reveals Shocking Reason Alabama Forester Fled Fall Tour*—and snaps off the television. She lies back against the couch, covering herself with a rumpled blanket half-spilled on the glossy tile, and closes her eyes.

She's been back in Nashville for two weeks, spending Christmas on the couch, torturing herself with daily viewings of sleazy tabloid shows like *Nashville Star On-Air*. Not satisfied with viciously maligning celebrities in print, as of last month, the *Star's* branched out and claimed the television business too. So far she's learned that Griff Greyson's been spotted at the Stillery with Mavis Banks, the Brothers Kincaid debuted a new music video; Dierks Bentley's opening a new bar on Broadway.

Everyone's moving on. Everyone but her.

Because she's still stuck in the fucking past.

She couldn't even go back to Clover. Griff ruined even that for her. Every time she closes her eyes, images of their time together play across her memory. That beautiful house, Griff's arms holding her close, making music like it was the end of the world.

No.

Alabama shakes her head as if that will dissipate the memories. She can't go there. Even if she still loves him. Her eyes bead with hot tears. Griff will never change. He's still running from her.

She wipes her eyes, her gaze drifting to the big floor-to-ceiling windows showcasing the gorgeous skyline of Nashville.

She knows Griff's out there, somewhere. They're in the same city, only miles away from one another, but truly so far apart they may as well live on different planets. Today, he'll be on a plane bound for Europe. She's not upset about missing the tour; she's upset about missing Griff. Upset about how she left things. She could have stayed and talked things through, but at that moment in time, Griff left her hurt and humiliated after Freddie's reveal. And instead of calmly discussing it, she let her worst flaw—her temper—take over.

She hurled every awful thing she could say at him. This time, she wanted to be the one to walk away first, before he did, but it's enough to make her wonder, would he have?

Alabama groans and buries her head in a pillow at the ringing of her phone. Faint, insistent chirping telling her to get up and move her sorry ass.

With a sigh, Alabama drags herself from her cocoon of blankets and goes to her small kitchen island, where the sound is coming from. She shuffles through bills and ketchup packets and finally finds her phone buried beneath her notebook full of songs.

She groans again when she sees who's calling: Holly. No doubt ready to give Alabama a sternly worded talking-to.

"Hey, Hol," Alabama says when she answers, her voice flat and dry.

Holly's bright voice greets her. "How's the self-pity going?"

"Oh, it's definitely in the wallowing phase." Alabama stares down into a melted carton of ice cream she's had for breakfast. "With a side of gluttony."

"Oh, baby, I wish I was there. You sound miserable."

"Yeah, but I'm miserable with ice cream, does that matter?" She grimaces at the ice cream and, before she can pick up the spoon to really seal the deal on her woe-is-me party, dumps the carton in the trash. "On a good note, my check came yesterday."

Holly whoops. "You got paid?"

"Yeah, I got paid," she says with a humorless laugh. "Too much."

"How much is too much?"

"Let's just say I won't need to sling hash at the tavern next year."

The money had covered her legal bills and then some. Although she was barely able to cash it; Griff probably had Freddie cut her a fat check to get their last conversation off his conscience.

"That's great, Al." There's a long silence, a clearing of her throat, then Holly says, "How about I raise your good news with some bad?"

Alabama pinches the bridge of her nose. "Lay it on me."

"Griff's house sold."

"Oh."

There it is. Now there's nothing to tie Griff to her, to Clover anymore.

"Buddy Green was over there yesterday mornin' takin' down the For Sale sign."

Alabama closes her eyes, her heartbeat a stabbing pain in her chest. "Holly."

"I know, I know. I'm supposed to keep my mouth shut about Griff." Holly's nails drum against the side of the phone. "But I figured you'd want to know. I swear, if some California city slicker moves in there I'm gonna stone 'em to death with their avocados."

Alabama chuckles. Her phone buzzes, telling her she has an incoming call. She glances down, and when she sees her father's name, her heart sinks. She hoped, wished, prayed, it would be Griff.

Not like it would be. After the way she treated him, she doesn't blame him for going straight no-contact.

As if Holly's read her thoughts, she asks, "Have you talked to Griff?"

"You know I haven't."

Absentmindedly, Alabama flips through her notebook. Pages and pages of songs she wrote pre- and post-Griff. The after-Griff songs are angry. Stomp-on-your-heart, put-a-boot-in-your-ass countrified blues.

"How can I after what he said?"

As if to prove her wrong, the notebook opens pointedly to "Find You Again," prompting a fresh sheen of tears to blur her vision.

"Al, you know I hate to disagree with you, but I have to bring up a strong and important point that you're failing to see."

"I thought you were on my side?"

"Just hear me out." A strong inhale of breath from Holly, and then a rambling, "Yes, Griff said a shitty asshole thing that doesn't endear him at all to me, but . . . he did what he had to do for his music."

Alabama scowls. "I don't see how any of this—"

"Like you did with Mort," Holly interjects. "And later, after you were in too deep, you realized it was probably a very, very, very, very, very—"

"Is this supposed to make me feel better?"

"—very, very dumb decision."

Alabama sighs.

Holly continues. "All I'm saying is, to Griff, it was a job. And then you were there, and then suddenly it wasn't. He probably never thought it'd go this far. But it did. And good thing too, because it was the happiest I've ever seen you."

Alabama shakes her head and crosses to the window. "Again, not on my side." She looks down on Nashville, pressing a palm against the glass.

"Hey, what can I say? I'm on love's side."

"Oh, so you're a romantic now?"

"After all those sappy country songs you made me listen to, hell yes, I'm a romantic."

Alabama bursts into a laugh.

Softly, Holly says, "Did he make you happy, Al?"

Alabama nods even though Holly's not around to see it. "He always made me happy."

"Then you should hang on to that." Holly's voice is filled with sympathy. "Right now, I guarantee he's goin' through the same thing you are. Absolute misery. So find you again, find him again, and make that second chance yours again."

A hitch of her breath. Her heart.

The words spark something inside Alabama. "I gotta go, Hol."

"Wait! Did you just think of a song?" Holly asks, her tone smug and excited. "Because if it's a song, I demand a cut of all profits—"

Alabama hangs up on her.

With a pounding heart, she grabs her notebook and a pen and settles herself on the couch. She flips to the tattered pages where her and Griff's song lives, her heart pounding out a melody in her ears. Her eyes scan the lyrics, then drop to the last verse.

*I reckon we're building on our present with the past

Maybe we're movin' too much, too damn fast . . .*

The one she and Griff just could not get right.

The words weren't working because she didn't know what to say. Because she was still holding fear in her heart. And it was that fear that had her saying those angry words to Griff, that had her believing the worst. But it wasn't the worst—it was Griff and she loved him. She still does.

The song isn't about loving the same person you knew, it's about loving the person they've turned into.

She's made mistakes; they've both made mistakes, and Griff still loved her despite them.

Alabama starts fresh, a new page, and soon she's scribbling furiously. She's in a trance. Nothing exists except their ending. A song that's bone-deep and aching and crying out to be heard.

An hour passes, and then another, and when she glances up her apartment is dim, but it feels brighter. She feels lit up inside, brought back to life again. That's what Griff did to her. He made her live. Better, bolder than she ever had.

And she found herself.

Reclaimed her voice.

Her song.

Her heart.

Finished, Alabama plops back into the couch. She glances once more at the page, at a song fixed, and her soul feels mended. Stitched together with song.

With a smile, she pulls out her phone and snaps a photo.

chapter
THIRTY-ONE

GRIFF SHOULDERS HIS BAG AND CLIMBS THE STAIRS onto the idling bus. From her perch on the couch, Freddie lifts her sunglasses to get a good look at him, her brow arching into space. "You're early."

"Don't got much else to do," he says, tucking his lank hair behind his ears.

Consider that his motto of the last two weeks. Since he got back to Nashville, he's buried himself in shit he's needed to do for so long, but nothing's been able to take his mind off Alabama. He's drunk himself silly, he's stayed sober. He's written shit songs, he's penned some good ones. He's willingly seen his label, he's told 'em to fuck off. Ain't nothing working. Ain't nothing chasing away the fact that he's still haunted by Alabama overhearing the conversation. Still haunted by how he treated her.

He should call her. Alabama's number one on his speed dial. One quick punch and he could be talking to her, apologizing. So why doesn't he do it? Because she's better off without him, that's why. Because he hurt her—and like the coward he is, he's running away.

Again.

He doesn't blame her for walking away. He was an idiot to keep the truth from her. Alabama valued honesty, valued her reputation, and what did he do? He lied to her. He fucking curb-stomped any hope he had at a second shot.

All the plans he had—the ring, Clover—up in fucking smoke.

Griff frowns as he settles onto the leather couch beside Freddie. "Where're we goin' again?" he asks, kicking a snake-skin boot up on the coffee table.

Freddie huffs a laugh but pulls out her iPad and runs through the itinerary. "We drive to New York today, where we have one show at Nita's Public House. Then tomorrow we board a plane for Amsterdam. Be excited, Griff. This will be a fantastic tour."

Normally, he'd relish the tour. It's the best form of distraction, hands down. But being three thousand miles away from Alabama has him uneasy. He wants to talk to her. Wants to make sure she's taking care of that arm. Wants to tell her he loves her more than anything on this fucking planet, but the memory of her face, angry and tear-streaked, won't let him pick up the phone.

He knows he shut down when she walked away. Hell, he's the one who let her walk away.

He should have taken her in his arms, made her stay and listen, gave her the best forgive-me kiss she's ever had in her entire life. But he couldn't. He couldn't shake that shit-awful feeling from years before. That he didn't deserve her. That she was better off without him.

But now—now he knows he was a goddamn fool.

"Here." Freddie hands him a printed itinerary. "Familiarize yourself."

As Griff runs a wary eye down the tour stops, a gut-wrenching need sweeps over him. How is he supposed to get through this without Alabama? Sleep, eat, fucking breathe? She made the last tour; hell, she *was* the last tour. She deserves this more than him. She should be here, beside him, singing her heart out on every stage in Europe.

"By the way, you never told me," Freddie's voice breaks through his reverie. "How was dinner with Mavis the other day?"

"That wasn't dinner, that was a date," Griff grinds out. "A fuckin' publicity stunt and you know it, Freddie."

A smile curls her lips. "Just getting you into prime fighting shape."

He rolls his eyes. His label had billed dinner with Mavis as a business meeting, but it really was a shameless setup. Nothing more than a distraction to get Griff's mind off Alabama.

His stomach twists, and he gives Freddie a wary look. "Right."

"I know you think I got you into this mess, Griff, but face it." Freddie glances down at her iPad. "You're better off. That man wasn't you. The old Griff Greyson suits you better."

His jaw clenches. He doesn't want to be the old Griff Greyson. He wants to be the man Alabama loves. That determined kid from Clover who had so much goddamn hope he'd bust down any wall in front of him to get what he wanted.

So what's stopping him now?

Freddie taps a nail on the table. "I want you to sing how you've been singing, Griff. Keep that sound you've built. It's good. The label loves it and can't wait to get you into the studio for your next album."

Griff scoffs. "That's some nice fuckin' hypocrisy right there, Freddie. You want me to sing how I've been singin', but you want the old Griff Greyson back." He crosses his arms. "Pick a lane."

Freddie sighs as Griff's phone vibrates. "We really need to discuss the sponsors," she says as he pulls it out of his back pocket.

When Griff looks down at his phone, his heart stops.

A text from Alabama.

With shaky hands, he swipes the unlock screen and reads the message. *Good luck in Europe. Give 'em hell.* The accompanying photo is a page in her notebook. The last verse and chorus of their song finished.

> What you did—how can I forgive you, how can I forget?
> All these feelings between us, they're once again lit
> I thought I had lost you, I thought our time was done
> But when I saw you standin' there all I did was come undone
> And I know I could be angry forever, but then
> I'd rather be makin' second chances mine again
> I reckon we ain't the same people we were

But we got the same love, and no more of the hurt
So I say let's keep the passion, those tangled sheets in
the bed
Because the cold hard truth is I don't love you like I did
Baby, I love you more than the way-back-then
I do, all because you're the one who finally found me
again.

Griff's throat bobs, heavy with emotion.

The song's perfect. Absolutely perfect.

And it's a sign. Alabama's way of telling him she's still in it.
If he is.

A shot of adrenaline surges through Griff. He rises abruptly, his boots hitting the floor with a loud thud. "I gotta go."

Freddie glances up. "What?" She scrambles to her feet when Griff moves for the door. "What in the bloody hell are you talking about?"

"I ain't doin' the tour," he says resolutely, no room in his tone for argument.

The song was never about their past. It was about their future. And Griff's changed. Alabama was right when she said he was the best man for her. He is. And starting right now, he'll prove it.

No more running. Not anymore.

"You can't—" Freddie palms her hands and takes a deep breath. "Come back inside and let's discuss this. Let's—"

"I'm done talkin'. I got a girl, and I got to go find her."

He pounds down the stairs, then stops and glances back at Freddie. Her arms are crossed, her face red, a small vein in her temple twitching. "You do this," she warns, "you're done, Griff."

"I know," he says with his typical swagger. "But hell, who am I kidding? The second she set foot on that bus, I was fuckin' toast."

chapter
THIRTY-TWO

LABAMA EXITS THE DOORS OF THE PHYSICAL THERAPY clinic, wincing at the pain in her arm. Her PT put her through the wringer, bending and twisting her arm in directions she never knew existed. Though she's not back to normal yet, and even using the arm hurts, she has more movement than she used to. She won't be able to hold a guitar for a while, but she's getting there.

She stares into the setting sun and breathes deep, resisting the urge to check her phone for about the hundredth time today. It's no surprise Griff hasn't responded to the message she sent yesterday. The things she said to him—she doesn't deserve a text back. By now, he's on a plane, bringing his rebel antics to Europe.

She smiles, finding herself happy for him. He should have all the good things in life.

And so should she. She's trying to pick up the pieces of her own life since she sent Griff that text. She and her father have been slowly texting back and forth. She doesn't know what will repair their relationship, but she's willing to work to get there. And the strangest of the strange, she had brunch with Sal Kincaid this morning. It was nice to talk to another woman who was fighting to get what she wanted out of life, despite every shit thing it had handed her. A year ago, if someone had told her that Sal would be the closest thing she had to a friend in Nashville, she would have told them they were crazy.

Now, she just calls it a second chance.

She pauses at her car, the purse over her shoulder swinging

awkwardly. "Damn it," she mutters, trying to dig around one-handed for her car keys.

"You need some help, sweetheart?"

She gasps and drops her purse, the contents and the keys spilling out over the asphalt.

She spins around, her eyes widening in surprise at the source of the voice.

Griff Greyson stands in front of her, looking roguish and disheveled, a smirk on his handsome face.

"Griff." She stares, then shakes herself awake. If her jaw got any lower, it'd be on the ground. "You should be on a plane right now."

He takes a step toward her, his eyes warm and searching. "Yeah, well, let's just say I had more important places to be."

Worry twists her stomach. "But the tour—"

"Don't you worry about the tour." Before she can say anything else, he dips down to retrieve her belongings. When he straightens up, he hands over her purse and says, "I don't like how we left things, Al." His voice is laced with regret.

"I know. I don't like it either." Alabama bites her lip. She's trembling as if all she wants to do is toss herself into his arms and stake her claim. But she forces herself to come down to earth, to focus on the man in front of her.

Griff's Adam's apple bobs. "I was hopin' I could have a chance to talk to you."

She nods. "Yeah, you can," she says, near breathless, near hope.

"Then c'mon. Take a ride with me." He tosses her a reproachful look. "You shouldn't be drivin' anyway."

On rubber legs, Alabama follows Griff to his pickup truck, a shiny black behemoth in need of a wash. He helps her in, then settles beside her in the driver's seat. "It ain't far," he says, catching her stare. "Just right around the block."

"Sounds good." She keeps her hands tucked in her lap, so they don't seek him out.

"How's the arm?" He glances over at her, his shrewd eyes taking in the absence of bandage, of sling.

"Sore, but it's gettin' there." She smiles. "Great recommendation on the therapist, by the way."

He nods and looks back at the road. In silence, they take the surface streets until, minutes later, Griff pulls into a parking lot. Alabama tilts her head when she sees the sign. Barn Door Studios.

She cocks her head to the side. "Griff. Why're we here?"

"Easy, woman." He cracks a mischievous grin. "I'll give you answers in a second. First, you gotta follow me."

Alabama lets out a growl of frustration but follows Griff's lead. They enter the front office, a small space with black-and-white photos of musicians on the wall. The cowboy-hat-wearing receptionist at the front desk raises her face and gestures to a clipboard. "You have a session booked?"

"Sure do," Griff says.

"Then please sign in and you can go on back to booth number three."

Alabama shakes her head when she sees the name Griff's put down on the sign-in sheet. The Copper Hounds. She reaches out and grips his forearm. "You ain't serious?"

His tawny eyes hold steady on hers. "You still got that song on you?"

All she can do is nod.

All she can do is silently follow Griff back to the recording booth. They enter the private room, padded with foam sheets and blackout curtains. Alabama and Griff lean back against opposite walls to face each other. She doesn't trust herself to move, to breathe.

Griff whisks his hands together. "We got an hour of time."

Alabama arcs a brow. "If you think I'm cuttin' a song with you when you're playin' mum, you got another thing comin.'" She crosses her arms. "Why am I here, Greyson? Talk."

"Okay, okay. Damn." A devilish gleam flashes in his eyes.

"First things first—I ain't doin' the tour. I walked away from Freddie yesterday." He gives a one-shoulder shrug. "Did you know there was an insurance clause in my contract givin' me that right? Think I even knew somethin' was fishy back then."

The room spins. "Are you crazy?" She pushes off the wall, stunned at his casual attitude. "You torpedoed your career, Griff. You were where you wanted to be. You finally had everything. You finally . . ."

She trails off.

Griff's shaking his head.

"I wasn't where I wanted to be, Al." He gives her a pointed look. "I was on that bus and all I could think about was how you should be there, beside me. Doing all this without you don't feel right." He lasers his eyes to hers. "It's never felt right. And I sure as shit didn't have everything."

He strides forward, moving so close to her she can feel the heat radiating from him. He reaches out to palm her shoulder. "I did a shitty thing makin' that bet with Freddie. For not tellin' you what was up in the first place. I never shoulda done that. I was wrong, Alabama. So damn wrong. And I'm sorry."

Alabama holds Griff's regretful stare. She nods, accepting his apology. An apology that means everything. "Thank you," she whispers.

"And I know you'd probably be better off without me, but I can't do it."

"Can't do what?"

"Can't walk away again."

Alabama closes her eyes and presses herself back against the wall for support. Unsure if her legs will hold, unsure if she can keep her hands to herself.

"I ain't makin' that same mistake." Griff's voice is thick with emotion. "I know what I want. And I know that I don't want to do this without you anymore."

Alabama opens her eyes. Griff's handsome face holds a

promise, a sliver of something she can't help but hope for, but want with every bone in her body. "What're you saying, Griff?"

"I'm sayin', let's start over, together." He reaches for her hand and gives her a smile that lights up the entire room. "I got nothin' if you're not right there with me."

They're the words she wants, the words she's craved since he left Clover. And they're better than any song, because Griff's the better—the best—man for her. Her chest heaves as she takes a shuddery breath, unable to help the tear that's slipped down her face. "Griff."

"Now I know I got a lot to make up for, but I'm workin' on it."

Her lips curve. "You are, are you?"

"I'm tryin'." He squeezes her hand, tangling fingers and angles his body to hers. "Like for starters, I called your daddy." Alabama's eyes widen, but he goes on. "He ain't happy about it, but he didn't give me too much grief when I asked him if I could marry you. I think he figures he owes you one."

"What . . . ?" She stares at him, her throat so knotted up she can't speak. Can't breathe. Can't do anything but gape at Griff.

"Oh," he says nonchalantly. "And I kept my mama's house."

"You did?"

"It's ours," he says softly. "If you want it."

Ours. The word steals her breath and jump-starts her heart at the same time.

She shakes her head, but she's smiling. "What're you thinkin', Greyson?"

"I'm thinkin' we keep it for summers, for holidays, for whatever. For when we go back to Clover, together." He wipes away a tear from her cheek. "We do it right this time."

Her voice breaks. "Oh, Griff."

Slowly, he pulls her into his chest and cradles her in his strong arms. "I still got the ring, and I still got the house. I just need a yes." His eyes, tender yet worried, waiting on her answer, search hers. "What do you say, sweetheart? Will you marry me?"

She knows her answer instantly.

She looks at this man, this boy, who's had such a claim on her heart for the last twelve years. No one makes her feel more alive than Griff. Lifting her up, supporting her, telling her she can do it and then some. Making her better. Protecting her. But the best thing he's ever done is believe. He never once doubted her, and he always took up for her. And this time, he came back for her.

This time they have their second shot. That find-you-again-kiss-you-until-your-knees-go-weak-need-you-so-damn-bad second chance.

"Goddamnit, Alabama. You're killin' me," Griff grinds out, his tawny eyes flashing with worry.

A sob-laugh tumbles out of her. "Yes," she says, smiling through her tears. "I want you, Griff." She reaches out and grabs him by his shirt collar, yanking him close. "I've always wanted you."

Griff, his too-cool-to care front shattered, lets out a cry of relief. He crushes his mouth to hers, his kiss like a torch. Hot. Dangerous.

Alabama winds her arm around his neck in a stranglehold grip.

He pulls away and wipes away her tears with the pads of his thumbs. "I love you so damn much, Al."

She frames his face with her hands. "I love you too."

Warm desire sparks in his eyes and Griff gathers her in his arms. He backs her against the padded wall, the two of them sharing a kiss that could rival molasses. Slow and sweet. A low heat curls within Alabama, her breathing jagged.

Because Griff's mouth is everywhere. Her lips, her throat, the curve of her breast. She gasps when she feels his hand drift beneath her dress. "I don't think this is the purpose of the booth . . ."

He pulls back, his grin roguish, his eyes hungry. "Hell, I paid for an hour and I'm damn well gettin' it."

"The song . . . ," Alabama tries, but words fail her.

Griff drags his teeth over her throat, and her neck tips back, her body arching into him as she gives up the fight.

Griff runs his hand over the curve of her hip, primal, claiming her as he leans closer. "The song can wait."

Alabama closes her eyes.

He's right. It can.

Because she finally has time.

Time to live her life, her way. With Griff by her side.

epilogue

Four Months Later

GRIFF TWISTS THE RINGS AROUND HIS FINGERS AND peers out from behind the curtain into the audience. The Bluebird Café, one of Nashville's most respected musician hangouts, is bustling. The crowd's loud and high-energy, voices filtering backstage. As he scans the audience, spying familiar faces and friends, Griff's hit by a shot of adrenaline. Excitement has him pumped for tonight. There's a strong need to take to the stage and pound out some scorching guitar licks. Not to mention, it's his and Alabama's first official performance as the Copper Hounds.

A slender arm snakes around his waist. "The crowd's gettin' restless."

He grins and twists around to face Alabama. Her smile's brighter than a spotlight, and so is the engagement ring on her finger. His gaze drifts over her, taking in the tight black skirt and equally tight corset top. She wears the cowboy boots Griff bought her, her long red hair combed sleek and glossy. She looks downright heart-stopping.

With a growl, Griff tugs her close, all kinds of heat rushing through him. "You wanna talk restless, just what are you tryin' to do to me, sweetheart?"

A look of amused adoration crosses her face. "Music, Greyson. Music is where your head should be at. Not me." She smiles, a mischievous glint in her eyes. "At least not yet."

"Somethin' tells me we ain't gonna make the after-party." He leans in to kiss her. "How are you feelin' about tonight?"

"Ready as I'll ever be," she says, reluctantly pulling away from the kiss. As she does, Griff sees her smile falter, her gray eyes betraying her nerves. But her jaw is set, her expression determined. "Besides, we got this."

He grins, a rush of pride filling him. "We do."

Over the last few months, he's loved seeing Alabama get into the music. How she let go of the stress of the past year and threw herself into her songwriting. She's more herself than he's ever seen her, and she ain't afraid. She's gonna kick the world's ass, and he'll be right there beside her.

Somewhere in the audience, a sharp whistle sounds.

Alabama peers past him to the stage. "That's Bobby." Her eyes narrow as she searches the darkened room for their manager. "He's in the front row. Or at least he should be. Who knows? With that guy, he's probably in the kitchen."

Her droll tone has Griff chuckling. She's right, though. Griff levels up with Alabama and finally spies their manager in the audience. After Griff broke his contract with Freddie, successfully claiming breach of contract, he looked up Luke Kincaid's new manager—Bobby Mazon.

Bobby's a kooky son of a bitch. Boisterous and scatterbrained. But he ain't some soulless money-grubbing suck of a manager. Bobby cares about the music and his clients, and Griff'll take that over Freddie any goddamn day of the week.

"No press," Alabama says, giving Griff a relieved look.

"Thank Christ." Griff wraps a protective arm around Alabama's shoulders. Even now, the thought of press lurking, taking her picture, has him on edge. Though the media attention has died down in the months since they made the Copper Hounds official, Griff ain't taking any chances. They're getting married in Clover. Small, intimate. No press.

Although if he had his way, he'd marry Alabama tonight.

"Oh, shit." Alabama rips the curtains closed. "My dad's out

there. Holly too." She looks at him horrified, eyes wide. "What did you do, Griff?"

He shrugs, a smile playing on his face. "I extended an invitation, is all."

"Now I'm *not* ready." She twists under his arm, but he just tugs her in closer. "You invited my dad," she hisses.

"What's he gonna do? Throw a tomato?"

"*Griff.*" Fixing him with a fiery glare, she parts the curtain and points a finger. "And what about that?" She nudges his shoulder. "Did Sal and Luke Kincaid get an invite, too?"

"No idea," Griff replies, straight-faced.

"Uh-huh." She props her hands on her hips, cocks her head. "Is your only goal in life to stress me out?"

"My goal is to make you happy. Very, very, happy," he says, nuzzling her neck, breathing in her silky hair, her coconut scent. Releasing her, he arcs a brow. "And maybe get you naked later."

Alabama laughs and playfully curls into him, her body like a brand against his. "So you're sayin' no encore tonight?"

The front of his pants is suddenly incredibly stiff. "Fuck an encore." Anything that keeps him away from Alabama longer than necessary ain't worth having.

"Whatever you say."

He slips her hand into his, willing himself to cool off. "You ready?"

Alabama stops him with a little tug. She's biting her lip. "What if they hate us?"

"They ain't gonna hate us," he says, reaching up to clasp her shoulders. "And if they do, who gives a shit? We got a number one song, and what do they got? Assholes." Alabama laughs, and he goes on. "We're doin' what we want. Screw everyone else."

When "Find You Again" released last month, it burned up the charts straight to number one. That tour he and Alabama did—it wasn't a fluke. The fans liked their sound.

And they're only going to give them more.

"You're right." Alabama takes a breath and palms his chest with a warm hand. "You're still a cocky SOB, but you're right."

"Yeah, and you love me."

She smiles. "Damn straight."

With that, he takes her hand, and together they step out onto the stage. The roar of the crowd sounds around them, Alabama's engagement ring glittering in the glow of the stage lights, and Griff's never felt more alive.

He's finally doing things his way, with the woman he's always loved beside him. He ran away years ago from everything that mattered, and tonight he's finally running toward what he wants—a future with Alabama.

He catches Alabama's smile as he pulls her in front of him and gives her a little twirl around the stage. This night is hers and he wants everyone to see her for the fierce force that she is.

Still holding Alabama's hand, Griff leans into the mic, and growls, "Y'all ain't ready for what comes next . . ."

After the show, after saying hello to friends and family, and an excitable Holly, who had stacks of wedding magazines under her arm, Alabama takes a breather in the hallway as she waits for Griff to finish signing autographs. While she loves the spotlight, Griff laps it up like a cat does cream.

Slowly, Alabama drifts down the hall, taking in the photos, the names scrawled on the walls. It feels almost as if she's intruding on the past, on the old Alabama. On all her mistakes, on every single heartbreak, on every song she sang.

She hasn't been back to the Bluebird since Mort discovered her. She was so new back then, so green and innocent.

She pauses in front of a dressing room, pressing her hand against the wooden door, fanning her fingers out across the nameplate.

She closes her eyes.

The past, the last five years of it, is so bright, so clear she can practically see it happening. Alabama, packing up her bags at the Bluebird, nearly in tears because she botched a cover of Dolly Parton's "Coat of Many Colors." Then that fateful knock on the door. Mort, asking her if she had a second of time, and she had looked at him with so much hope in her face, he probably knew right then she'd do anything he'd ask.

Well, not anymore.

She thinks about how signing with Mort changed her life. For the bad. For the good. She used to think she would do it all over again, but now, now she wouldn't change it for the world.

Shaking off the memories, Alabama continues down the hall, a smile on her face.

She's finally made it out of the papers, finally made peace with an industry that's tried to throw her under the bus more times than she could count. Tonight was her one foot forward, her second chance at the woman she came to Nashville to be.

She's been chasing her ever since she left Clover, and tonight, she finally found her.

A photo of Dolly Parton has her stopping. As she takes in her idol, her hand absentmindedly caresses the shiny piece of flesh on the curve of her shoulder.

It's small, but she'll always have a scar.

She's glad for it too. It'll always remind her not to be afraid to take risks.

"Hey," a gravelly voice behind her says. "I've been lookin' for you."

She turns around, smiling brightly as she takes in the gorgeous gruffness that is Griff Greyson. She can't stop marveling at how lucky she is. At this man who has always known her and loved her for who she was. He was on fire tonight; they both were. Eyes and heart locked as they sang the soul out of the song that brought them together once again.

"Just takin' a walk down memory lane."

Seeing her hand on her arm, he frowns, worry clouding his tawny eyes. "Everything okay?"

She has to smother a grin at the surly, overprotective bastard he is. Even months later, he still won't let her carry a guitar case. "Everything's great," she says, stretching out a hand. "C'mere."

She lets out a content sigh as he takes her in his brawny arms and clasps her to his broad chest. Her heart flips over in her chest at the heated kiss he gives her.

"You were amazing tonight," Griff says, his eyes holding steady on hers.

"Mmm," she says, wanting more of his kiss. Her hands drift low, curling around his belt buckle. "I think they liked us."

"I like you." He kisses down the curve of her throat, his lips moving lower to her collarbone.

Alabama closes her eyes as a deep heat pulses low within her, spreading out like a warm glow. She lets loose a throaty moan as Griff nips at her neck, making a mark that's both primal and protective.

Griff pulls back and looks at her, his grin as cocky as the devil. As if he knows just what he's doing to her and enjoying it too damn much. "What do you say we get out of here?"

"And go where?" she asks, even though she already knows the after-party's got no chance in hell.

"Anywhere." Griff presses a kiss to her lips. His voice warm, his eyes serious, he tenderly cups her cheek, his rings tangling in her hair as he stares into her eyes. "As long as I got you."

Alabama stares up into his gorgeous gold eyes and smiles. "You do," she breathes.

His words have her going molten. Because she sees he means it. Again and again, Griff's showed her she's the most important thing to him. This man, who always makes sure she knows he loves her, has never wavered in his commitment. In his heart.

It's their very best love song.

A song of second chances, of being found again.

A song that will last forever.

Here's a special sneak peek at *Love You Always*,
a *Nashville Star* Novella

chapter
ONE

NO, SHE THINKS. *No, no, no.*
Sal Kincaid sits in the bathroom stall, staring at
the dark smear on the inside of her underwear. She
bites her lip, frustration building in her until she finally wipes,
flushes the evidence and stands.

Another month, another hope down the literal drain.

With a heavy sigh, Sal exits the stall. She washes her hands,
the water warm over her trembling fingers, and dries them on
scratchy paper. She meets her reflection in the mirror and winces.

She has to tell Luke.

Again.

There's still no baby. And at the rate they're going, there
might never be. For the last year, they've been trying. Except for
her first pregnancy, she's never made it past eight weeks. Sure, a
few stuck, but they all ended the same. In blood. In loss.

She never thought it would be this hard. She and Luke had
had enough heartbreak, she thought the universe would cut her
a break, make wishing for a tiny baby easy, but it's like running
headlong into a brick wall over and over again.

A voice over the hospital loudspeaker calls for Doctor Yates.
Sal takes down the loose braid she wears. As much a part of her
uniform as the starchy paramedic garb she sports. She combs
her fingers through the dark strands and gives herself a *get-your-
shit-together* scowl in the mirror. She's a fighter.

After all the hard knocks on the baby front, she has to remind herself about everything she has. All she has to be grateful for. Her life, for instance.

It was only two years ago that Sal was in a plane crash, leaving her friends and family to think she was dead. She was left with no memory. Left living with a madman who manipulated her into believing he was her husband for nine months. But then Luke found her. And he brought her back to their life—and their love.

She and Luke—they've overcome so much. Both before her memory loss and after.

Henry.

Sal closes her eyes. The name of her first baby, a baby she miscarried at four months in an awful car accident before she went missing, haunts her. She can't remember him. And it kills her. It absolutely kills her.

Shaking her head, she chases away the weary thought. Better to focus on all the good things in her life. Everything she's rebuilt. Everything she can hold on to. Her health. Her friends and family. Her job.

Slowly but surely, she recertified her paramedic's license. Her skills, her knowledge, held innate for so long, became automatic the second she started classes. It was like muscle memory. Like a blessing. And though her memory still hasn't fully returned, Sal's determined to live her life to the fullest. This is just her life now, and she's okay with it.

She's fucking Sal Kincaid, and she came back from the goddamn dead.

Exhaling a resolute breath, Sal opens her eyes and wipes a long strand of chocolate-brown hair away from her face. *Let's go home*, she thinks to herself as she exits the bathroom and walks down the long hallway of the hospital.

After staying with a patient for the last three hours until they were admitted, she's bone tired. Ready to get home. A glass of wine. A shower. Luke. A smile tugs at her lips. Even now, miles apart, he still has her knees going weak. Sal never knew you could crave a person. Food, sure. Sleep, definitely. But Luke. He's a soul quench. A fierce force of love. And at the end of a long day, there's nothing better than the sight of her hot as hell husband taking her in his muscular arms and bending her over—

"Whoa, sweetcheeks, where you goin'?"

Sal's jolted to a stop as a hand snags her arm. Tawny Reynolds, the other half to her paramedic team, stands in front of her. All biceps and black ink tattoos, Tawny's a boss, takes no shit, and she and Sal always have each other's backs when it came time to step up.

"Home," Sal says, giving her partner a smile. "You know that warm and cozy place where relaxation beckons."

Tawny shrugs. "Can't say I've heard of it."

Sal laughs. "That's because you live in a gym."

"Truth." Tawny cocks her head. "You finally get that patient admitted?"

"Yeah. Only took three hours." She moves to the side, getting out of the traffic of the hallway, and Tawny follows suit.

"Damn." Tawny shakes her golden lion's mane of hair. "That's rough. Which is why I feel like an asshole for asking this right now."

Sal lifts a brow. "What's up?"

"I need a really big favor. Nurse Buntin's got a patient in exam room two who's clamming up."

Sal sighs, knowing what Tawny wants. She thinks of Luke, on his way home from the studio. Though her husband's been nothing but supportive since she went back to work months ago, he worries when she's late. A throwback to last year. A never-healed wound from when Sal went missing.

Tawny's brown eyes are all apologies. "I know you're on your way home to your handsome husband, but. . .please? No one can get her to talk. And we all know about that magic touch of yours."

Sal smiles slightly. Since she's been back on the job, she's learned she has a rep around the hospital as someone who takes their time with the patients. Makes them feel as comfortable as possible. Having firsthand experience with hospital stays, she knows it's important for them to be listened to and understood even while in their most painful moments.

Tawny's serious face morphs into a pleading smile. "Pretty please?"

"Fine." Sal groans, but grins back at her. "Lead the way."

Through the exam room window, Sal sees a young girl, huddled in a corner chair, her legs pulled up to her chest. She's waifish with a short red pixie cut and a wary expression. Nurse Buntin leans over, giving Sal the details. "Molly Banks. Twenty-two. She was brought in complaining of stomach pain but now won't let anyone examine her."

Sal nods. She's seen her share of non-compliant patients. Most lie because they're embarrassed to tell the truth, or want to avoid being judged or scolded. It's her job to coax the truth out of them so they can be safely treated.

"Molly?" Sal says as she enters the room.

The girl looks up, her face full of bewilderment.

"Hi, my name's Sal and I'm a paramedic." Molly's watches with suspicious eyes as Sal walks further into the exam room. "I hear you're having some trouble. I don't blame you. No one likes it here."

The girl's face softens.

"Nurse Buntin says you came in with stomach pain. You want to tell me about it?"

"Not really."

"Are you sure?" As she gets closer, a familiar chill steals over Sal. Though Molly's tried to cover it with makeup, her right eye is black and blue. Sal's eyes drift. More bruises. On her wrists this time.

A long pause. Molly tightens her arms around her legs, resting her chin on her knees. "I feel better now. Really. I can go home."

"Well, we'd hate to send you home if something was wrong." Sal kneels beside the chair. She keeps a soft voice. "Are you here because of that eye?"

Molly shifts uncomfortably. "No."

"Because if you are, there's nothing wrong with that."

Molly doesn't reply, staring off into space, her attention diverted elsewhere.

The girl's a wall, and Sal needs to break through.

She searches her mind and has the answer. It's not her favorite, but it's honest. And hopefully, it will work.

Taking a breath, chasing away the nerves bubbling up, Sal forces herself back to the past. "Believe me, I've been where you have."

Molly squints at Sal, her stare disbelieving. "I doubt that," she sniffs. Her face is like a wounded animal, distrustful, bitter.

Sal nods. "I have. It was about two years ago and it was awful. I was with a man who didn't treat me right at all. Who hurt me."

Molly lifts her head, straightening up.

"There were days when I didn't want to exist, days when I didn't know what to do, when I felt all alone." She licks her lips. Her throat wants to shut down at the words she's saying, because they feel foreign, they're not her life anymore, but she pushes past it. Pushes herself. "Finally, I made the decision to get out, and it was hard, Molly. So damn hard. It won't be easy for you, but I understand what you're going through. I really do."

Molly's gaze tracks Sal, a small flicker of belief beneath her hard exterior.

Sal's breath is held tight in her chest. Hope. Hope Molly's listening. She meets the girl's brown-eyed gaze. "No one's saying you have to do anything now. All I want to do is make sure you're okay. That's what's important."

Molly shakes her head, thinking on it, worrying, but then she whispers, suddenly, "He doesn't know I'm here.

"Who doesn't?"

Her eyes well. "My husband. Chris. He found out I'm pregnant. And. . ." Molly trails off. Unfurling her legs, she lifts her shirt. What Sal sees has her blood turning to fire. The imprint of a shoe sole branded on Molly's stomach. "He doesn't want me to have it. Doesn't want there to be anyone else." She draws her legs back up, closing herself off. "I don't want it either. I can't. I can't have it."

A pang hits Sal at the mention of a baby, a baby no one wants, but she checks her own feelings, her judgment. What Molly's saying is horrifying, but Sal lets her talk. The girl needs to get it out, needs someone to listen to her, because right now, as Sal knows, Molly's mindset is that this is normal. That she's the one who did something wrong.

Molly stares at Sal. Hurt in her eyes. "And the cops don't help. They always come but they never listen to me. They leave me there. They don't do a thing."

"I understand," Sal says carefully. "They didn't help me very much either." She smiles, even though it takes all her strength. "How about I help you?" She holds Molly's eyes. She can see the girl relenting, giving in to someone who gives a damn.

"I'm scared." Her eyes dart to Nurse Buntin, who is hovering in the hall. "I don't want to be alone."

"You won't be. I'll be right there with you."

She sniffles. "You will?"

"Of course, I will." Sal wants to give this girl just a moment of tenderness. Hell, she once was this girl. Trapped with Roy. Desperate. Confused. The memory is ruthless and Sal's stomach churns. Everything from the past rushing back, hitting her hard like a rogue wave, ready to wreak havoc.

Molly shifts on the chair. "No needles?"

Sal chuckles. "No needles."

"And you won't go?"

"No, I won't."

But she thinks of Luke at home. Wondering. Worrying.

"I just need one second, okay?" Standing, she pats Molly's hand. "How about you hop up on that table and I'll be right back?"

As Molly reluctantly climbs up on the table, Sal steps outside the room. After giving Nurse Buntin a brief rundown on

Molly's condition so far, she says, "I'll stay for the exam. Make sure she gets through it okay."

"You're a saint."

Ducking into a corner of the hall, Sal pulls out her phone to send a quick text to Luke.

She smiles, her heart lifting as she writes the words.

I'm late tonight. I love you. Bet you a beer I still beat you home.

Coming April 2022

books by

AVA HUNTER

Babymoon or Bust

The Nashville Star Series

Know You More – a Prequel
Sing You Home
Find You Again
Love You Always – Sal & Luke's Novella
Need You Now
Bring You Back
With You Forever – Lacey & Seth's Novella

acknowledgments

To my readers: a massive, massive thank you for all your support. Every eyeball that has read my book, every minute you've spent on my words, I appreciate it more than you know. I am sending you air kisses and all my love. Please never leave me. I only say this somewhat jokingly.

My husband and daughter: thank you for putting up with me when my mind is on my writing and I can't be bothered with anything else. Not even dinner. I love you.

My beta readers: Chelsea, Michelle, Chrissy, and Tammie. Y'all are godsends.

My sister: You know what you do. You keep me sane. You kick my ass. You cheer me on. I love you!

Bookstagrammers and ARC readers: Wow, wow, wow. You give it your all—all your heart, all your time, and all your energy. Thank you for taking a chance on indie writers and reading our books. I just really adore you guys.

To coffee: Yes, I'm yours forever.

about the
AUTHOR

Ava Hunter is a strong believer in black coffee, red wine, and the there's-only-one-bed trope. She writes contemporary romance with healthy amounts of angst, where the damsels are never quite damsels, but the men they love (good, bad and rugged) are always there for them. Her first series, *Nashville Star*, centers on sexy country singers and their honky-tonk drama-filled lives. When Ava isn't parked in front of the computer writing, she is mom-ing, reading, traveling, drinking wine, baking and watching good TV. She writes from her home in Arizona, where she lives with her husband, daughter, and a very chonky cat.

Find her at www.authoravahunter.com

Printed in Dunstable, United Kingdom